Please Don't Leave Me

Please Me

Emma Pathy

Meraki Creations

Published by Meraki Creations LLC

Cover Design by Love Lee Creative

Editing by Deliciously Dark Editing

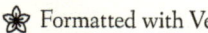 Formatted with Vellum

Author's Note

Dear Reader,

This book contains sensitive topics that may be harmful to your mental health. Please proceed with caution. Your mental health matters to me.

Emma

———

Trigger Warnings:
Recreational drug use, descriptive sexual content, sexual assault, parental conflict, pet loss, suicide attempt, and suicide.

Dedicated to my Pepin

Playlist

The songs on this playlist are each related to specific events in the book. They are in order of the way those events play out. If you think it will be a spoiler for you, then wait until you finish the book to listen, or play as you go along.

Enjoy!

1. **Sister** - K.Flay
2. **To the Moon** - JNR CHOI
3. **Peer Pressure** - James Bay, Julia Michaels
4. **For Me** - Lo Nightly
5. **Neither Do I** - Stwo, Jeremiah
6. **Man I Feel Like a Woman** - Shania Twain
7. **iSpy** - KYLE ft. Lil Yachty
8. **Waves of You** - Surfaces
9. **Just Like Autumn** - Jordy Searcy
10. **Electric** - Alina Baraz feat. Khalid
11. **Stupid Deep** - Ion Bellion
12. **Better Off Without Me** - Matt Hansen
13. **I Still Think of You** - Promoting Sounds
14. **Holiday** - Lil Nas X
15. **Hide Away** - Daya
16. **If I Could** - Ashley Kutcher
17. **Strangers** - Ashley Kutcher
18. **Breathe** - Kansh
19. **Time Of Your Life** - Kid Ink
20. **Haunt You** - Social House
21. **Girls Like Us** - Zoe Wees
22. **I Can't Breathe** - Bea Miller
23. **Hold On** - Chord Overstreet
24. **Close To You** - Gracie Abrams
25. **The One That You Call** - Mackenzy Macay
26. **Seamless** - Chris Grey
27. **Imagine-Acoustic** - Ben Platt
28. **At Your Worst** - Calum Scott
29. **Share Your Address** - Ben Platt
30. **It's You** - Ali Gatie

Prologue

LOUISA

"I need to tell you about the time I tried to kill myself," I say in a hushed and embarrassed tone, knowing full well he knows nothing of what I'm about to tell him. This conversation has been weighing heavy on my mind for months now, but I need to tell him. No more waiting.

I'm holding my breath for what seems like minutes, waiting for him to respond. In reality, it's probably only been a couple of seconds.

He sits up a little straighter. "Okay."

He pauses, waiting for me to continue. But I can't seem to get the words out.

"You don't have to if you don't want to," he reassures me.

My body heats like a furnace, and I can feel the sweat running down my sides. The baggy sweatshirt I'm wearing does nothing to soak it up.

"Well, I don't particularly want to, but I think it's important for you to fully know what you're getting into with me.

"I'm all ears, Lou."

I take a deep breath that almost makes my lungs explode and let it back out. Lifting my glass to my lips, I take a sip of my drink, letting it burn on my tongue for a moment before swallowing.

I start at the beginning...

Chapter One

ONE YEAR EARLIER

LOUISA

I walk through a sterile feeling hallway lined with cages, waiting for one of them to speak to me. Not that I expect a dog to literally speak to me but in a metaphorical sense. I've never adopted a pet before, and all of a sudden, I'm feeling the pressure to choose the right one and hoping they'll choose me back.

"Hey, little cutie patootie. What about this one over here, Lou?"

My sister insisted on coming with me today to pick out, in her words, her niece or nephew. I guess she's just as nervous about me making the wrong choice as I am. Then again, B doesn't get nervous about anything.

I've never known someone as confident and carefree as my little sister. Briella, who solely goes by B, is younger than me, and we could not be more opposite. As kids, it caused us to fight non-stop. But eventually, we got old enough to realize we were on the same team. We've been close ever since.

"I told you, I don't want a little ankle biter."

3

"But just look at that face." She leans down to where the dog is trying to lick her through the cage and gives me huge puppy dog eyes.

"No, I want a bigger dog that won't scream at the door every time one of my neighbors is in the hallway."

"Fine." She gives up and walks down the hallway to where I stand in front of a cage holding a black lab wagging its tail so hard it knocks over its water bowl. "You're so boring."

"I'm being practical." Before I continue walking, I tug on her long lavender braid slung over her shoulder. B has had colored hair since she was fourteen. I still remember the first time she dyed it.

She came with me to get groceries and snuck a box of hair dye into the cart without me noticing. An hour later, our mom ran into our bathroom after hearing screams to find B crying. She had left the bleach in for too long, and it burned her scalp. At that point, my mother, bless her heart, wasn't going to make her go to school with yellow bleached hair, so she helped her with the rest of the coloring. That blue hair made her stand out like a sore thumb at our small private high school. But B did not give two shits about what people thought of her, and she still doesn't.

A worker comes in to check on us. "Let me know if you find one you like, and I can put them in our meet-and-greet room for you."

"Actually, I do have a question about this guy." I point to the old-looking, full-size doodle mix in front of me. "It says here he's ten years old. Any idea why he was given up at such an old age? He seems so chill."

"Are you looking at Pepin?" Her face lights up as she jogs down the hall to where we stand. "Apparently, the family was having their seventh kid or something like that, and they didn't have time for him."

B mumbles under her breath and rolls her eyes. "Yeah, because six children are *way* more manageable than seven. Damn rabbits."

As Pepin and I stare at each other, something in me feels drawn to him.

"Could we spend some time with him?"

"Sure! Head out that door at the end of the hall, and I'll meet you in room three; it should be open."

"Thank you."

———

"WELL, Pepin, welcome to your new home."

Staring into my 900-square-foot apartment, I start to wonder if he's as unimpressed with it as I am. He gets up and starts wandering around, inspecting the place. I really hope he's as docile as he seemed at the rescue. Regardless, I'm just glad to have a companion.

I've been wanting a dog for over a year now, but my ex always said no. Now that he's out of the picture, I can do whatever I want. Although I've only been living here alone for a couple weeks, I was starting to get really lonely. Most of my college friends live out of state, and my family lives in a small town over an hour from Minneapolis. After Jay left, I've been in this city mostly by myself.

"So, have you found a new roommate yet?" B asks with a mouth full, eating the last of my Oreos. "Because I've been thinking maybe I could move in with you. It'll be just like old times."

We haven't lived together since I left for college five years ago, but I honestly think having her around could be good for me. I don't do well alone. And as great as having Pepin around will be, some consistent human interaction will make the transition to being single easier.

"Yeah, I think that would be great. But I thought you were going to live with your college friend once you move to the city?"

"She decided to take that job in New York instead. She called me this morning to tell me she got us out of our lease. So I guess Jay dumping you works out great for me," she says with a sarcastic grin on her face.

I roll my eyes at her. "Yeah, I'll find out his new address so you can send him a thank you card."

She walks over to where I'm standing and tackles me onto the couch. "You know I'm just messing with you. By the way, how have you been? I haven't heard much from you since you called me two weeks ago to tell me that Fuck Face let the greatest thing that's ever happened to him slip through his fingers." She has always been my biggest hype girl, giving me way more credit than I deserve. I appreciate the constant support and confidence in me more than she'll ever know.

"Better, now that I have a roomie. And I'll be even happier when that new roomie signs a contract promising not to leave her dirty dishes in the sink."

"Hey, I always wash them *eventually*!"

We laugh and hold each other on the couch for a moment before I get up, hoping she won't catch the single tear I let slip from my eye.

I really haven't taken the breakup as hard as I thought I would. Yes, I'm sad. But I'm less sad about losing Jay than I am scared of being alone. The last time I was single was in my junior year of college. Before that, I dated a few other people. Needless to say, I haven't spent much time on my own.

Jay never really felt like the one, but I think I got complacent and settled for what would keep me on track with my life goals as opposed to what was best for my heart. He wasn't bad; he just wasn't great. And after watching my parents growing up, I know that great love exists. I was just too blinded by ambition and stubbornness to be honest with myself.

Jay had fit into my plans. I wanted to be engaged and a homeowner by 25, on my way to becoming a great architect. Now, here I am, 24 years old and single, about to move my little sister into my janky apartment.

I hope this pause in my plans doesn't last long. I am less than a year away from taking my licensure exams and becoming an architect. And now I have a dog, which wasn't a part of the original plan due to the shitty ex-boyfriend, but it definitely seems like a step in the right direction.

Pepin trots over, jumps up on the couch, and curls up next to B, where I left her lying there. "Looks like Lou is getting two new roommates, huh, Pep." The side eye he gives her sends both of us into a fit of laughter.

This is going to be good. And everything is going to be okay.

Chapter Two

LOUISA

The interesting thing about moving back in with my sister after five years apart is that not much has changed. B started moving in her crap this morning, and I'm already questioning my decision. While I am neat, organized, and focused, B is messy, chaotic, and scatterbrained.

"How do you have this much shit?"

"Mom and Dad made me take all my stuff out of my bedroom at home so they could turn it into a library."

"They also had me clean out my room when I graduated last year. And you know what I did? I sorted through everything and got rid of what I didn't need."

She drops a box of what looks like yarn and shoots daggers at me. "Not all of us are as type A as you, Lou. I'm sentimental."

Reaching into the box she just dropped, I pick up a half-crocheted dishcloth. "And what sentimental value does this hold?"

She flinches when I throw it back into the box as if I just slammed a door on her heart. Her eyebrows scrunch together, and her lips press tight together. She really is quite the drama queen at times.

Deep down, I know that my type A ways drive her just as crazy as her chaos drives me crazy, so learning to live together again will be a challenge. One thing that I am definitely up for if it means I don't have to live alone.

And you should have seen the look on my mother's face when we told her B was going to be moving in with me. You would have thought I told her Barnes & Noble was having a two-for-one sale on self-help books. She would not stop telling us how lucky we are to have each other and how she wishes she would have had the opportunity to live with her sister again.

I actually believe her when she says that. My mother and her sister would leave their husbands in a heartbeat and live off-grid on a hobby farm together if the opportunity presented itself. B and I have always idolized them, and I guess you could say that they are a big part of why we are so close.

Walking around the box of yarn, I wrap my sister in a big hug, squeezing her until she begs me to let her go. I plant a big kiss on her forehead and free her from my bear hug. I put my hands on her shoulders and look her in the eyes. "I love you, B. And I'm really glad you're here. We'll find room for all your shit, even if it means we have to stack boxes to the ceiling." Which is saying a lot, given that these are ten-foot ceilings. Her smirk lets me know that I am forgiven and we can continue on with the unpacking.

Pepin trots over with a plush toy in his mouth and squeezes his way between B's legs, trying to get her attention. With a smile now on her face, she reaches down and grabs his toy. She's about to throw it when I stop her.

"No, wait. He doesn't want to play fetch. He just wants to show it to you."

"Really?"

"Yeah, he just wants you to be proud of him and tell him how cool his toy is."

A little chuckle escapes, and I barely hear her mumble as I walk into the other room, "Sounds like someone else I know."

"I heard that!"

———

AFTER WHAT FELT like thousands of trips up and down the stairs, since the old building doesn't have an elevator, we finally got everything out of the trailer. I give myself permission to take a break and plop my butt down on the couch. B comes in a moment later with two seltzers in her hand. She sits down on the couch next to me, cracks one for herself, and hands the other to me. I hate the watermelon flavor, but I'm so exhausted that I am not about to get up and walk to the fridge to grab a new flavor.

"So, how's this going to work? Are we on a rotating schedule for who gets to bring hot dates home? Or is it a first come, first serve type of thing?"

Leave it to B to be the first one to bring up sex. Like the rest of her personality, her sexuality is wild and free. Though she has never had a serious long-term relationship, she has had her fair share of hookups and even the occasional situationship.

I used to live vicariously through her when I was in my relationships. Lucky for me, she's an open book and spares no dirty details about her sex life, and it's only going to get more interesting with her new job.

B got hired by Daniel Perez, an art curator for celebrity clients. His job requires him to travel all over the country and even internationally to collect art. They met at a night-club here in the city when B was visiting me last fall. She had the balls to climb up a railing to the bottle service booths just to tell him she loved his jacket.

Apparently, this jacket was part of some rare collection that used art graphics from the 70s. I honestly would have thought it came from the half-price bin at a thrift store had B not told me it was worth over $4,000. She knew exactly what it was, and he was impressed. He then invited her up to his booth, and they spent the rest of the evening talking about rare art and fashion, which are all things I know nothing about.

At the end of the night, he gave her his business card and told her to call him if she was ever looking for a job. She took him up on his offer this spring when she graduated. Now, she's his personal assistant and will get to travel all over with him.

She has already told me she plans to hook up with a new person on each trip. When I asked her what her boss would think of that, she just said, "Daniel is a self-proclaimed glut, so he'll be getting more dick than me." The confused expression on my face had her explaining that glut meant 'gay slut'. When in Rome, I guess.

The only response I have for her is an uncomfortable laugh because, if I'm being honest, I haven't even thought about having another man back in the apartment that I used to live in with Jay.

"Lou, you need to get back out there ASAP! I'm serious; we need to get a dick in you before it gets old and dusty."

"Excuse you! It's only been a couple months."

"Tooooo long." She sets her drink down on the coffee

table without a coaster and bends over till her head is between my knees. "Yep, exactly what I feared. The cobwebs are already taking over."

Slapping her head away, I yell, "Okay! We need to set some ground rules. Starting with personal space and off-limits topics, including my vagina."

Her laugh makes me roll my eyes and eventually join in. We both know that there is no such thing as off-limit topics with us.

I reach out and put a coaster under her drink.

"And aren't you the one who always tells women that they don't need a relationship to be happy?"

"Who said anything about a relationship?"

I've always been a long-term relationship girl, so I don't have experience in the casual one-night stand department. Luckily, I have a live-in expert.

"Don't you ever worry about STIs?"

"I mean, sure, but that's what condoms and Ruthie are for?"

"Ruthie?" I ask.

"Ruth is my bestie at the clinic where I got tested regularly when I was in school. I would see her just about every Tuesday."

This girl! How are we possibly related?

Chapter Three

LOUISA

It's Friday night, and B's childhood best friend, Iris, is visiting us in the city. Iris is a junior at the same university B just graduated from. The two of them have been inseparable since we were younger, despite being two grades apart.

Iris's older brother, Liam, and his wife, Evie, graduated high school with me. The five of us are all going downtown to celebrate Iris's 21st birthday.

I poke my head into B's room and find the floor scattered with a million pieces of clothing. A thick red head of hair and a wavy mane of purple hair are squished together, taking pictures in the mirror.

"Are you guys ready to go yet?" I just got home from work an hour ago, and I'm already dressed. They have been getting ready for the past 3 hours, so in theory, they should be as well. But are they?

"No! This kind of perfection takes time," B yells at me without even turning around.

"How much longer do you two need? Liam and Evie said they're picking us up for dinner at 7:00."

Iris turns around and gives me a big smile, and I can already tell she's a little tipsy. "Louisa," she's the only one who calls me that, "do you think this outfit says 'it's my birthday, buy me a drink'? B says it looks like I'm about to walk on stage at the strip club."

"I never said that was a bad thing!" B defends herself.

I giggle to myself, knowing she definitely meant that as a compliment. Iris is wearing a bodysuit with two strips of fabric coming up from her skirt, crisscrossing over her chest and tied around her neck, leaving her stomach and back completely exposed. On the bottom, she's wearing a skin-tight skirt that shows every curve on her petite little body. The ensemble doesn't leave much to the imagination, and I'm very curious how Liam is going to react to it.

"You're very sexy and beautiful, Iris," I say, even though my sisterly instincts are to throw a big sweater over her and shield her from the world; she's a big girl and has autonomy over her own body. Plus, if anyone tries to get handsy without Iris's permission, B would kick their ass.

"Have you finally decided on an outfit, B?"

"No. I think I tried on everything in my closet twice. And since I gave the birthday girl my best outfit, I have nothing to wear."

Of course that top belongs to B. "I think what you have on looks great."

"Says the girl wearing a sweater out to a bar. Seriously, Lou, you're not wearing that. You're supposed to be getting some dick tonight. That sweater screams, 'I'm boring in bed,' and I won't let you go out like that because I love you." She starts rummaging through the endless pile of clothes on her floor.

———

"B, I'm not comfortable in this." I look at myself in the mirror, admitting that I look hot. But I'm not comfortable being seen out in public with this much skin showing. She put me in a black crop top with a delicate chain around my hips and a skirt.

Pepin barks from the bed and gives me a disapproving look.

B notices him and comments. "Pepin, there are enough old men in the world giving their unsolicited judgments; we don't need you against us too."

He lays his head down on his front paws as if giving up the fight. Even he knows there's no winning when B is on her feminist soap box. "I told you, Lou, this is what people wear. You're not going to stick out. If anything, you'll actually blend in more."

"Fine," I concede because we are really running late, and I hate being late.

———

DINNER WAS GREAT, but I barely ate anything because I was so nervous about potentially finding someone to hook up with. B kept reminding me there was no pressure and then, in the same breath, was reminding me that I needed to get laid.

I'm standing here on a rooftop bar downtown with just enough liquid courage to possibly talk to someone outside of our group. It's not that I'm shy; I just haven't done the whole dating thing in a while. But even if I do find someone to flirt with, I probably wouldn't be able to hear them over the loud music. I lean over and yell into B's ear, "I need to pee."

"Okay, I'll come with you."

We make our way inside and down the stairs to where the bathrooms are. She's holding my hand as she trails behind me; otherwise, we'd likely get separated in the crowd. We get there, and of course, there's a line for the women's and no line for the men's.

After several minutes of the line moving at a snail's pace, B says, "Screw it!" She drags me out of the line and into the men's bathroom.

"B, what the hell are you doing? We can't just barge in here!"

"There's basically no one in here."

Umm, there very much are people in here, and they are staring at us over their shoulders from the urinal. I accidentally make eye contact with a brown-haired guy with shockingly blue eyes. He smirks at me, and I immediately turn my head away, praying that this will be over soon.

We cram both of us into a stall meant for one person and take turns peeing. Once we finish, I high-tail it out of there, hoping that we don't draw any more attention. I saw some hand sanitizer on the wall outside, so I don't bother wasting time washing my hands.

Part of me is glad she dragged me in there because I really had to pee. When I turn away from the hand sanitizer hanging on the wall, I'm confronted by the attractive man who smirked at me only minutes ago.

Shit. I was trying to forget about that. He clearly hasn't.

He confidently walks up to me and says, "Hey, what's your name?"

I glare over at B. She tries to suppress a laugh, but it comes out in bursts of squeaks before she runs back up the stairs, leaving me alone with the mystery man. She is likely going to find Iris and tell her what happened. At the top of the stairs, she turns back and mouths, "Are you okay?" and flashes me two thumbs up. I nod but try to tell her with my eyes that I'm not happy.

"I'm Louisa," I say, turning back to the bathroom guy and reaching my hand out to shake his. Fuck. Do people shake hands when they're interested in someone? Based on the grin on his face and how slowly he lifts his hand to mine, I'm guessing they don't.

"Your friend abandoned ship pretty quick there." He's clearly referring to B's disappearing act.

"That was my little sister." I lean in when I'm talking to him because even though it's quieter back here than out by the bars, I still can't really hear him over the bass. "And I'm going to kill her when we get home. That was her idea to barge into the men's room."

"She's smart. The men's line is always way shorter than the women's. They really need to do something about that."

Agreed. Yet another one of B's feminist rants that I quietly agree with.

"In hopes that she never does that to me again, I'm not going to tell her you said that."

He laughs and takes a step closer to me. I can smell his cologne. It smells like Axe, which reminds me of middle school, but it's not bad. God, I forgot how horny I was.

One moment I'm looking into those blue eyes, and before I can even process what I'm saying, words start coming out of my mouth. "Want to come back to my place?"

Oh my god, why the hell did I just ask him that? We literally just met.

"Uh, yeah. I'd like that. Do you live close?"

"Just a few blocks that way," I say, pointing to what is

likely the wrong direction because we're inside, and I'm clearly tipsy.

"Great! Let's go tell your friends where you're headed and then get out of here." Well, that just made me feel better about going home with a complete stranger. But also, I think I could take him if I needed to.

"Good idea. Are you here with anyone?" Figured I should ask in case he's here with a girl.

"Just came here with some coworkers. I'll shoot them a text to let them know I'm heading out."

After finding my group and letting them know I'm walking home, we make our way toward my apartment. The fact that no one seemed shocked when I walked up with a stranger tells me that B had already filled them in and likely made some assumptions about how my night was going to go.

We make small talk, and I find out that he works at a nature center doing environmental education, which makes sense. His outfit and shaggy hair were definitely giving granola vibes.

His name is Darrah, by the way. I awkwardly learned that in front of everyone else when I went to introduce him and realized I never asked.

———

I WAKE up to the sound of Iris and B giggling and stumbling. There's a crash, and I'm pretty sure they just broke a lamp.

"Shit! Lou is going to kill me. I'll find some glue and put it back together before she notices."

Before she makes a huge mess, I go out there to stop her. "B, just go to bed. I'll clean it up in the morning."

"I'm sorry, Lou." One side of her lip curls up, and she shrugs her shoulders. "Wait. Is he in there?" She points to my room, and I assume she means Darrah.

"No, he left a couple hours ago."

Eyebrows scrunched together, she looks at her phone to check the time. "It's only 2am. You left the bar around 11:30."

"Exactly. Unfortunately, Mr. Darrah was a two-pump chump." Though I feel bad labeling him like that, it really was not great, and I've been dying to tell B about it.

Iris slaps her hand over her mouth, "Spill all the details!"

Before sitting down on the couch to share the dirty details, I grab the girls some water. They are going to be violently hung over tomorrow based on how much they're both slurring their words.

As soon as I'm seated, B starts chanting, "Tea. Tea. Tea. Tea."

I UNLOCK THE DOOR, and he follows me inside. Pepin immediately greets us upon entering. Well, he greets me. Darrah did not receive the same warm welcome I did. Pepin's tail stops wagging, and he lowers his head, growling at Darrah.

"Pepin, stop that! Sorry, he's usually super friendly." Grabbing him by the collar, I gently guide him to B's room and shut the door. I feel bad, but I'm not about to risk him growling at my guest all night.

"It's alright. Maybe he doesn't like men."

That's unlikely because he loves Liam and my dad. He must just be grumpy because I've been gone for several hours. Since getting Pepin, we haven't been apart for more than a few hours, since I mostly work from home.

I turn from the door and am immediately greeted with warm lips on mine. One of his hands works its way to the back of my head, entangled in my hair, and the other on my exposed midriff. I may be rusty at flirting with strangers, but this I know how to do. I pivot us and walk backwards toward my room, reaching my hand behind me to find the doorknob.

His lips move wildly over mine, and I part mine slightly, inviting him in. When he doesn't respond, I continue mimicking his patterns. I guess he isn't a tongue guy, so closed-mouth kissing it is. I giggle to myself, thinking about how his kissing matches his cologne—very middle school. But I'm not in the mood to be anyone's teacher right now.

Once we make it to the back of the room, I part from him for a second to drop down onto the bed and shimmy my way up to the pillow. He follows, laying on top of me between my spread legs. I can feel how hard he is through his jeans rubbing against my center. God, I didn't realize how much I'd been craving another person's heat between my thighs.

A small gasp comes out of my mouth as his cold hand glides from my waist to under my tube top. After giving my breast a small squeeze, he pulls his hand out, grabs the top seam of my shirt, and pulls it down to expose both of them now.

He works his way down my neck with frantic kisses all the way to my nipple. A more audible gasp comes out this time, and I can feel him smile over my stiff peak, clearly pleased with the fact that he drew it out of me.

If I'm being honest, I just haven't been touched by anyone in a while. Jay and I stopped having sex a few months prior to breaking up. What I thought was a dry spell was actually our slow, dragged-out ending.

I am a big foreplay girl, but I've been nervous about this for days and just want to rip the bandaid off, so I pull his face back up so our lips connect again. Then, reaching down, I pull up the hem of his shirt and help him pull it off over his head. Before we reconnect, he reaches down and starts to undo his belt, then the top button of his jeans, then his zipper.

He reaches behind him and pulls out his wallet from his back pocket. He shuffles through some cards and bills before pulling out a condom. God knows how long that's been in there for. I'm currently very glad I've been on birth control since I was 15.

This guy is starting to seem more like a virgin with every second that passes. Against my better judgment, I reach out and help him pull down his pants along with his boxers. I think I saw little Darth Vaders on them.

His size is average, which is what I'm used to. I have yet to experience a "breath taker," as B so lovingly calls well above-average dicks. Luckily, I'm wet enough without much foreplay, so he lifts up my skirt and slides right in.

Leaning back down on top of me, he braces his forearms on either side of my shoulders and presses his cheek to mine so his hot breath is right in my ear.

Now, people will think I'm exaggerating this part, but I swear I'm not. He makes a max of ten good pumps before he grunts into my ear, and I can feel his upper body shaking on top of me. The worst part is that he fakes a few more pumps, probably hoping I didn't catch the fact that he just came. But I can feel him already getting soft inside me.

IRIS AND B are in a fit of laughter, and once B catches her breath, she finally gets out the only words she has, "You're joking!"

"I really wish I was," I say as I close my scrunched-up eyes and shake my head from side to side. I can't decide if I'm more embarrassed for him or for myself.

Iris finally catches her breath and wipes the tears from her eyes. "So, then what? He just left?"

"Yep, pretty much. He threw the condom in the trash, pulled up his pants, and left. And no, I did not ask for his number, and he didn't ask for mine." I run my hand down my face as if trying to wipe the memory from my mind. "After he left, I was still so horny, so I whipped out my vibrator and took care of myself."

B exhales after taking several gulps of water and fist pumps in the air, "Good for you, girl!" It's followed up with a big yawn, which spreads to Iris, then to me.

"Okay, I'm about to pass out, so I'm going to brush my teeth and go to bed." She scoots over on the couch towards me and wraps her arms around my neck. "Sorry your first time back in the game was such a blowout. Or whatever sports people say."

I chuckle and hug her back. "Honestly, I'm glad it wasn't that great because I'm not ready to find my husband yet. I just want to play the field for a while, then hopefully find Mr. Right. I want to enjoy being single for a while."

B lets go of my neck and puts her hands on my cheeks, squishing my face. Her eyes are blurry, so I'm not sure if she'll remember this in the morning, but I can tell she means what she says next. "I'm so proud of you, Lou. You've had boyfriends for so long, and there's nothing wrong with that. But I really want you to enjoy being single with me, at least for a while. Because we may never get this again." She gives me a soft smile, and I rest my hand on top of her hands, which still rest on my cheeks.

The smile suddenly disappears, her lips form a thin line,

and her eyes get big. Oh shit, she's about to barf. I quickly grab her empty water cup off the coffee table and put it under her chin. She gags, but nothing comes up yet, so I drag her to the bathroom as quickly as I can and put her head over the toilet. She gets there just in time to yack up the entire contents of her stomach.

After I finally get B settled into bed, I go out to the living room and find Iris passed out on the couch. She looks relatively comfortable, so I cover her with a blanket, put a pillow under her head, and leave her.

I can't help but mother them, so I put a fresh glass of water by each of them, along with a couple pills for when they wake up with headaches tomorrow morning. I've always been the mom of the friend group, especially in college.

Don't get me wrong, I definitely had fun too. But Jay was always so particular about how much I was allowed to drink because he said he didn't want to be embarrassed by me. So, by the end of a night out, I was usually sober enough to take care of everyone.

I walk back to my room and crawl under the sheets. Pepin jumps on the bed and curls up next to me. I always keep it colder in my room so I can snuggle Pep and sleep with a weighted blanket without burning up.

The pressure from the weighted blanket and Pepin pressed up against my side is comforting. After sharing a bed with Jay for the last two years, those first few nights after he left were terribly lonely. My legs were restless, and I felt so cold. I went out and bought this weighted blanket the next day. It helps, but Pepin helps the most. He's so attentive and knows exactly when I need a little extra love.

I roll onto my side to face him and stretch my arm out to scratch behind his ear. He lets out a little huff and nuzzles his head into my chest. "Guess you were trying to warn me about that guy, weren't you, buddy?" He lets out another little grunt in confirmation. "Alright, next time, I'll listen. But if you do that to every guy who walks through this door, I'll start to get suspicious."

I smile at my own joke and kiss his big, soft head. "Goodnight, Pepin. I love you." He wiggles a little closer into my body to say he loves me too. I truly will never understand how anyone could give this sweet boy up.

Chapter Four

LOUISA

 I wake up the next morning before B and Iris—no shocker there—so I run to grab some coffee and bagels for the three of us. The coffee shop is just around the corner, so I throw on some joggers and a hoodie to go over my nightshirt. My hair is thrown up in a messy bun on top of my head, and I still have my glasses on.

 Needless to say, this was not how I'd want to look if I ran into a super hot, well-dressed British guy with meticulously twisted hair and light brown skin. But the universe had other plans for Louisa Blake this morning.

 I don't even notice him at first because I'm scrolling on my phone. The line is long and snakes back and forth through the ropes leading to the register. He's several people ahead of me in line but right across the barrier to my left.

 "Grumpy old bear?"

 I look up, not knowing what's going on. I look over and lock eyes with this gorgeous man who was clearly talking to me. I'm confused. "Excuse me?"

He looks down, nodding his chin toward my chest. "Your jumper."

"Oh, yeah," I say, looking down at B's sweatshirt, which I just grabbed off the chair by the door on my way out of the apartment. It has an image of a bear smoking a pipe on it; his face is scrunched in a way that definitely makes it look grumpy. The text surrounding his head says 'Grumpy Old Bear' in bold letters. "It's my sister's. She has very...unique taste in clothing."

He chuckles and says, "Well, I think it's funny, and it looks good on you, so you should keep it."

I try to tone down the grin that tries to take over my entire face, straining my cheeks till they hurt. "Thanks, maybe I will."

He reaches out a hand to introduce himself. "Matt."

See, people *do* shake hands! "Louisa. But you can call me Lou."

"Looking forward to it." His smile is so soft and confident it makes my heart melt.

What does he mean by that? I don't think about it too long because I'm distracted by the feel of his hand in mine. His hands are so strong and so gentle at the same time. The skin of his palm is soft like butter, and I suddenly get self-conscious about my man hands, which are probably rough in comparison. Butterflies start to erupt in my stomach, and my body heats up.

The line starts to move again, separating us further and forcing us to let go. With the way the line is formed, we won't get another chance to pass by before he gets to the front to order.

My mind starts racing, and I try to process what just happened. Did I just hit it off with someone in a coffee line? And not just someone. A very attractive man who looks like he has his life together. Of course, this is just speculation since the only thing I know about this man is that his name is Mark. Wait, no. Was it Matt? Shit, I was too distracted that I didn't process what he said his name was.

It's his turn to order, and I can hear his sweet honey voice talking to the barista, but I can't make out what he's saying. I close my eyes, and an image pops in my head of him pressing me up against a wall and talking sweet nothings to me with that voice. It has my vagina fluttering.

When I come back to reality and open my eyes, I realize the line in front of me has moved significantly, and I rush forward to fill in the gap. When I look over at the register, I see that he's no longer there. Looking down the counter to the pick-up station, I see him waiting there and talking to someone. I can't see who it is because they're hidden behind the espresso machine. Probably some well-dressed, hot blonde who doesn't look like they just rolled out of bed.

It's my turn to order next, so I step forward, and despite my best efforts, I can no longer see either of them. Damnit.

"Welcome to Mad Hatter's. What can we make for you today?"

I turn to the young girl at the register and order what I know to be B and Iris's go-to orders, a cafe miel for me, and a variety of bagels with cream cheese.

I finish ordering and wait for her to say the total. Instead, she takes my name and directs me toward the end of the counter where I can wait for my order.

"Sorry, I didn't pay yet. I must have missed the prompt on the screen." Digging into my purse, I fish out my credit card and hold it up to the card reader.

"It's already been paid for, ma'am. Someone in line ahead of you told me to charge it to their tab."

The confused look on my face makes her giggle. "Next!" She waves the person behind me forward.

Oh my gosh, he probably just meant to buy me one drink. He likely didn't intend to buy three drinks and half a dozen bagels. I feel terrible.

I quickly walk down to the pick-up station where I last saw him standing to thank him and apologize. When I get there, I find he's gone, and my heart deflates a little. That was so sweet of him. He must be a regular here if he has a tab. I'm surprised I haven't seen him here before.

I really hope I run into him again, preferably when I'm more put together. I laugh to myself, wondering if he'll even recognize me.

"Louisa," a worker calls out to let me know my order is ready. I grab the drink carrier and box of bagels and head back to the apartment, still thinking about that beautiful man and all the things I'd kill for him to do to me.

———

As I'm unlocking the door to the apartment, I can hear the TV on, so I know the girls must be awake. I'm greeted by two barely functioning lumps on the couch and a very spoiled Pepin snuggled between them. "You guys will not believe what just happened to me at Mad Hatter's." They both perk up slightly at the smell of coffee and the sound of a good story.

"Here, I got coffee for you guys. What kind of bagel do you want? I can throw them in the toaster for you." I hand out their drinks and display the bagels for them to choose from.

Iris leans forward and picks out a cinnamon and sugar bagel. "Have I ever told you you're the best sister, Lou?"

"She really is," B says with her mouth full of blueberry bagel. I guess she didn't care to wait for the toaster or the cream cheese. "So what happened at the coffee shop?"

I stand up and walk into the kitchen to prepare a bagel for Iris and myself. "I met a guy."

High-pitched squeals come from the living room, and I know I just got their hopes up only to let them down.

"Don't get too excited. I didn't get his number, and I'm not even totally sure I heard his name correctly. I think it was Mark or-"

"Matt?" B cuts me off.

"Could be, but I honestly can't remember what he said because I was too distracted by how hot he was." The girls start to giggle. Wait. "How did you know his name might have been Matt?"

I walk into the living room to figure out what they're giggling about. I almost run into B when turning the corner because she was on her way into the kitchen to find me. She stops abruptly and shakes her disposable coffee cup in my face.

I can't believe what I'm seeing. Written in marker on the side of B's cup is the name 'Matt' and a phone number. It's written in the same girly handwriting as the coffee order, so he must have had the barista put it on one of my cups when he paid for my order. I can only imagine how he described me to her: 'I want to pay for the girl who looks like a hot mess in the dumb bear sweatshirt.'

All I can do is stand there, staring. B shakes me. "You have to text him!"

"I don't know. Maybe he was just doing it as a joke. He was talking to someone else after he ordered. I bet they were in on it together."

Iris rolls her eyes from the couch and says, "You're being

ridiculous, Lou. He wouldn't have given you his phone number if he didn't want you to reach out."

"He also paid for our whole order."

"Okay, see. He definitely wants to get in your pants." That's some very B logic right there.

I finally grab the cup from her hand and put the number in my phone so she can finish her coffee. I put him in my contacts as 'Matt Mad Hatter' because I have several Matts in my phone, and I don't want to embarrass myself by texting the wrong one.

"Should I text or call him?"

"I don't know. How old was he?" B asks.

"I would guess early to mid 30's, but I'm not totally sure. He looked like a *man*, not a boy, if that makes sense. He was dressed well and had one of those nice wool peacoats. And he had this deep voice with a sultry British accent." I'm getting wet just thinking about it all over again.

"Then definitely call him," B advises. "If he were younger or seemed less mature, I'd maybe suggest texting, but what you're describing seems like a phone call kind of guy. Plus, then we'll get to hear that sultry voice of his."

"You do *not* get to listen in on our conversation."

"Oh come on, Lou. That's no fun. You can't tease us like that. Iris and I can be here to coach you so you don't say something stupid."

I flinch at the thought of messing this up. I suddenly get nervous about hearing his voice again. "Fine. But keep your mouths shut. If you need to tell me something, hit the mute button so he doesn't find out someone else is here with me." They're both so giddy right now you would barely believe that 5 minutes ago, they were violently hung over.

We all curl up on the couch together, with me seated in

the middle. Pepin sits on his favorite chair across from us and stares lovingly at me, like he always does.

My finger hovers over the call button, and I can feel my hands getting clammy. B taps the top of my hand, forcing my finger to press down on the screen, and the phone starts ringing. Against my better judgment, I quickly put it on speaker so they can hear.

After a couple rings, he answers, "I was wondering when you'd call."

"Hey, it's Lou." Why am I so awkward?!

"I'm glad the barista gave the cup to the right person. I was worried she would accidentally give it to another pretty brunette with brown eyes."

I can feel my cheeks turning red, and I don't know how to respond to that. I've always been horrible at taking compliments.

Luckily, he continues so I don't have to. "Are you busy next weekend?"

He's straightforward, and it takes me by surprise. Of course, I was hoping he would ask me out on a date, but I was so sure this was a joke that I hadn't thought of what I would do if he actually asked.

B reaches over and taps the 'mute' button. "Say something! You're not busy next weekend."

I unmute the phone before saying, "No, I'm not busy next weekend."

"Great. Would you like to go to dinner with me on Friday night?"

My heart is racing, and I'm about as giddy as Iris and B are on either side of me right now. I can tell they're trying to hold in their excitement so they don't make any noise. "Yeah, I'd really like that."

"I'm glad. Text me your address, and I'll swing by to pick you up around seven."

B reaches over again to press the mute button and misses. "We'll need way more time than that to get you ready after work."

"Sorry, I missed that. What did you say?" Oh my god, he heard her say that.

I shoot a death glare over at B, and she sucks air through her gritted teeth before mouthing the word, "Sorry."

"Nothing, seven works great!" I stumble to recover. "Is there a dress code for where you'd like to go?" I figured it was a safe question to ask since he clearly likes nice things. I didn't want to show up to a fancy restaurant wearing jeans, but I also didn't want to show up in a little black dress and heels to a burger joint.

"I got us a reservation at Orion's, so whatever you deem fitting for that."

"I'm sure I can dig something up that's nicer than what I was wearing at the coffee shop."

"Well, anything *or nothing* would be just fine with me." I can hear his smile through the phone, and I'm instantly wet again, thinking about wearing nothing under him while he makes me scream.

"Noted. I'll see you Friday."

"See you then."

Chapter Five

LOUISA

It's Friday evening, and B has been doing my hair and makeup for what feels like hours. I'll hand it to her, though; it does look really good. She does her finishing touches and then walks over to my closet to grab the dress I bought earlier this week.

"And now, it's time to put on the dress!"

"You're acting like it's my wedding day, B. Try to remember that this is just a date."

"Yes, but it's your first actual date since Jay. And I have all the confidence in the world that Mr. Sexy Voice is going to make it a good one." She takes the dress off the hanger and opens up the hole for me to step into. "I mean, he's sending a car for you and taking you to dinner at one of the hottest restaurants in the city. No way it won't be amazing."

Matt texted me earlier this week saying that he has some business to attend to before our date down by where the restaurant is, so he's going to have a car sent to get me. I told him I was perfectly fine driving myself or taking an Uber, but he insisted.

When he said he had a reservation at Orion's, I was shocked. Reservations are nearly impossible to get there, especially on such short notice. Either he had this reservation for someone else, and it didn't work out, or it was a situation where he knows someone who knows someone.

I looked up their menu online so I wouldn't have to panic about what to order when I'm there. While on the website, I saw that there is a dress code, so he was setting me up to fail when he told me to wear whatever.

There's a knock on the front door as B grabs shoes for me out of her closet. She tosses them into my room and yells at me to hurry and put them on before running to get the door.

Still standing in front of the mirror in my room, I put them on and take a look at myself. We decided on a knee-length, emerald green, satin dress with a low-cut back that hugs my hips. The cowl at the neckline disguises my smaller boobs. My butt has always been one of my better features.

B slicked my hair up in a high pony and braided it. The makeup she did makes my eyes look big and bright. I put on the last of the jewelry she put out for me and make my way to the front door, where a man in a suit waits for me.

"Ready," I say, smiling and trying to act like being picked up by a strange man in a car is normal. "B, you have my location if you need to find me." One can never be too safe. And if this is a ploy to kidnap me, I want him to know that someone is going to come looking for me if I disappear.

———

I walk into the restaurant and am immediately escorted to a table way in the back where Matt is already seated. Like a gentleman, he stands up to greet me with a hug. He embraces me and then takes a step back, scanning me up and down. "You look absolutely stunning. I'm not going to be able to take my eyes off you the whole night."

"Thank you." I smile as he pulls out my chair for me. "This place is even nicer on the inside. I've walked by it so many times but have never actually eaten here."

"Well, I am glad I get to be with you the first time you experience it." He grabs the wine list from the table and asks, "Are you a wine drinker? They carry some very nice bottles here if you want to try some."

"That would be great. I'll let you pick since you seem to know what you're doing." I've never been a huge wine drinker, but I'll be anything he wants me to be.

When the waiter comes over, Matt orders a bottle of some sort of red wine that I've never heard of.

"So, how was the work stuff you had to do tonight?"

"It went well. I was just securing some properties in the area for future development."

I'm assuming he means for whatever company he works for. Matt and I didn't text much this week other than details for tonight. And I couldn't stalk him on the internet because I don't know his last name, so I don't know anything about him.

"What do you do for work?"

"I work in the restaurant and entertainment space. What about you?"

Ah, so that's how he was able to get this reservation. He probably has connections to all sorts of places in the city.

"I graduated with my architecture degree, and now I'm just working towards completing my experience hours before I start taking my licensure exams next summer."

"That's great. Do you like it so far? Think you chose the right career path?"

"Yeah, I do. I'm nervous about the exams, but I loved what I learned in school, and I'm starting to find more of what I like in my current job."

"So if you're able to take your exams next summer, then that makes you...25?"

I'm surprised he knows that it's typically a five-year degree instead of four. "I actually just turned 24. I was able to complete a lot of college classes in high school, so I got it done in four years instead of five."

"Impressive. And how do you feel about being with older men?"

We are getting right into it. "I've honestly never dated someone older than me, but I am getting a little sick of immature boys. So, I definitely see it as a plus." I want to ask how old he is, but that seems rude, even if he is clearly hinting at our age gap.

He smiles knowingly. "In the spirit of being mature, I always like to be very open and honest with the women I get involved with. So, if I may, I'd like to just lay out some expectations for you so you're fully aware of my intentions."

Finally! A man who knows what he wants, isn't afraid to ask for it, and has clear communication skills. Matt is going to be a complete breath of fresh air compared to my past relationships.

I nod and say, "Of course. I always appreciate honesty."

"That's what I like to hear." His smile fades ever so slightly. "I'm not looking for anything serious. I'm 34, I've been single for over a decade, and I know that the lifestyle I live works best when I'm not tied down. I tried to wrestle with that for several years and realized that it was not fair to the women I dated, so I just decided that long-term committed relationships aren't for me."

Well, that just took the wind out of my sails.

He continues, "If you are looking for something serious and don't want to continue with me, I completely respect that. But, if you're up for playing out a more revised role, then I'd love to have you on board. I'm just looking for someone with whom I can have a very casual relationship. We have fun together occasionally with no commitment and an understanding that it will never lead to more than that. I have a lot of events I go to, and it always looks best when a businessman has a date, so I like to bring women with whom I have formed a connection to make events less boring. Fun, Lou. It's just all about having fun. And at any point, if you want to terminate the situation, that is completely your call."

He's given me a lot to think about. On one hand, I have never done anything remotely close to this, so that scares me. On the other hand, I did just tell B that I didn't want to be tied down yet and that I just wanted to enjoy being single. Maybe this is the perfect situation presenting itself. Hot guy who just wants to fuck me and show me off; I guess that doesn't sound so bad.

After pausing to think it through, showing him that I am seriously considering what I'm getting myself into, I respond, "I think that is exactly what I need right now. I just got out of a long-term relationship, and I don't want anything too serious."

A mischievous grin spreads across his face, and I know I'm in trouble.

———

THE REST of dinner was great. We got to know more about each other and talked about life. After the start of our conversation, I was expecting him to keep everything very surface level. But to my surprise, he actually wanted to get to know me.

After our waiter took away our dessert plates, I was expecting him to bring the check. These things are always so awkward. I like to at least attempt to pay for my meal so I don't seem greedy, but with how he has treated me tonight thus far, I'm guessing that's not going to happen. The waiter never brings us a check, which I find odd, but maybe he already gave them his card when he went to the bathroom earlier. I saw a guy do that in a movie once, and I have always wanted someone to do that for me.

"If you're tired and want to go home, I can have my driver take you. Otherwise, if you're up for having the night continue, there's a cocktail bar I'd love to take you to."

I am not tired one bit. It might be the espresso martini I had with dessert, but I'm guessing it has more to do with the fact that the sexual tension between us is consistently sending electricity through my body.

"I'd love for the night to continue if you're not sick of my sarcasm yet."

He laughs and shakes his head. "Let's go; the car should be out back."

I stand and turn to walk toward the front door when he grabs my hand and tugs me back. "This way." He inclines his head toward the door that I believe goes to the kitchen. I give him a confused look but allow him to guide me through it.

We walk through the kitchen, where none of the staff even bat an eye at us, except for a woman who looks to me like she's in charge back here. We veer over toward her workstation. She wipes her hands on her apron as Matt introduces me, then introduces her. "This is Lana, the head chef here at Orion's.

"Nice to meet you." I shake her hand. "The meal was delicious."

"I'm glad you liked it," she says in a thick accent I can't quite place.

"Have a good night, Lana." I take that as our queue to leave. Matt tugs on my arm again, guiding me to the exit.

We step out the back door and are greeted by the cool night air. My short dress isn't doing much to keep me warm, and I didn't think to bring anything to cover up with. My body breaks out in bumps from the cold, and my nipples harden, my satin dress giving me away. Luckily, the car is right outside the back door.

The door of the black Escalade opens, and Matt guides me in, shutting the door behind me and running around to get in on the other side. The car is already warm, and the seats are heated as well. It takes a few seconds for my body to heat back up, and the pebbles on my skin start to fade. My nipples are the last thing to return to normal. As soon as they fade from plain sight, Matt leans over and whispers in my ear, "I'm sad to see them go. Maybe we should turn on the A/C and get them back."

My breath hitches, and I start getting wet between my thighs. The car starts driving out of the alley, and I can see a smirk on his face, knowing he's gotten a rise out of me. It's only a few minutes before we pull into another alley. We stop and a man opens my door for me and helps me down.

Matt is right there to offer me his arm, and he escorts me down the alley. I look around, unsure why we aren't stopping at any of the doors back here. When we get to the end of the alley, I start to ask what we're doing, but I'm cut off by him leaning into me. Did we really walk all the way down here to make out against the back wall of the alley?

Right as I'm about to lean into him, I realize he's not

leaning in; he's reaching across me. There's a small string hanging out from between two of the bricks, visible only if you know it's there. He pulls the string, and I can hear a small bell ring. Then, a lock clicks from the other side of the brick wall. I jump backwards, startled by the brick wall in front of us as it swings open.

I can tell he's getting a kick out of surprising me. He must do this with a lot of women. I wouldn't blame him because this shit has me wanting to give him everything.

He takes my hand, and we walk through the opening in the brick that was not there seconds before. We still haven't spoken a word since getting out of the car. I'm just following him blindly, trusting that he's not leading me to my demise. It's kind of thrilling, and he knows it.

At the end of a dark hallway, we are greeted by a server in a uniform who takes us through another door. This second door opens up into an elegantly decorated speakeasy bar with dim lighting. It's a cozy space, and there are so many nooks and crannies that several of the tables and booths have their own private area. It makes me think that if mob bosses still exist, they would definitely conduct business in a place like this.

We're guided by the same server to the back of the room and seated in a half-moon booth only big enough for two. The table is situated so it's isolated from the rest of the bar room—very private.

I just realized that Matt still hasn't said anything. How did the server know who he was or that he had a reservation? This is definitely an establishment that requires reservations well in advance, like Orion. Especially since I haven't even heard of this place. I thought I knew all the hot spots in the city.

Finally breaking the silence, Matt says, "Welcome to The Hallows."

"Am I about to be forced to swear a blood oath to a mob boss and then thrown in a trunk with a bag over my head? Because those are the vibes this place gives off." I'm obviously joking, but it really does.

"I'll tell Jillian you think her design works well for the intended concept."

Should I know who Jillian is? Did he mention her earlier tonight, and I just forgot her name? I really need to get better at remembering people's names.

The waiter comes over, and Matt orders for us after asking what my favorite spirit is. I said vodka because it seemed the safest. "I'll take Tracey's Old Fashion, and she'll have a Sex Under the Mountain."

"Is that drink's name by chance in reference to a trending fairy smut book?"

"I believe so," he says with a nod and that devilish grin he's been giving me all night.

The music is loud enough in here that you can't hear the conversation of the table adjacent to you but quiet enough that you can converse easily with the person directly next to you. Why can't all places keep their volume at this level?

The song "For Me" by Lo Nightly is playing, setting a vibe in the room that makes my skin tingle. After I'm done scanning the room and taking in all the details that some people might miss, I turn my head back to him. He looks at me with darkened eyes, making my heart race. I want him so badly. I wish we were in private so I could act on these urges.

Matt leans into me, brushing his lips on my cheekbone. I can't help but roll my head to the side to give him access to my neck. His lips graze my skin softly, working his way down my neck to my collarbone. Meanwhile, his hand slides across the velvet cushion and onto my exposed thigh. I feel my body responding to his touch, and I can't help but give in to him.

His lips leave my neck, and I immediately miss their warmth. His free hand grabs the side of my face and brings my lips to his. They are so soft and warm. His tongue sweeps across mine, and I let out a small moan. The sound makes him grip me harder, and he slides his right hand further up my thigh, slipping under my dress.

The clink of glass hitting the table breaks me from his spell. My heart races with a combination of arousal and surprise. My head pulls away from his, trying to act like he didn't just have his hand up my skirt or his tongue in my mouth. Matt seems completely unfazed though. "Thank you, Jeffery." I look into his eyes, and he can sense my hesitation. "There's no need to worry or be embarrassed."

"They're going to kick us out of here if we keep going where I want this to go." I pick up the drink and take a sip, trying to cool myself off.

"They can't, love. I own the place."

I choke on my drink but recover quickly and say, "You...what?"

"The Hallows, Orion's, and several other bars and restaurants around the city. Jillian is my cousin, and she designs the interiors of all my locations."

I relax a bit, relief washing over me. And he can tell.

"I can tell you've been noticing odd things throughout the night but didn't say anything." I nod, affirming his suspicion. "I don't like to bring it up if I don't have to, but I definitely am not letting the opportunity to please you right here slip through my fingers." He leans in close again, those full lips teasing mine with soft touches. "Jeffery won't be interrupting us anymore. And neither will anyone else."

I lean forward, crashing my lips into his, and part mine for him. His hand that remained on my upper thigh this whole time continues its way up to my panties. His knuckle grazes my center, applying just the right amount of pressure. It takes my breath away, and I pull my lips away from his for a second to collect myself. I know he promised me privacy back here, but I'm sure the other patrons would prefer not to hear me moan.

He takes the break as an opportunity to lean in. "You're so fucking wet, Lou. Have you been this wet all night?"

I press my cheek against his and let out a breathy reply, "Pretty much."

"Good girl."

My breath hitches again, and I clear my throat, trying not to fully melt into my seat.

His hand under my dress has been working on me, and I can't handle it anymore. I need more of him. As if he can read my mind, his finger loops around the edge of my panties and pulls them to the side, allowing himself full access to me. His finger teases my entrance before slipping inside. My arm flies up and clutches the sleeve of his dress shirt, and I suck in a deep breath.

My body melts into his as he adds another finger and plays with me so well. Heat starts pooling in my belly, and I can feel it coming. God, it's been so long since a man has made me come. Grabbing the fabric of his shirt tighter and dropping my head into the base of his neck, I try to suppress my moan as I fall over the edge. I can feel my pelvic muscles contracting and clenching his fingers inside of me.

I'm just coming down from that high when he pulls his fingers out and sticks them in his mouth, licking them clean.

"I knew you would taste amazing." I lean in and kiss him again, this time slow and soft to ease myself down. I can taste myself on his lips, and I don't mind one bit.

Once my breathing levels out, I start to feel bad that he hasn't gotten anything from me. I reach my hand over to his lap and slide it up his thigh. He grabs my hand and smiles at me. "No need. Tonight was about you."

"But...?"

"If you go on a second date with me, then we can explore that side of things. For tonight, I wanted you to see what this could be. But I want you to really think about if this is something you want without having fully committed to it already."

I narrow my eyes like I'm skeptical. "I thought your whole thing was about *not* committing."

"You know what I mean. Think about it and let me know if you want to stay in touch. If not, there are no hard feelings. But until you officially tell me no, I'll be dreaming about how wet you were tonight and how good I know it's going to feel to be inside you." He grips my chin between his fingers and kisses my forehead.

"How many days do I have to decide?"

He chuckles. "There's no timeline. Take all the time you need."

Chapter Six

LOUISA

After my first date with Matt, I was riding the high for a few days. I had never experienced something so thrilling. The practical side of me brought me back down and reminded me that this is not the end game. This is only temporary and purely for enjoyment.

Matt made that very clear, and I'm not self-loathing enough to think I can change his mind. But just being touched by him and having his attention is enough for me at this point in my life. And it doesn't hurt that he's fun to hang out with.

The highlight of my night was getting off, but the rest of it was also very enjoyable. I've decided that if he asks to go out again, I'm going to say yes.

LOU

Hey, Matt.

MATT

Well hello, beautiful.

LOU

I've made up my mind.

MATT

And...?

LOU

I would love to continue seeing you.

MATT

I'm glad to hear that. Are you sure?

LOU

Yes

MATT

Good girl.

It's been a couple of weeks since I messaged Matt, and I haven't heard anything. To be fair, I haven't messaged him either. I've been extremely busy with work, and in my free time, I've been either going on walks with Pepin or scrolling on a dating app B forced me to sign up for. So far, nothing has come out of it. I'm pretty picky, and B reassures me that's not a bad thing.

I'm currently sitting in the living room watching a show with Pepin and B when my phone dings on the coffee table. I lean forward to pick it up. When I see it's Matt, my heart starts to beat a little faster.

MATT

Hello, gorgeous.

LOU

Hi, handsome.

MATT

I'm having a Halloween party at my place next weekend, and I want you to be there.

> **LOU**
> Can I bring a guest?

MATT
As long as I don't have to share you with them.

> **LOU**
> Unlikely, as it would be my sister.

MATT
Sisters are always welcome in my bed.

> **LOU**
> Ha Ha

MATT
Of course you can bring your sister and anyone else who won't try to steal you from me.

> **LOU**
> Okay, I'll be there.

MATT
Lovely. I'll send a car for you.

I tried to tell him that wasn't necessary, but he again insisted.

———

Tonight is Matt's Halloween party, and B might be more excited than I am. But she will be ditching me the second half of the evening to attend her boss, Daniel's, party.

I look at myself in the mirror and slightly regret letting B pick out my costume. She chose to make me a classic angel. Of course, it's slutty; I knew that when I conceded, but I didn't think I could feel confident in something so revealing.

The little white dress barely covers my ass and is low cut—to show off the little cleavage I have—with spaghetti straps. B's my counterpart with her tiny red leather dress and horns. I'd much rather wear a headband with devil horns than these itchy angel wings, but I lost that battle. B is curvier than I am, and the angel dress did not have enough support to contain her tits. Not that her leather dress is doing much better, but I think she likes it that way.

I had a pair of baby blue heels from years ago that B said were okay to wear with my costume; they make my legs look a mile long. I'm nervous I'm going to be taller than Matt. At 5'6", I'm considered above average height for a woman, and wearing heels makes me as tall as average-height men. Matt isn't short, but he's only a few inches taller than me. If I had to guess, I'd say he's probably 5'9". I was the same height as him on our first date, which made me nervous he would be self-conscious, but he didn't seem to be bothered. He is a very confident man.

"Are you ready to go? The car should be here in a few minutes."

B yells from her bedroom, "Yeah, just touching up my makeup." I walk into her room to check that she's telling the truth, and she spots me in her mirror. "Damn, you look hot! Matt is for sure fucking you tonight."

I roll my eyes at her and walk to the kitchen to fill Pepin's food and water bowl before we leave. He does really well when we're gone for several hours, but I always feel bad leaving him alone, so I put a little pumpkin in his bowl to make up for it. He immediately runs when he hears me and sits like a good boy, waiting for me to finish preparing it.

He came out of the box perfectly trained. It took me a

few days to figure out what commands he knows, but after that, he's been so easy. I couldn't have asked for a better first dog.

As I'm putting his bowl down on the ground, he starts licking my face lovingly, as if to say, "Thank you, Mom."

"Pepin! Quit ruining my masterpiece."

I spot B standing in the doorway to the kitchen. Busted. She spent a long time perfecting my makeup, glitter and all.

"How bad is it?" I ask, standing up and allowing her to inspect the damage.

"Actually, it's not too bad, but Pep is definitely going to be shitting glitter for a while." We both giggle and look down at him chugging water, likely regretting his decision.

B touches up my left cheek, making sure they're even before we head down to the entryway to wait for Matt's driver. I felt bad that he had to come up and get me last time, even though I know that's his job.

———

WHEN WE ARRIVE at Matt's building, the doorman greets us and asks for our names. He checks his list and then walks us to the elevator. Matt didn't give me an apartment number, and I still don't know his last name, but clearly, the doorman knows where we're going. I feel a little silly dressed like this in such an elegant historic building.

The doorman inserts a key into a slot and presses the 'P' button. Of course Matt lives in the penthouse. It's a long ride up 30 floors. B and I look at each other, and I giggle. I'm both nervous and excited. B has been to parties like this before, but I haven't.

The doors open, and it's one of those apartments where the elevator opens directly into the unit. We're instantly greeted with music, lights, and people dancing. It's like a club in here. I look to my right, where the DJ booth is, and see a young man with bleach-blonde hair behind the table. He's cute, but he looks like he may bat for the other team.

To our left is a large kitchen with an island the size of my bedroom. It's filled with hors d'oeuvres and little Jack-o-lantern decorations. Next to it is a bar with two bartenders mixing up drinks. They're both dressed in costumes, but you can tell they're hired to help and not guests by the professional way they carry themselves.

Straight in front of us is a dance floor in what I'm assuming is usually the living room. But it looks like all the furniture is relocated to the back of the room and arranged so there's a sitting area by the big glass doors leading out to a terrace. There are a few hallways branching off of the main area, likely leading to bedrooms, offices, and that sort of stuff.

The architecture in this historic building is amazing. I can't stop looking at it and admiring the craftsmanship.

"Let's grab a drink first," I lean over and say in B's ear.

As we make our way over there, I see a staircase in the back left corner, behind the bar, that I didn't spot the first time. It leads up to a loft, and you can't see what's beyond that. My eyes keep darting from one unique detail to the other.

"I knew you'd like it."

I startle and turn around to see Matt standing very close behind me in a toga costume; he looks like a Greek god.

He knows I have an admiration for great architecture. "It's beautiful."

"As are you, my little angel." He takes my hand and lifts it above my head, guiding me to spin so he can see my whole outfit.

"Matt, this is my sister. B, this is Matt."

"Damn, Lou, you weren't lying. He's hot." She says it loudly so that not only Matt but also the bartenders and people in line behind us can hear it.

He gives one of his deep, sexy laughs, and I blush.

"And you're as bold as she said you are."

B straightens her shoulders, and I know she took that as a compliment. "I find it exhausting to be filtered and ashamed. I don't know how Lou does it."

He tilts his head to the side and looks at me with a knowing smile. "We've been working on that, haven't we, Lou."

My face heats. "One could say that."

He gestures toward the seating area in the back of the room and invites us to sit. "Why don't you guys join me? I was just chatting with an old friend of mine you might know." He says that directly to B, so I'm curious who it could be.

We walk over, and he introduces us to a person I've never seen before, and I don't recognize their name.

But apparently, B does. "Oh my god! I love your music."

Matt can tell I'm lost, so he clarifies for me. "Stevie is the lead singer in the band Grumpy Old Bear."

"That sweatshirt is for a band?" I direct my question to both B and Matt. "You never cared to mention that?"

They both laugh at my ignorance, and I realize that I admitted to this stranger that I have no clue who they are, nor did I know that was the name of a band. I want to shove my foot in my mouth right now.

"Yes, Grumpy Old Bear is a band. I knew right away you had no clue who they were even though you were wearing their sweatshirt. Stevie and I go way back, and they're in town working on their next album."

Stevie looks over to B, who is fangirling so hard right now. "You could stop by the studio sometime this week if you want to meet the rest of the band."

"I think I'm going to die," B says, leaning over on me, acting as though she's going to pass out. "Yes, I would love that!" Then she lifts her head to look at me and says, "You need to meet more hot strangers at coffee shops because cool shit keeps happening to me when you do." To that, we all burst out laughing.

As we're walking away from Stevie toward the terrace, B leans in and whispers, for once, "I have such a crush on them! I'm going to wear my hottest outfit to that studio session. Maybe they'll ask me out. I really would die."

Oh, B. Whatever am I going to do with that girl?

The night air is chilly out on the terrace, but there are fire pits and heaters scattered all over to keep people warm. Matt said he had to run and handle something quickly but to meet him out here.

B and I are standing in line at another bar to get a fresh drink. The cocktails they're serving taste so good. I guzzled my first one down so fast, and I'm already starting to feel it. B and I pre-gamed prior to coming here, so that is also contributing to my buzz.

We get our new drinks and stand by a heater to wait. "You know what, I'm going to let you and Mr. Sexy Toga Man have some alone time. I'm going to get Stevie out on the dance floor." Without waiting for a response, she bolts inside.

I'm not standing alone long before I see Matt walking through one of the large glass doors with a drink in his hand. It looks like one of those old fashions he had on our date or some sort of dark liquor on ice.

"Sorry about that. The DJ asked to add a guest to the

list, so I had to call down to the concierge." He's standing close to me, and I can feel his body heat warming my skin. Or maybe it's just the heater we're standing by. Either way, I'm so horny around him. As if he read my mind again, he asks, "Would you like a tour...of my bedroom?"

I look at him through thick lashes. "I would love to see your bedroom. But first, can I get a full tour of the place? I'm dying to know what the rest looks like." As much as I want to run to his bedroom and pounce on him, my curiosity is getting the best of me.

Matt agrees and takes me inside.

The rest of the house is just as glamorous as the main living area, complete with crown moulding and handcrafted woodwork. At first, I pegged Matt as a sleek and modern industrial-style man, but now I see how well he fits in a place like this. Classic, timeless.

By the time we get to his bedroom, which he conveniently saved for last, the sexual tension is at an all-time high. His bedroom is up the stairs behind the loft I spotted earlier.

He opens the bedroom door and allows me to enter first. It's full of antique furniture and looks straight out of a design magazine.

"I know I've said this about a million times by now, but WOW."

"I'd like to keep you saying that all night long." He steps closer and wraps his arms around my waist, pulling me into him.

I heard him lock the door on our way in, and there's a security guard by the stairs, so I know we won't be disturbed this time. I place my hands on his chest and wrap one fist in his costume, pulling his face closer to mine. I may have been a little timid at first, but I want him to know that I want this.

I nod, and to make sure he knows, I whisper on his lips, "I want you."

He takes that as his queue and connects his lips with mine, kissing me with passion and urgency. My breathing is heavy, and I can feel liquid heat pooling between my legs. He walks me backwards until my legs hit the edge of the bed, and l fall back onto it.

I expect him to crawl on top of me, but instead, he kneels down, positioning himself between my legs. He slides his hands up both my thighs and pulls down my panties. My dress has already ridden up over my ass, so I'm exposed to him now.

"God, she's beautiful."

He wraps his arms around my legs and pulls me toward the edge of the bed so his face is right in line with what he wants. His tongue sweeps up my center, and I whimper, reaching my hands down to grab his hair. His twists are pulled back into a ponytail, so there's nothing for me to grab. Instead, I wrap my fists in the blanket I'm lying on.

His tongue works in long strokes at first before picking up pace around my bundle of nerves. My legs start shaking. He tightens his grip on them and places his palms on my lower abdomen to hold me still. A finger finds its way to the most sensitive part of me and slowly works in circles while his tongue goes back to long, firm strokes.

"Right there!"

He continues a pattern that has me holding my breath. My hands grab hold of his arms wrapped around my legs, and I squeeze as I tip over the edge. My upper body lifts a few inches off the bed as my abs flex with pleasure.

He slows his movements, and I catch my breath as I come down. He unwraps his arms and lifts himself to a standing position between my legs as they dangle off the bed. I'm breathing heavily as he strokes my thighs.

"Good girl."

A tingle runs down my spine at his praise. I never knew that was a thing I liked till he did it at the speakeasy.

He walks over to a dresser on the far wall, and I roll over on my stomach, my eyes tracking him. He reaches into the top drawer and pulls out a long rope.

"Have you ever played with rope?"

I still haven't quite caught my breath, so I just shake my head.

"Want to try something new?"

Again, I use my head to communicate. I nod with a smile on my face.

As he gets closer, I get a better look at the rope. It looks like twine, and I'm a little scared it's going to hurt.

"Roll over onto your back."

I do as I'm told, scooting myself so I'm more in the center of the bed. He crawls to where I'm laying and grabs my legs one at a time, bending them so my feet are by my ass and my knees are by his chest.

"This should feel tight and bite a little, but let me know if it hurts or feels like it's cutting off circulation, okay?"

"Okay."

He gently wraps the rope around my leg, starting at my ankle and upper thigh all the way up to just below my knee. He was wrapping it in a crisscross pattern that I wasn't paying attention to. He tucks the loose ends into one of the Xs and moves to do the same thing to the other leg with a separate piece of rope. My legs now look like candy canes, and I can only move them at the hips. I'm still not entirely sure what this is supposed to be doing.

He backs off the bed and undoes the clasp holding up

his toga on his left shoulder, letting it drop to the floor. All he's wearing now is his boxer briefs, and I can see how hard he is beneath them. I'm instantly wet again. He opens his nightstand and pulls out a condom. Finally, he pulls down his underwear, leaving him fully naked in front of me.

He skillfully rolls the condom on and positions himself over me so his tip is resting at my entrance.

"Let me know if you want me to stop or to untie you. Got it?"

"Yes." My voice comes out more assertive than I thought.

He presses into me, and I can feel him fill me a little at a time, going slowly in and out until his hips meet my feet that are strapped to my thighs. My instinct is to wrap my legs around him and pull him even closer, but I realize I can't. Interesting.

His first full thrust in and out makes me arch my back and moan. When I look back up at him, he's smiling. He knows exactly what he's doing to me.

My hands find their way to his face, and I pull him down to kiss me. He puts one hand behind my head while the other braces him up. He starts thrusting in and out at a slightly faster pace for a while. After his tongue has thoroughly explored mine, he lets go of my head and sits up while keeping himself inside of me.

He rests his hands on my knees and spreads my legs wider. My feet are still tied down in a spot that restricts him from entering me all the way to the base, but he's hitting the perfect spot. His thrusts quicken and get more aggressive, making me start to build toward another orgasm.

The pressure keeps building, and I throw my hands over my head to grab the edge of the mattress. He's thrusting so hard, and I start to realize the point of binding my legs in this way. If I was fully spread in front of him with no restrictions, he would be destroying me right now.

The realization that he intentionally did this for my comfort and pleasure sends me over the edge. I try to extend my legs, but the rope restricts them, giving me something to tense up against. This time my orgasm is more intense than the first, and all I can do is yell, "Fuck! Fuck! Fuck!" as I come all over his cock.

I start to get extremely sensitive, and I'm nervous he'll continue at this pace, but he slows down and comes right along with me.

After a moment, he slowly pulls himself out and starts untying my legs. "Fuck baby, you're so hot when you come like that."

After I'm free, I sit up and stretch my legs.

"Were they too tight?" he asks, looking at my purple-striped legs. Surprisingly, they don't hurt, but that could be because my body aches all over.

"No, it was kind of nice."

He gets up off the bed and walks toward a door leading to the bathroom. "Come on, you can shower here."

He hands me a towel and points me in the direction of his massive tile shower with floor-to-ceiling glass panels and *three* shower heads. I strip off my dress before selecting a shower head and rinsing off.

After my shower, I walk out of the bathroom to find him sitting in a chair by the window, waiting there for me. He hands me my phone. "B tried to call you."

"She was probably just trying to tell me that she's heading to her other party."

"I'll have my car take you back so you don't have to ride home alone."

"You really don't have to do that."

He grips my chin and kisses my forehead. "But I'm going to because I want to make sure my new plaything gets home safe."

I know he's only partially joking, so I roll my eyes and playfully punch him in the shoulder.

————

ON THE RIDE HOME, I had 20 minutes to think about what all went down tonight. I ended up calling B, and she tried to beg me to go to Daniel's party, but I'm so ready to crawl into bed. She finally gives it up, but I'm guessing that has less to do with her admitting defeat and more to do with the person calling her name in the background.

Tonight was amazing, and Matt was amazing. In a fairy tale, he would be the bad boy that I change, and he would fall in love with me. But the reality is that Matt was very clear about his intentions, and I have to respect that. I am not about to be a "pick me" girl and pine over something I can't have.

I walk up the stairs to my apartment and am greeted by Pepin at the door. His tail wags and I'm just as happy to see him as he is to see me. I wash my face, brush my teeth, and snuggle into bed, Pep by my side.

I mindlessly scroll on the dating app, mostly swiping left with the occasional swipe right.

"Goodnight, Pepin. I love you." I plant a kiss on the top of his head, and he nuzzles into me.

Chapter Seven

LOUISA

It's a Saturday morning, and I have nothing to do. B is out of town for a work trip and will be gone for a week. I went to college in a different state, and most of my college friends stayed there while I moved back to my home state to be closer to family. And working from home isn't very conducive to meeting new people. So when B is gone, it's pretty much just Pepin and I.

I usually do lots of reading, study for my licensure exams, and take Pepin on walks. He loves walks and insists on at least one a day. I'm not exactly sure how that's going to work in the winter, but that's a problem I'll figure out later.

I open the dating app and start mindlessly scrolling. So far, nothing good has come out of it. A few messages here and there, but I easily get the ick, so they tend to not go anywhere.

Zach: Ew, another guy holding a dead fish. Left.
Seth: Confederate flag hat, no thank you. Left.
What is this app's problem? Either I've scrolled through

all the eligible bachelors in the Twin Cities area, or the algorithm needs some updating.

Brandon: Likes the outdoors, 25 years old, has pretty eyes, full head of hair. Right.

Ethan: Assault rifle in the first picture, seriously, dude? Left.

Kevin: Likes plants, 24 years old, enjoys intramural sports... Mormon. Left.

Sam: Likes dogs, 26 years old, has a picture with a Pride flag, and is a small business owner.

Before swiping right, I linger on his page for a minute. He looks vaguely familiar, but then again, he sort of has that basic, All-American look to him. Brown curly hair, 6'2", and dresses well, but not so well that he'll judge my clothing. I can't tell what color his eyes are; they present differently in every picture. He has one of those kind-looking faces where you know he's nice to his mom. And bonus that none of his photos are a shirtless mirror pic at the gym.

Right.

———

SAM

Work has started to slow down now that it's fall, so I find myself bored more often. That's how I let my younger brother, Quinn, talk me into signing up for a dating app. I was really hoping I would find someone the organic way, but that hasn't panned out so far. So here I am on a Monday afternoon, scrolling on my phone when I decide to check if there's anyone new is on the dating app.

Quinn pretty much set up my entire profile for me. I made my own at first, but he asked to see it and immediately took charge, changing everything. Literally, everything.

Except for my name and age, I guess. The version of me he put on here is accurate; it's just a more curated version of me.

I swipe left on six women in a row, and I almost swipe past her out of habit, but I stop myself in time. She's stunning. Shoulder length, straight brown hair, gorgeous brown eyes, very naturally pretty. She's an aspiring architect, lives in the city, has a dog. She can't be real. I swipe right before I accidentally mess this up. There's no way we're going to match, though; she is way out of my league. But the screen lights up saying, 'It's a MATCH.'

"Shut. Up."

My heart races, and I suddenly feel the pressure to say something good. I've never been this nervous to message someone on here. I tap 'Message Louisa Now' and freeze. After twelve different drafts, I finally send one, and it's not even clever.

SAM

Hey Louisa. Is that a standard labradoodle in one of your pictures? He's adorable.

I lock my phone so I stop staring at it, waiting for her to reply. A walk to the kitchen will distract me. I make myself a sandwich and sit on a stool by the island to eat it. I sit there waiting for it to buzz, but it doesn't.

I successfully ignore my phone for the next hour while watching a show. Then it dawns on me that I never turned on notifications for that app. I jolt forward and knock my phone off the coffee table while trying to grab it. I pick it up off the floor, and the screen unlocks to my face. The last thing I had open on the phone was that app, so it's the first thing to pop up. One message notification. I click it and pray that it's her.

SAM

Hey Louisa. Is that a standard labradoodle in one of your pictures? He's adorable.

LOU

I adopted him, so I don't know for sure, but they think he is a labradoodle. His name is Pepin, and he's 10 years old.

I can't believe she responded.

SAM

How long have you had him?

LOU

I just got him in August.

SAM

What made you adopt an older dog?

LOU

I honestly don't know. He was so sweet when I met him at the shelter, and I just couldn't leave him there. Originally I wanted a younger big dog to take on long walks with me. But surprisingly, Pepin loves to go on walks. Actually insists on it, daily. So it all worked out.

———

LOUISA

We talked until I fell asleep last night and throughout the day on Tuesday. Mostly just small talk and getting to know the basics. He's so cute and so far checks a lot of boxes—accomplished, kind, and ambitious. Not to mention handsome as hell.

I had to pry it out of him, but I learned that he runs his own landscaping company. I am a very goal-oriented person, so it's important for me to find a partner who has goals.

Partner...look at me jumping ten steps ahead. Why do I always do that? Chill out, Lou; you literally just met the man. For all I know, he could just be another good lay like Matt and nothing more. But something in my gut tells me Sam isn't the "hit it and quit it" type.

I'm running out of basic questions to ask him, and I don't know what to do because I've never gotten this far. Then I remember B has a card game she's obsessed with that asks the players deep questions. I go to the living room, where we store all of our games on a shelf. Scanning through them, I finally spot the little red box.

LOU

Are you up for playing a game?

My sister has a card game that is full of random questions.

SAM

I'd love that. What's it called?

LOU

We're Not Really Strangers.

SAM

That sounds like the perfect game for two people who meet on an app lol.

LOU

Great. So there are three levels and the depth of the questions increase with the level.

I'll start with Level 1.

What does my wallpaper tell you about me?

I send him a screenshot of my lock screen. It's an image of Pepin and B on the couch in our apartment

SAM

It tells me that you love your dog, which I already assumed about you.

Is that your sister, B?

LOU

Yes, it is. What gave it away?

The purple hair?

SAM

Haha, yes.

LOU

Without looking, what color are my eyes?

SAM

Caramel brown

LOU

Wow, that was fast!

SAM

It was one of the first things I noticed about you.

LOU

Well, that was the next question, so I guess I'll draw another card.

Do you think I'm usually early, on time, or late to events? Explain.

SAM

Definitely early. I mean this in the best way possible, you give off Type A energy.

LOU

You are not wrong.

Rate your dancing skills on a scale of 1-10. It says we both need to answer this question, so at 10:55, send your answer.

5

SAM

8

LOU

8!? Wow, now I need to see those dance moves.

SAM

Haha, hopefully someday you will. I'm sure you're better than a 5, you look pretty athletic.

LOU

I guess you'll have to find out for yourself. But you can't say I didn't warn you.

What do you think my go-to car karaoke song is?

SAM

Man, I Feel Like A Woman by Shania Twain

LOU

That's a great answer. I wish I would have thought of it myself. But, being truthful, my answer is iSpy by KYLE and Lil Yachty.

Lots of great memories associated with that song.

SAM

Now THAT was unexpected.

I like this game!

LOU

Make an assumption about me.

SAM

You sleep with socks on.

LOU

How dare you. I am NOT a psychopath.

Of course I do not sleep with socks on.

Do you?

SAM

I do not.

LOU

Thank god.

Ooo interesting. This card just says, "Reminder: Let go of your attachment to the outcome."

I feel like the universe is out to get me with that one.

SAM

How so?

LOU

As you guessed correctly earlier, I am very Type A. I guess that leads me to put a lot of pressure on myself. I'm very goal-oriented and try to control the outcome of my life as much as I can.

SAM

I think having goals is great. You're obviously a very accomplished person, Lou.

I hope someday you allow yourself to not feel so much pressure.

LOU

Thanks, Sam.

> Okay, I'm getting pretty tired but I'll draw one more card.

> Do you fall in love easily? Why or why not?

SAM

Yes and no. No, I don't because I know what I want, and I don't want to waste anyone's time if I don't see a future. But yes, when I know something feels right, I fall hard and fast.

Do you?

I'm shocked by how unashamed he is of being honest and talking about emotions.

LOU

> I guess I do. I've pretty much been in long-term relationships for most of my teen and young adult life with a small amount of time in between where I was single.

SAM

You say that like it's a bad thing?

LOU

> My sister thinks I need to take more time and enjoy being single.

SAM

She's not wrong.

But if you find someone who makes you happy, why stop yourself just because of some arbitrary timeline?

LOU

> I think it may be the arbitrary timelines that push me towards relationships.

SAM

Care to elaborate?

LOU

Maybe some other time. I'm really tired.

Goodnight, Sam.

SAM

Of course. Night, Lou.

I lock my phone and place it on my nightstand. How does this man have me almost telling him my biggest insecurities? He makes me feel like I can trust him, like he'd understand and wouldn't judge me.

I roll over and snuggle into Pepin, who has been curled up by my side for the last hour. I pepper him with kisses from his snout to his head. "Goodnight, Pepin. I love you."

SAM

The next morning, I roll over in bed, and the first thing I do is check my phone to see if Lou has messaged me. I see a message notification on the app, and I get excited. When I open it, I'm met with disappointment because the message isn't from Lou; it's from someone named Kirsten, who I don't even remember matching with.

KIRSTEN

Hi Sam. You're so cute, and I was wondering if you wanted to go get coffee sometime?

I click out of my phone and decide I'll respond to her

later. You can't see if someone has read your message or not on this app, so I don't have to feel bad about leaving her on read. I always respond to people because I feel guilty if I don't. I mean, I did swipe right on them, so in theory, I should be interested. But sometimes, I find myself not as into someone as I originally thought. The last thing I want to do is hurt anyone's feelings, but sometimes I message them for too long, and then I'm a jerk because I'm leading them on.

It's different with Lou, though. I'm excited about her, and I'm worried she's going to stop talking to *me*. I need to keep this game going so I can learn more about her, and so she'll keep talking to me.

I throw on some jeans and a plain black T-shirt, brush my teeth, and throw on a hat since I'm just running down the road to Target. My curls are a little unruly if I don't wash them and put product in my hair. Growing up, I used to always keep my hair cut short because I didn't know how to manage my frizzy curls, nor did I care to. Eventually, my younger brother Quinn forced me to grow them out and taught me how to take care of them. He made me buy products and even wrote out the order in which I needed to use them. I don't need to reference the guide anymore, but it still takes time. And on days when I'm too lazy, I just throw on a hat.

I hop in my pickup and pull out of the driveway. The neighbor kids are playing in a big pile of leaves, and it makes me smile. I remember when my brothers and I were little, we would bury each other in leaf piles and try to scare our mom. We never dared try to scare Dad; he always had a short fuse. Correction: *has* a short fuse. He beat Jacob, my older brother, one time for pulling a confetti popper in the house. And the memory that started off happy turned dark.

That tends to happen when I reminisce about my childhood.

My dad is a corporate lawyer, so I grew up in an upper-class family. Joel Carlyle. What a fucking dick. My parents divorced when I was in middle school, and it couldn't have happened soon enough. I'm a firm believer that "staying together for the kids" is a load of crap. If you hate each other, split up so your kids don't have to witness your train wreck of a marriage for too long.

Jacob had it the worst, though. He ended up having to care for my mother when my dad left; she was a wreck. He became the "man of the house" at the ripe age of 14. And no matter how responsible he had to be at mom's house, he was still treated like a little kid when we went to visit Joel.

Before I know it, I'm in the Target parking lot. I quickly run inside, find the game section, and check out. When I get home, I tear open the package and open the little red box. I open the packs of cards labeled Level 1, Level 2, and Level 3.

Lou has been asking me questions from the Level 1 deck. I wanted to buy it so I could contribute to the game and ask her more questions. I crave talking to her, and any excuse to continue it, I'm in. I could tell she didn't want to dive into whatever insecurity she was referring to last night, so I won't push it. She can tell me when she's ready.

I shuffle the Level 2 deck and draw one from the top.

Chapter Eight

LOUISA

My phone buzzes on my desk, the notification says I got a message on the dating app. I hope it's Sam. I was too nervous to message him first after I cut him off last night and didn't answer his question.

> SAM
>
> What title would you give this chapter in your life?

Last night, I browsed through the Level 2 cards to see if they were too intense to ask Sam. I recognize this as one of them.

> LOU
>
> Did you go buy the cards last night?

> SAM
>
> No.
>
> I went this morning. I didn't want you to be doing all the heavy lifting here.

LOU

That's so cute, Sam.

SAM

Chapter title?

LOU

Oh, right! I would probably call it 'Learning to let go'. But I'm still in the very beginning of that chapter.

SAM

Learning to let go is a really hard thing.

Anything in particular you're trying to let go of?

LOU

Nothing specific. I'm a little high-strung, so I've been learning to just go with the flow more and let things happen in my life, even if it's not a part of my plan.

SAM

I think that's great.

LOU

Thanks, Sam.

Next question. Have you changed your mind about anything recently?

SAM

Dating apps! I was about ready to give up on it. I'm really glad I didn't.

Aka, I'm glad I matched with you.

LOU

I'm glad B talked me into this and that I stuck with it for a bit. I almost deleted it, because I was meeting more guys in the real world than on here.

SAM

Oh? I find it so hard to make connections organically these days. I also don't go out very much, so that's probably it.

LOU

Well, I wouldn't call them "connections" per se. They were singular interactions, if you know what I mean.

SAM

I catch your drift. I could use an interaction like that. I'm in a bit of a dry spell. (That is not me asking you to hook up; that would be tacky).

LOU

Haha, that would be tacky.

How long is this dry spell you're in?

SAM

Honestly, I think about a year. I've been putting a lot of my energy into work.

LOU

Understandable.

If I'm being completely honest, sex was rare in the last year of my relationship with Jay. He was never in the mood, which made me frustrated and then that also made *me* not in the mood. It was a negative feedback loop that we never got out of.

Sam and I talked for the rest of the day, going back and forth answering Level 2 questions.

SAM

What is your mother's name? Tell me one thing about her.

LOU

My mother's name is Eden, she's a middle school social studies teacher.

SAM

That must take an incredible amount of patience.

LOU

She is the most patient person I've ever met.

Well, maybe tied with my dad. That super power must have skipped a generation because my sister and I have none.

SAM

I don't know how to respond to that without implicating myself.

LOU

Smart man.

———

SAM

"How do I ask her out on a date?" I hand Quinn a box of screws and hold the board level.

He grabs a few out and fastens the shelf to the wall. "Just fucking ask, man."

"We've been talking for a week now. If she wanted to go out with me, she probably would have said something by now, right?"

"She's probably saying the same thing about you, idiot."

Quinn always makes everything seem so easy. Just because he goes on 2 dates a week doesn't mean the rest of us have his level of game. But he has a point. Neither Lou nor I have really done this online dating thing before.

"Well, I don't know the rules."

He drops the drill down on the counter and turns toward me. "There isn't a set of rules, Sam. You like the girl, right?"

I nod, a little embarrassed. "Yeah."

"Then ask the girl on a damn date! The worst she can do is say no."

I hate when he's right. "What should I even-"

"Give me your phone!" He grabs me and starts feeling my pockets for my phone. I try pivoting and backing away from him, but he easily corners me in the small bathroom. He eventually gets a hold of it and runs out to the dining room, distancing himself from me on the other side of the table.

"Quinn, don't you dare!"

"What's your password? 1234?"

I run around the table, and he maintains the distance.

"Dude, you need to change your password. You've clearly never had a nosy girlfriend."

"Shut up. Give it to me, Quinn. I'm serious."

———

LOUISA

"What does one wear on a first date to an apple orchard?"

It's 6:00pm in London right now, and B is getting ready to go to a work dinner while I get ready for my first date with Sam. I asked her to FaceTime me because I'm freaking out.

"Are you planning to get laid?"

"At the apple orchard? Seriously, B."

"I meant *after,* but that would be sexy, too."

75

I roll my eyes at her. "We didn't talk about hanging out after. We just planned to meet there at 2:00."

"Invite him over after."

"Let's take this one step at a time. What if I don't like him in person?"

"Who said you had to like him to fuck him? I mean, did you forget about Darrah."

"Yeah, because that went soooo well."

She's off-screen at the moment, but I can hear her cackling in the distance. "You got me there."

I've been waiting for her to come back so I can show her the outfit I picked. "What do you think?"

"I was ready to shut down your first pick, but honestly, Lou, you look damn good! I've taught you well."

"Sure, take all the credit, you brat."

"Love you!" She blows me a kiss through the phone.

"Alright, I have to go. Have fun at your work dinner."

"I will! There's this really cute blonde on their marketing team. I'm going to convince her to take me clubbing after."

"Good luck."

"Honey, I don't need luck tonight; you do."

She's right. I really need all the luck I can get. I've never gone on a date with someone I met online, and I've heard such horror stories. My nerves are through the roof. But if he's the same way in person as he is online, I think we'll have a good time. If anything, he may just end up being another friend, which is always good to have.

Chapter Nine

LOUISA

I pull into the parking lot of Penelope's Apple Orchard. It was a 30-minute drive from my apartment, giving me plenty of time to freak out. I almost turned around three times, but my curiosity about this man kept me driving.

Sam and I finally exchanged cell phone numbers. It's been a lot easier than messaging on the app. I was tired of getting notifications from other guys and getting my hopes up that it was Sam.

LOU

Just got here. I'm the brunette standing by the entrance.

SAM

Be right there. I'll be the guy looking for the cute brunette.

My heart races, and even though it's a crisp fall day, I'm starting to sweat. Shit, there he is! Breathe, Lou. As soon as he spots me, a big smile stretches across his face.

"Hey, Lou."

"Hi, Sam."

As he walks up to me, he stretches out his arms and wraps me in a hug. I'm completely swallowed up by this man. And god, he smells so good. His grip on me loosens, and I step back, taking in the sight before me. How is he even hotter in person?

He's wearing a green long-sleeve shirt and over it a light-weight wool jacket in a tan color. His dark jeans hug his muscular thighs. And his stylish white sneakers round out the outfit to make him look like an Abercrombie model.

"Thank you for not being a catfish."

He laughs and rubs his hand down his cheek and jaw. "Same. You look great." That smile still hasn't left his face, so I believe him. "Wanna go in?"

When I turn and walk through the gate, I feel him gently place his hand on the small of my back. He's so calm, cool, and collected. It makes me less anxious than I was two minutes ago.

SAM

She's just as beautiful as she was in her photos, if not better. Those eyes, though darker in color, sparkle when she smiles. Her outfit shows off her figure, especially her butt, which looks amazing in those jeans. She's wearing boots that add a little bit to her height, but I still tower over her.

We start off by going into the gift shop to get a drink. I buy myself a hot chocolate, and she orders a hot apple cider, which I pay for, despite her protest. It was my idea to come here, so I'm going to use that as my excuse to treat her to everything today if she tries to put up a fight. Actually, it was Quinn's idea, but I won't bring that up unless she does.

"So what made you choose this place? Have you been here before?"

Busted. "Actually, it was Quinn's suggestion. He gets out a lot more than I do. When I told him I wanted to take you out on a date, he suggested this place."

"You were talking about me to your brother?"

"Ummm, yeah." I'm a little nervous, so I rub the back of my neck. "We pretty much talk about everything. We're really close."

"That's sweet. Are you as close with your older brother? Was it...Jacob?"

"Yeah, Jacob. And no, we aren't as close. Quinn gets himself involved with everyone's business, and Jacob mostly keeps to himself."

"B and Quinn sound like they would get along well. But boy, would they cause trouble." She laughs. "Does Quinn have a girlfriend?"

"Women aren't Quinn's type. But no, he's single."

"Got it." She nods with no hint of judgment on her face. Not that I would expect it from her anyway.

We're walking around the orchard, talking, when we come across a maze. It's made out of rectangular hay bales stacked high enough where even I can't see over them.

"Wanna try it?"

She looks little nervous. "Sure."

"We don't have to if you don't want to."

"No, I want to."

We toss our empty cups in the trash and walk to the starting entrance.

"Have you done one of these before?"

As we start the maze, she walks a little closer to me, her arm brushing up against mine. I use it as an opportunity to take her hand in mine. She doesn't look up at me, but I can see she's smiling now.

"Yeah, they always have one at the county fair near my hometown."

"Makes sense. I forget you're from a small town."

We continue chatting as we walk. She tells me all about her small town and how even though she loved her child-hood, she never wants to move back there. I start to notice that the further we get into the maze, the less talkative she gets. Ten minutes later, Lou grabs my arm with her other hand that isn't locked in mine.

"Are we lost?"

"No, I'm pretty sure we just reached the center of the maze," I reassure her.

"I was *not* expecting it to be this big. It's going to take us 20 minutes to get out of here." Her breathing becomes quick and shallow, her eyes darting around us in every direction.

I turn towards her and cup her chin in my fingers. I tilt her head up to look me in the eyes. "You okay?"

"Yeah, I'm okay." She does her best to fake a casual smile.

Her breathing slows a bit, but I'm not quite convinced. I drop my hand from her chin and slide it to the side of her neck. My thumb swipes back and forth on her cheek and she leans into it.

"You seem a little stressed."

"I got lost in one of these as a kid. Haven't done one since."

I let go of her face and turn around to assess the options, keeping my fingers on my other hand laced with hers. I guide us out of the center circle toward where I'm pretty sure one of the exits is.

After several twists and turns as well as a couple dead ends, we finally see the exit. I can see her sigh with relief as soon as we turn the corner. She picks up the pace of her strides and I follow suit.

Once we get out, she's still holding my hand, and I'm not going to be the one to break the contact. She turns towards me, looking up.

"Okay, I lied; I was very anxious back in the middle."

"I know."

"It's dumb, I know. But all of a sudden I was 8-year-old Louisa stuck in the corn maze at the county fair, screaming for my mom. Oh god, this is so embarrassing. Please just forget that that ever happened. I would love it if—"

She stops mid-sentence when I reach my free hand up to tuck a loose piece of hair behind her ear.

She swallows, hard. "What I mean to say is thank you for being so calm."

"You don't have to thank me. I could tell you were nervous; I just didn't want to make a big deal of it."

We're still facing each other, and I can feel my heart beating against my chest. I know I want to kiss her, but I'm frozen. I really don't want to screw this up. There's still a piece of me that thinks she's way out of my league and that any wrong step will scare her away.

After a long pause of silence where we just stare at each other, she asks, "Do you want to come back to my place?"

Thank god. I would invite her back to my house, but it's a bit of a construction zone right now with all the renovations I'm doing. Not that I'm embarrassed by that, but it's not the most romantic setting.

"I'd love to. But...I'm starving. Would it be okay if I ordered takeout and picked it up on my way over?"

She gives me a soft smile and nods. "That would be perfect."

Chapter Ten

LOUISA

I sprint up the stairs and into the apartment to start cleaning. It's not dirty; there are just certain things I'd rather not have Sam see on our first date. For example, my box of vibrators on my dresser or B's copy of the Kamasutra that she leaves in the living room as a conversational piece. In fact, let's just shut B's bedroom door and pretend it doesn't exist.

That reminds me…I kneel down in front of Pepin's chair so we're eye level. "Pepin, there's a man coming over. You better be nice because I like this one. But I mean, if he gives you red flags, then by all means, let me know. I'll actually listen this time." He licks me on the cheek, and I kiss the top of his head and scratch behind his ears.

I haven't had a guy here since Pepin growled at Darrah incessantly the night of Iris's 21st birthday. Let's hope Pepin's behavior was truly Pepin's judge of character and not a jealousy thing. If that were the case, it would be this dog's only flaw.

After I'm done hiding things, I run to the bathroom and

rip off my sweater. I'm worried my nervous sweating made me stink, and I don't want to turn Sam off. I quickly wash my pits in the sink and reapply deodorant before changing my shirt.

I change into a long-sleeve shirt and swap my jeans for some leggings. As I spritz on some perfume, I hear a knock at the door. Damn, that was fast!

But when I open the door, it's not Sam.

"Hi Louisa, do you have two eggs I could borrow? I completely forgot to get some when I ran to the store earlier, and I already started cooking, so I can't run out."

"Hey Sarah, of course. I'm pretty sure I have some. Come on in while I run and check." Sarah is my upstairs neighbor. She's a young single mom with 3 kids, and we've only met because she frequently sends one of them down here to apologize for the noise.

Sarah steps in, and I run to the kitchen to check the fridge. I grab three eggs and bring them out to her. "Here, in case one breaks or has gone bad."

"Thank you, you're a lifesaver!" She says that a lot. When I watch her kids while she runs out for a second, when I borrow her things, or even when I water her plants when she's out of town. All very simple things, but to her, they seem to make a big difference. I can't imagine raising three kids on my own in the city. The thing I tell *her* all the time is that I don't know how she does it.

"Of course, any time."

I go to open the door for her, but she stops me. "Are you having company over?"

"Huh?" How could she possibly know that?

"The glasses and bottle of wine on the coffee table. I noticed them when you ran into the kitchen."

"Oh, right. Yeah, I have a date coming over."

"Someone you've met before?"

"We actually just had our first date earlier this afternoon."

"Is B out of town again? I haven't heard her in a few days." I've gotten so used to the noise that I sometimes forget how thin the walls and floors are in this old building.

"She's in London for a week."

"Okay, well, if I hear shouting, I'll assume something is either going horribly wrong or wonderfully right." She winks at me with a smirk on her face.

Oh no. Now that's going to be on my mind if things go there tonight. I laugh awkwardly and go to open the door again. "I'll yell out your name if I'm getting murdered."

She steps toward the door, rolling her eyes, that smirk still on her face. "Sounds good. Thanks again, Lou. You have fun tonight."

As she steps out, she almost runs into a wall of muscle standing outside my door. "Jesus! Oh hello. You must be the date." She whips around and raises her eyebrows so they're up to her hairline and mouths, "Good job." I think if she didn't have eggs in her hands, she'd be giving me a thumbs up too.

Sam stands in the hallway holding brown bags full of our takeout food. "Sorry, didn't mean to startle you. Someone let me in the front door."

When I texted him my address, I included the apartment number so he could buzz me to let him in. "All good. Sarah was just leaving."

"I had to borrow some eggs to feed my gremlins."

Sam laughs at her bad joke and he steps aside for her to walk around him.

Sarah yells back at me as she takes the stairs two at a

time. "See you later, Lou. And hey you—" she pauses, looking directly at Sam.

"Sam," he tells her, assuming she's waiting for his name.

"Sam. Please don't murder my friend."

"I promise."

Sarah continues up the flight of stairs, and Sam looks at me with a sheepish grin.

"Don't mind her. She just worries about me when I'm here alone."

"She's a very good neighbor for that. And it appears you are, too. I didn't know people still did that. You know, borrow their neighbors a cup of sugar." He says it in a teasing tone, so I know he wasn't put off by her comment.

"I didn't think so either until I moved in below Sarah." Remembering that he's still standing in the hallway, I side-step. "Sorry, come in! You can set the bags on the coffee table as long as you don't mind eating in the living room. This place is too small for a table, so we eat most of our meals out here."

He walks past me, and I can smell his cologne again; it's intoxicating. "Doesn't bother me." He sets the bags on the coffee table and looks around. "Hey there, Pepin."

After initially greeting Sarah, Pepin went back to his chair, where he currently sits. I almost forgot about him and how nervous I was that he would growl at Sam. He seems quite unbothered. Sam walks over and squats down to pet him on the head. Pepin leans into his hand and starts panting.

"I'm glad he likes you."

"Does he usually not like men?"

"He didn't really like the last guy that was here. For good reason."

———

SAM

I try not to think about the fact that there was a "last guy" she had over here. I know she's been seeing other people because she told me, but that's not really what I want to be thinking about right now. I can tell she regrets saying it, and she quickly pivots by offering me some wine.

We eat the Indian food I picked up on my way here and chat about this and that. When we finish, she carries the dishes to the kitchen, and I pack up the leftovers and put them in her fridge, which is organized to a T. No surprise there.

Now we're sitting next to each other on the couch, finishing the bottle of wine she opened, and I just want to be closer to her. But at this point, we've been sitting here for a little while, and I can't find a good excuse to get closer to her.

"I'm going to run to the bathroom; I'll be right back."

"No problem. It's the middle door down the hall."

I set my wine glass down and walk to the bathroom. It's just as tidy as the rest of her place. There's a painting of the ocean hanging on the wall. The signature in the bottom corner is barely legible, but after a second, I can make out the name Eden Blake. Her mother, I remember. She's very talented. I flush the toilet and wash my hands to make it sound like I actually had to use the bathroom.

"Did your mom do that painting in the bathroom?"

"She did. She paints a lot during her summers off."

"It's really good. Do you do any art?"

"I draw from time to time, but B is way more artistic than I am."

When I get to the couch, I make an effort to sit as close

to her as possible without it being weird. My leg grazes her bent knee on my way down, and I make no effort to move it once I'm seated. Neither does she.

"Where were we?"

I lean in a little closer. "I think you were just about to spill all your deepest, darkest secrets to me."

She narrows her eyes at me and smirks. "I don't think so, Mr. Smart Ass. You're not going to get secrets out of me that easily."

"Worth a shot."

Her tongue peeks out, wetting her soft lips, and she bites her lower lip for a brief moment.

"I think you were about to kiss me." It was a bold move, but I'm dying to feel her lips, and I think she wants it, too.

"Oh, was I? I thought you were going to kiss *me?*"

I take her wine glass out of her hand and set it on the coffee table. Then I adjust myself on the couch and lean over; she meets me halfway. I cup the side of her head with one hand and put the other on her inner thigh.

Our lips are so close I can feel her warm breath on mine. I lick my lips to wet them and press them to hers. They're so soft and warm. She parts her lips for me and makes a small moaning noise when I sweep my tongue across hers.

That moan sends me into another gear, and I wrap my hand around the outside of her thigh and pull her onto my lap. Both my hands are on her ass now, and I give her a gentle squeeze. At that, she grinds her hips forward on my lap, making *me* moan this time. She's so intoxicating and I want to pull her close enough that there's no space left between us.

My hand migrates up under her shirt and explores the soft skin of her back. She leans forward into me, pressing her front flat against mine. I can feel her chest rising and falling against mine. We haven't come up for air since our lips first touched, and I'm perfectly happy to suffocate under her like this.

———

LOUISA

I pull my lips away from his to catch my breath, and he immediately starts kissing down my neck to my collarbone and back up. I tilt my head, and his hand comes up to sweep my hair out of his way. His lips leave my skin wet and tingling with every kiss.

The sexual tension has been building between us for weeks now through messaging. I'm surprised we made it a whole afternoon of being around each other without a single kiss. But now, the dam has broken, and the floodgates are open. Figuratively and literally. I'm so wet I can feel myself soaking through my panties.

My hands explore his thick, curly hair, and I can tell he likes it by the little noises he's making. His hands were exploring my back before resting on my waist. He subtly plays with the hem of my shirt. I nod, letting him know he can lift it up. But before he does, he pulls his lips from mine and looks at me. "You okay with this?"

I nod again, but he waits. "Yes," I say, giving him the verbal approval he's clearly waiting for.

I lift my arms to assist him, and he lifts my shirt off over my head. Typically, I would be self-conscious about being this exposed with all the lights on, but I don't care. I just want him.

To even the score, I tug at the hem of his shirt and pull it over his head. He's solid muscle. I run my hands down his chest, over his abs, and then back up his arms, devouring him with my eyes. I press my body into his. The feeling of his skin on mine sets me on fire, and I just want to be closer to him.

"Do you want to go to my bedroom?"

"If you'd be more comfortable there."

I nod and start to lift myself off of him. He puts his hands under my thighs, stands up, and wraps my legs around him. He must be incredibly strong to have done that so smoothly. I'm not sure how it's possible, but I'm even more wet after that.

He heads down the hallway, walking slowly since my lips are locked to his, blocking his view. "Last door on the left," I say against his lips.

He turns left, and my back hits the wall. At first, I think he turned too early, but this is intentional. He presses his body against mine to hold me up, and he reaches out his right hand to open the door. Before taking me in, he holds me against the wall for a second. Pulling his lips away from mine to look at me, he says, "I need you to tell me if you ever want me to stop."

How does this man manage to make consent sexy? "I will. But I won't." He gives me a skeptical look that makes me giggle. "I promise I will let you know if I want you to stop. But I really don't see that happening," I clarify for him. "I want you." Not being able to wait any longer, I press my lips to his, and he responds with a rumble from the back of his throat.

Our pace quickens as he tears me off the wall, walks into my room, and throws me on the bed. No one is going to be coming into the apartment, so I don't bother telling him to shut the door.

I'm lying horizontally on my queen-size bed, with the

lower half of my legs dangling off the side. He crawls over me, supporting his weight with his forearms so he's not crushing me. We lock lips again, and his left hand runs through my hair while his right picks up my leg at the knee and hugs it close to him. I arch my back as he grinds his hips into mine.

I run my hands down his front and grab him through his jeans, wanting to rile him up more.

It works. I feel his smile on my lips. "Are you trying to kill me, Lou?"

I giggle. "Maybe."

He lifts himself off me and kneels on the floor in front of me. He tugs on my arms to help me sit up. Reaching around me, he grabs the waistband of my leggings and looks up at me for permission. Instead of answering him, I reach my hands around, place them over his, and lift my hips. Guiding his hands down my ass, we slowly remove my pants, leaving my panties on. I scoot forward to the edge of the bed because I can only pray I know where this is going.

He places his hands on my knees and gently spreads my thighs, positioning himself between them. He looks up and kisses me softly on the lips. His lips continue traveling down my neck, my chest. He reaches up, slips a bra strap off my shoulder, and pulls down my bra to expose my nipple. It's peaked from all the arousal. He plants his lips around it and swirls his tongue. I moan because it feels so good. He lets go and slides my bra strap back on my shoulder.

He leans down and starts grazing his lips up my inner thigh, running from my knees to my center. Then he repeats it on the other side. This time, when he gets to the center, he loops his fingers around my thong and pulls it down my legs. I'm fully exposed to him now and so worked up that I was pooling in my underwear. He runs a finger through the soaking crease and moans.

————

SAM

She's so wet, and I want to be inside her. But not yet; I want to taste her first. I sweep my tongue up her center; she tastes amazing. Her hands fly to my hair and grabs it as she gasps. After a few seconds, she sighs and releases my hair.

I place her legs over my shoulders to give me better access to her. She completely surrenders and throws herself back down on her bed.

I slide one finger in while my mouth still explores her folds. She's so ready for me that I know she can take another one. I add one more finger, and she shudders. I curl my fingers and feel around till I get the reaction I'm looking for to know I'm in the right spot. I know it's different for every woman, so I try to read their body language as best as I can.

I continue, gently tugging, licking, and sucking. I can feel little pulses starting to build, so I keep doing what I am doing. Her hands find my hair again and grab hold. Her body tenses, and eventually, her muscles contract around my fingers as she comes for me.

I slowly remove my fingers and remove her legs from over my shoulders. Before I can wipe my face, she surprises me by quickly sitting up and grabbing my face, slanting her open mouth over mine, and sweeping her tongue in. I answer with a sweep of my tongue, then gently bite her lower lip.

We both stand up, and she pivots us, so now my back is to the bed. She reaches down and fusses with my belt for a bit before I reach down and do it for her. "Sorry, it's got a little lever on the bottom."

"You were setting me up for failure there."

"When I got dressed for our date, I didn't quite think it through this far."

She smiles up at me as she undoes the button on my jeans and then my zipper.

———

LOUISA

Already, I can tell he's bigger than I've ever had before just by what's straining against his boxer briefs. I pull down both those and his jeans at the same time. I have no patience left. I need this man inside me. The orgasm he gave me only made me needier.

He kicks his pants to the side, runs his hands all the way up my arms, and cups my face in both hands, kissing me. I place my palms on his shoulders and lower him into the bed.

I'm a girl who likes to please, and after what he just did to me, I'm extra eager to show him what I can do to him. It's such a turn-on for me when I make a man have to fight not to come.

He watches me as I bend over to grab a condom out of my nightstand. I can tell he's staring at my ass, and I love it. After I tear one off of the pack, I stop. I don't think this is going to fit. These are leftovers from when Jay and I were together; he didn't need magnums.

I turn to him, embarrassed to ask, but what choice do I have? "This isn't going to fit, is it?"

He rubs the back of his neck and winces. "I really don't

mean to sound like a douche, but probably not. It'll likely go on, but I don't want to risk it tearing."

An idea pops into my head. "I'll be right back!"

I run two doors down to B's room. She's *got* to have something bigger in here. I frantically dig through her drawers. I'll apologize to her later, but let's be real: B would be mad at me if I *didn't* look for one in here.

Bingo! I grab one out of the box and then grab another, just in case. Running out of the room once is embarrassing enough; I don't want to risk having to do it again.

I come back in and hope that he's not over it. Judging by how hard his dick still is, I'm going to say he still wants this as much as I do.

"Found one in B's room."

"Remind me to thank her later."

I hand him one, toss the other in my open nightstand drawer, and shut it. By the time I turn around, he's already got it on.

I walk over and put my arms around his neck, leaning into him. "Where were we?"

"I'm not entirely sure. You seemed to be taking charge."

"Yes, I was." I smirk and straddle him one leg at a time, seating myself on his lap.

I grind my hips, rubbing myself up against him. I'm still soaked from earlier, so I slide right along him. Reaching around my back, I unclasp my bra and toss it to the floor. I see his Adam's apple bob as he swallows.

I lift myself up just enough to hover over his tip and slide down onto it. I can only take a little bit at a time, so I bob up and down, letting him enter me a little more each time. His hands are on my hips, guiding me slowly.

When I'm fully seated, I feel so full it takes my breath away. I have to pause a second to adjust to him. I know there are other positions where he could get even deeper, and I can't imagine how that's going to work.

After a moment, I start grinding my hips front to back, moving him inside of me. His tip hits a spot that makes my thighs squeeze on either side of his hips. With his hands still on my hips, he closes his eyes and tips his head back. "Fuck, you feel amazing."

I use my arms around his neck to help lift me up as I ride up and down on him, moving my hips. As I continue, I feel pressure building again. His thumb finds my clit and rubs as I move. I climax again and lean into him, pressing my forehead into his shoulder. He wraps his arms around me and holds me tight while my body shakes.

My breathing is heavy, and I need a minute to collect myself. I rest my cheek on his shoulder, and my hair falls into my face. He notices and tucks it behind my ear. I'm glad because now I can breathe without swallowing hair.

I lift my head and start to slide off his lap when he wraps one arm around me and flips us on the bed. I lay on my back, and he hovers over me, running his eyes down my body and back up to my eyes. "You're so beautiful."

My heart skips a beat.

He reaches over, grabs a pillow, and places it under my hips. I run my hands across his chest and over his shoulders, pulling him closer to me. As I kiss him, I feel him reach his hand down and grab the base of his cock to guide it back into me. Even though I just had him in me, this different angle makes it feel new again.

He moves his hips faster and kisses my neck, sucking on it and gently biting. His movements get wild, and the slapping of his hips on my thighs echoes through the room. He's so deep that it borders on pain but feels so good.

Sitting up slightly, he adjusts the angle so he can reach

his hand down and rub my clit again. The sensation sends me through the roof. I'm already so sensitive from coming twice. His hand moves slow and steady as his hips move fast, a lethal combination that has me tipping over the edge yet again. This time, he comes right after me.

Now, it's his turn to catch his breath. He collapses on top of me, but not with his full weight. I can feel his heart hammering through his chest on mine before he slowly pulls out of me. He peppers my neck with kisses and then hovers his lips over mine, just barely touching. I run my fingers down his cheek, across his jaw, and touch his lips.

It's the least sexual thing we've done since entering my room, but for some reason, just being right here with him seems very intimate. I almost forgot that this is technically still our first date. No one has ever worked my body the way he just did on the first try, if ever. Was I just that horny, or are we that good together? I can't wait to find out.

Chapter Eleven

LOUISA

"It was that good?"

"B, it was amazing."

She lets out a high-pitched shriek that makes me pull the phone away from my ear. "I'm so happy for you."

"I'm happy for me too."

"So, did he go home right after?"

"No, it was super late by the time we checked, so he actually spent the night. Then, this morning, we took Pepin on a walk to get some coffee. He just left a little bit ago."

"So, basically, your first date lasted almost 24 hours, and you didn't get sick of him, in addition to coming *three* times? Marry that man. Right now."

I laugh and start to tell her to chill out, but she cuts me off.

"No, wait! What happened to enjoying being single for a while? Lou, you're not supposed to meet your dream guy this soon. You haven't sucked enough dick yet."

"How was I supposed to know he'd end up being so

great? I honestly wasn't even that blown away by his profile. I think I almost swiped left because I was getting so frustrated."

"Do you guys have plans to hang out again?"

"No, we didn't talk about it. And with the holiday coming up, I'm sure we won't see each other until after."

"Speaking of which. I'll be home on Tuesday. Are we driving back home together on Wednesday?"

"That's the plan. Mom said she wanted us there on Tuesday, but I told her you weren't getting in till later, so we would just leave sometime on Wednesday."

"Sounds good. Thanks for making the plans. I'll be crazy jet lagged, but I'm hoping Thanksgiving dinner will put me in a food coma and give me a hard reset."

"Sounds like some flawless logic to me."

I hear a door slam on her end. "I have to go to a meeting, so I'll talk to you later."

"Wait," I stop her before she hangs up, "I was talking about me so much I never asked how your night went. Did you hook up with that marketing girl?"

"No. Poor girl thinks she's straight."

"Maybe she actually is straight, B. You do know that not everyone is gay, right?"

"Keep telling yourself that."

"Alright, love you."

"Love you too. Congrats on getting laid." She hangs up before I can throw back a snarky reply.

———

THE OTHER NIGHT, after Sam and I finished, he threw his boxer briefs back on. I put on my silk pajama shorts and matching tank top, and we curled up in my bed and talked for a bit before we fell asleep. Pepin, of course, joined us on the bed since it's his spot, and Sam was just a guest. The three of us snuggled up in my queen bed looked like a clown car, but I loved it. Sam was the big spoon, I was the middle spoon, and Pep was the little spoon.

I don't even remember what we were talking about when I dozed off because all I could think about was Sam's hand on my bare waist. His hands are strong and calloused from all the physical labor he does. Last night, I learned that Sam's company doesn't just do landscaping in the summer; it also does snow removal in the winter. Makes sense, I guess, since you can't do landscaping year-round in Minnesota.

He also bought a house a couple of years ago and has been fixing it up with the help of his brothers, mostly Quinn, since Jacob is in dental school.

He talks about his brothers a lot, which I think is really sweet, and I've told him all about B and her adventures. He hasn't told me much about his parents other than they're divorced, and I've gathered that he's not his dad's biggest fan.

This week is Thanksgiving, so B and I are headed back to our hometown to spend time with family. We'll be staying at our parents' house, and some of our extended family will join us for dinner on Thursday.

Holidays are pretty typical at our house. My aunt loves to ask questions that are way too personal. My grandfather is getting dementia and says some very out-of-pocket things that are usually insensitive. My mother worries that everything isn't going to get cooked on time, and my father tries to help, but when he gets shooed out of the kitchen by my mother, he joins everyone else in the living room and watches the parade or football.

————

SAM

Happy Thanksgiving, Lou.

LOU

Happy Thanksgiving to you too! Where are you headed first, your mom's or your dad's?

SAM

My dad's. We typically don't stay there long, so it's easier to dip out if we have the excuse of going to my mom's.

LOU

Makes sense. Don't you get super full eating two Thanksgiving meals in one day?

SAM

Yes. Now that I'm not a teenager though, I've gotten better at not overindulging during the first meal. I still typically end up passed out with my brothers on the couch at the end of the day.

LOU

I love that for you.

SAM

What are your Thanksgivings usually like?

LOU

Nothing too crazy ever happens, but there's always something going on. I'll keep you updated if anything interesting starts happening.

SAM

> I would love that. My dad's place is usually pretty boring, so I would love to hear about what's going on at your place.

LOU

> Consider me your personal Thanksgiving entertainment.

———

SAM

Quinn and I decided to carpool today because the odds of both of us being able to stay sober through this are slim. We have an unspoken rule that whoever is getting targeted by Joel the worst gets to get drunk, and the other one drives, and if it's pretty even, we play rock paper scissors.

Jacob's car is already here when we pull into the driveway, and I wonder how long he's had to endure our dad without us.

Quinn inclines his head toward a car next to Jacob's that I don't recognize. "How old do we think Joel's girlfriend is this year?"

"Who knows. My bet is 35." I know that's wishful thinking.

Our dad tends to attract women who are significantly younger than him. He always swears it's not because of his money, but that's hard to believe when they're half his age and wearing designer clothing that they clearly can't afford with their waitressing job.

I'm not judging the women, good on them. If my dad is desperate enough to shell out that much money for pussy, then that's his choice. I just don't like when he expects us to take their relationship seriously and treat her like she's going to be our new stepmom. That's a little hard to do when they flirt with me at the dinner table.

I knock on the door and wait. My dad answers with his new toy at his side.

"Boys, you know you don't have to knock. This is your home, too. Just come in next time."

"Mmmmk, Joel." Quinn can't help himself; he just has to poke the bear.

He steps aside and welcomes us in. Recently, we've been showing up empty-handed because any time we try to be helpful and bring something, it's always the wrong brand, or he has a better one, or it's too cold. He always has an excuse to throw it in the trash when we're not looking, and sometimes, he's not even that considerate.

I take off my coat, and Denise, our dad's housekeeper, takes it out of my hands. Denise is a 50-year-old Colombian woman who barely spoke English when she started here. Either he pays her a lot of money, or she's desperate, because she's been working for him for 15 years now, despite him treating her like shit. At first, he tried to hide it, but over time, the facade went away. "I can hang up my own coat, Denise; you don't have to."

"That's what she's paid to do, son."

Prick.

Denise grabs Quinn's coat too, and before heading off to the coat closet, she reassures us, "I don't mind, sir."

I hate when she calls me that. I don't want her to think of me like my dad, and that's what she calls him. "Sam, please call me Sam. We've known each other long enough."

"Okay, Sam." She smiles before turning to leave with our coats in hand.

Finally acknowledging the woman standing beside him,

my dad introduces us. "Boys, this is my girlfriend, Holly." She looks no older than me.

"Hi Holly, I'm Sam." I wait for Quinn to introduce himself, but he's looking off in the distance, pretending not to be a part of this conversation. "And this is Quinn."

"I've heard a lot about you guys."

Sure she has. I doubt my dad has told her more than our names and a list of the top 10 things we've done to disappoint him.

"Where's Jacob?" Quinn asks.

Joel is clearly annoyed that Quinn is ignoring Holly, but he chooses to let it go. "He's here somewhere. Probably already raiding the bar."

Quinn takes off down the hallway, leaving me behind. "Great! I'll join him."

I start walking through the foyer with my dad and Holly, heading toward the living area.

"So, Sam, how's the kitchen renovation coming?" I'm surprised he remembers that.

"I finished that a couple of months ago. I'm onto the master suite now."

"It's taking you forever to finish that place. How do you live like that? I don't know why you didn't just let me give you my guy's number and have him handle everything. He could have had it done a year ago."

"Because I like doing it, and it's a lot cheaper if I do it myself."

"Are you hurting for money? Is that it?"

"No—" He cuts me off.

"I told you that lawn mowing business wasn't going to get you the lifestyle you grew up with. You should have taken your degree and gone to law school like I told you."

"I don't mow lawns."

"What's that now?"

Of course, he didn't hear me; he's too busy listening to the sound of his own voice. I'm genuinely surprised that anyone in his industry puts up with him. But maybe all corporate lawyers are like that.

"I said, I don't mow lawns. It's a landscaping business."

"Yeah, landscaping, that's what I said."

No, it wasn't.

I hope to god Quinn brings a drink back for me. Maybe we can both get drunk tonight. Ubering an hour to Mom's house may be worth it.

———

Joel won't shut up about his new yacht that he just purchased and how it's better than some other rich man's yacht. I lost at rock paper scissors, so I'm the sober driver tonight. Quinn is already drunk off our dad's expensive scotch, which is dumb because he doesn't even like scotch. I think he's just drinking it because he knows it pisses off Joel when he "drinks it the wrong way."

SAM

Any funny stories yet?

LOU

Nothing yet. Unless you count my grandpa falling asleep with a KitKat bar in his lap and it melting all over his pants.

SAM

Oh, that definitely counts. Was he mad when he woke up?

LOU

He's still sleeping. And probably will be until he hears my mom yell that dinner's ready. How's it going at your dad's?

SAM

Quinn is already drunk, and Jacob hasn't said much all night. My dad keeps yapping on about how much money he has and his new girlfriend is 25.

LOU

25?! That's only one year older than I am. And a year younger than you. Yikes!

SAM

I give it another month, two tops.

LOU

Very generous of you.

Oh my god. My aunt just asked me how my sex life is. She has no boundaries.

SAM

Just out of curiosity, what did you tell her?

LOU

Oh, wouldn't you like to know?

SAM

That is why I asked.

LOU

My mother chimed in before I had to answer and told her it's none of her damn business.

"No texting at the dinner table, Jacob." When I look up, I see Joel looking at Jacob with a stern look.

Jacob doesn't put his phone down and continues with

whatever he was previously doing. "We aren't even eating yet."

"Well, it's still rude. You could engage in the conversation."

Jacob throws his phone down and his hands up. "What could I possibly have to contribute to a conversation about vacation homes in Tuscany? Plus, no one can get a word in when you're going on and on about yourself."

"Fine, Jacob. You want to talk about you? How are your graduation requirements coming? I heard from my friend at the dental school that you may be falling behind."

"That is none of your damn business. And Dr. Mayes better watch what he says. It's against school policy for him to discuss my grades with you. I'd hate to have to report your *friend*." I can tell Jacob is starting to lose his cool.

"Are you avoiding my questions because you're embar-rassed?" Joel presses.

Jacob hasn't hung out with Quinn and me for several months now. Is it because he really is falling behind? I know he was stressed about requirements last spring, but I figured he would have caught up by now. With only one semester left, he doesn't have much wiggle room. He also failed one of his board exams and had to retake it. From what I under-stand, it's not uncommon for students to fail at least one board exam due to how subjective dentistry can be.

Jacob has always put a lot of pressure on himself. I think being the oldest plays a part in it. He always felt like he had to set a good example for us. Jacob took our parents' divorce the hardest. Quinn and I were young enough that the memories of that time are foggy. Jacob remembers it all. And for some reason, our dad has always been toughest on Jacob. He was the one always telling Jacob to do something useful with his life, so Jacob went to dental school. Our dad put similar pressure on Quinn and me, but we both said "fuck it" and did what we wanted. Jacob didn't have that option.

Jacob didn't get in the first time he applied to dental school. Again, his classmates that I've met tell me that's very normal, but Jacob saw it as a huge failure. He spent that whole gap year studying to retake his DAT and working at a dental office to boost his resume. He didn't get in the next year either. It's likely because he wasn't pursuing it out of passion.

If my dad was upset about the first time, he was *livid* about the second. He straight up told Jacob he was an embarrassment and that even with him pulling some strings, Jacob still dropped the ball. I've never seen Jacob more upset in my life. Right now might top that.

"Fuck you!" Jacob stands up so fast that his chair tumbles backwards, and the table moves. "You were the one that pushed me into this. And in the same breath, you told me I'd be nothing. Maybe if I had a little more support, I wouldn't be so stressed or put so much pressure on myself to the point where I don't eat or sleep anymore."

I could tell he hasn't been doing much of either lately by the bags under his eyes and the gauntness of his face. Jacob has always been athletic and lean, but with him now standing over me, I can see how much weight he's lost. Damn, when was the last time I saw Jacob?

Quinn and I were so busy this summer with work, and then once fall came, we got sucked into my house projects. Of course, we texted Jacob and asked him to join, but neither of us ever checked in on him.

"Those are excuses, Jacob. If you want to blame someone for your failures, look in the mirror."

That's it. That was Jacob's last straw. I see his face go from angry to completely defeated and empty.

"Happy Thanksgiving, everyone." With that, Jacob turns and storms out.

I go to pick up his chair and see that his phone is on the floor. It must have fallen out of his pocket when he jumped up. I pick it up and check to make sure the screen isn't broken. Thankfully, it's not.

"'ll be right back." I jog toward the front door. "Jacob, wait. You left your phone."

I run out the door in my socks, not wanting to bother with shoes and risk missing him. When I get to the driveway, I see he's in his car, about to back out.

"Jacob!"

I wave to get his attention. He sees me and stops, rolling down his window. I'm slightly out of breath when I get to his car. "Your phone was on the floor." I reach out and hand it to him.

"Thanks." He grabs it from me. That empty look is still in his eyes, and there is no real expression on his face.

"I know this is a dumb question, but are you okay?"

"I'm fine."

I know he's lying, but I don't know how to get him to talk to me without prying. "Okay, drive safe. I'll see you at Mom's."

"I'm not going to Mom's."

"What? Jacob, don't let what Dad said ruin Mom's Thanksgiving." I immediately regret it after the words come out of my mouth. He stares at me and starts rolling up his window. I catch it with my hand, and he stops. "I'm sorry, Jacob. I shouldn't have said that. If you need to be alone, then do that. I'll explain it to Mom and make sure she gets over it."

"Thanks."

"Text me if you need anything or if you change your mind, okay?" I remove my hand from the window, and he continues to roll it up. When it's all the way up, I can't help but stand there. He looks so hurt, and I don't know what to do to help him. I've always attempted to be the peacekeeper of the family, and right now, I feel like I'm failing. All I can think to say is, "I love you."

He looks at me, and tears fill his eyes. I've seen my brother cry before, so that's not what jars me. It's that he just shakes his head and backs out of the driveway. Once he's gone, I walk back into the house, nervous about the shit-storm I'm about to walk into.

Quinn is grabbing his coat from Denise, and she's holding mine as well.

"Joel says we aren't welcome here anymore because we didn't have his back when Jacob was being a big meany to him." Quinn pantomimes a baby crying.

"Fine by me." I say that, but I know I should try to smooth things over before we leave. "Go get in the car, and I'll be right out." I hand Quinn the keys and walk toward the dining room.

Joel sits there with his glass of scotch in one hand and the other around Holly. He seems so unbothered by what just happened, and that pisses me off.

"That was a little uncalled for, don't you think?" I know I'm not going to get anywhere with him, but I can't sit by and let him beat up on Jacob like that when he's clearly in a vulnerable state.

"I think everyone is getting too sensitive these days. You little millennials or Gen Z, whatever you are, get so butthurt when people tell you the truth." I look at his girlfriend to see if she's offended by his comment. I can tell she's holding back her wince and trying to act supportive.

"Happy Thanksgiving, Joel. Holly, it was nice to meet you. I hope for your sake we don't see you at Christmas."

On my way out, I grab my coat from Denise, who is still standing in the entryway holding it. "Denise, my offer to hire you at my company still stands. If you ever change your mind and want out of here, I can help you."

She nervously looks over my shoulder to see if my dad is within earshot. "Thank you, Sam."

"You have my number, right?"

"I do."

"Happy Thanksgiving, Denise." I wrap her in a hug. Partially for her, but when she squeezes me back, I admit to myself that maybe I needed it too.

———

LOUISA

Laughter echoes from the dining room as I step out of the bathroom. They better not be laughing at my expense. When I enter and reclaim my seat, I look around at my family. We're partially through dinner, which started three hours later than my mother wanted due to a turkey fiasco. Half the family blames my cousin; they think he accidentally turned off the oven when he was changing the clock to the correct time. The other half swears there was a brief power outage that was so quick no one else noticed. Either way, the turkey is now fully cooked, and everyone is sitting around our big table enjoying their meal.

"Where did you run off to? Calling your boyfriend?" My aunt is relentless.

"Auntie, like I said earlier, I don't have a boyfriend."

"Then who are you texting? You've been smiling at your phone all day."

To be more accurate, I was smiling at my phone all afternoon. Sam hasn't responded in a couple of hours.

"Nobody," I say with a not-so-convincing smile.

My mother catches wind of our conversation and ditches her conversation with my grandpa about his BINGO girlfriend to chime into ours. "She's right, Lou. I haven't seen you that giddy over your phone since you found out your phone had a calendar with time blocking."

"Mom, I said it's nothing. I don't want to talk about it. If it turns into something, you'll be the first to know."

"Excuse me. I better be the first to know. I live with you!" B glares at me from the other end of the table.

My mother, ever the peacekeeper, corrects me. "Of course, B will be the first to know. But I'm assuming she already knows who it is, so I'll be the first *new* person to hear about it." She glances down at B as if she can get her to spill my secret to her later.

B knows that look, but she isn't taking the bait. "My lips are sealed, Momma. Sister code."

I'm pretty sure she just made that up, but I'm grateful she doesn't have a big mouth. I'm also grateful for my mother dropping the subject and diverting my aunt's attention to another topic.

I pull my phone out of my pocket and check again to see if Sam has messaged me back, even though I just checked it in the bathroom, and I didn't feel it buzz. No messages. I go to slide it back into my pocket and stop when I feel it vibrate. I quickly unlock it to see who it is.

SAM

Sorry it's taken me a while to respond.

Family stuff.

LOU

No problem at all. I've been very busy, too.

No, I haven't Unless you count having a mini marsh-mallow eating contest with my cousins as being busy.

SAM

Any other fun stories? Don't even ask me, because the answer is no. We left my dad's house early.

LOU

Apparently, my grandpa has a girlfriend at the BINGO hall he goes to every Tuesday.

SAM

Good for him. I hope I still have that much game when I'm his age. Obviously, I hope I don't have to be. But if I find myself a widower, then it wouldn't hurt to still be able to flirt.

LOU

I think it's more transactional than that. He said she has the best BINGO dobbers.

SAM

That's hilarious.

LOU

How's your mom's house?

SAM

It's good. My brother Jacob had to head home after my dad's, so my mom is bummed about that. But otherwise, it's been good. I'm Quinn's sober cab tonight so he is having a great time.

LOU

How did you end up landing that role?

SAM

Lost at rock paper scissors.

LOU

You're joking.

SAM

I really wish I was.

LOU

I'm dying. Maybe I'll start playing that with B to see who has to vacuum.

SAM

I feel like you would just end up doing it after her anyway...

LOU

I hate the fact that you're not wrong.

SAM

Does your family drink?

LOU

Like FISH. My uncle makes his own apple pie, which is a homemade moonshine drink. It's so delicious and so strong, which makes it very dangerous.

SAM

I've never heard of that before.

LOU

It's a staple in my hometown. But my uncle makes the best. I'll have to bring some home for you to try.

SAM

Pretty presumptuous of you.

Assuming I'm going to ask you out on a second date.

LOU

Well, are you?

SAM

I think so.

Quinn is pretty drunk, so I'm going to take him home. I'll talk to you tomorrow.

Enjoy the rest of your evening.

LOU

Drive safe.

And Sam...I'd really like it if you asked me out on a second date.

Chapter Twelve

SAM

When I got to my mom's house yesterday, Jacob had already called her to tell her he wasn't feeling well and that he wasn't coming. Quinn and I drove around the block a few times to cool off before going in. I needed it more than he did. I think he's so used to being disappointed by Joel at this point that he's learned to get over it. I, on the other hand, still hold on to the idea that my dad can change, even though deep down, I know he won't.

I spent an hour or so talking with my mom about what went down at Dad's and begging her not to drive over there to yell at him. That would help no one in this situation, especially Jacob. Because then my dad would just call him and tell him he's a whiny baby for running and telling our Mom. He's way too predictable at this point, and all I could do was try to convince her to continue with dinner so we could enjoy the rest of our evening.

I wanted to text Louisa all night, but my mom kept asking if I was texting Jacob and asking if he was coming over. I didn't want to get into the whole Louisa thing with her, especially this early on, so I just told Louisa I had to go. My mom is a hopeless romantic who is constantly confused about why her perfect boys are all still single. She seems to forget that getting married in her early 20s didn't really work out for her and that maybe her sons don't want to repeat her mistakes. I'll never understand what she saw in him or how she stayed married to him for as long as she did.

The rest of the evening was uneventful. Quinn was the life of the party, as usual. He loves being the entertainment; that's why instead of helping me with snow removal in the winter, he DJs at clubs and parties for rich people. If you looked at him, you'd see the DJ side of him, with his bleach-blonde hair and stylish clothes. What you might not see is the guy who does physical labor and loves to get dirty. He's multifaceted, as he will gladly tell you.

Jacob never showed up. But I sent him a text to make sure he was okay.

SAM

Sorry Joel was a total dick to you tonight. If you're up for coming over to Mom's, Aunt Janet made her pecan pie. I know it's your favorite.

He never responded, but I'm sure he's turned off his phone and is ignoring everyone for the rest of the night.

It's the morning after Thanksgiving, and I'm up early working on drywalling the master bedroom. Joel was right; these projects are taking a lot longer than they should. I've made good progress with the busy season over, but the snow is coming. When that happens, I'll get busy again, and these projects will have to be put on hold.

I don't hear my phone vibrating on the table at first over

116

the sound of my drill. I take off my gloves and pick it up to see that it's a call from an unknown number. I never usually answer calls from numbers I don't have saved in my contacts, but some delusional part of me thinks it might be Lou calling from B's phone or something. I haven't texted her this morning since I got up so early and didn't want to wake her.

I think twice about it and realize how stupid that is. If she didn't have her phone on her, she wouldn't have my number. And why would she call instead of text? I put the phone back on the table, waiting for it to stop ringing. It does. But then, a few seconds later, it vibrates again. I pick it up and see it's the same number as before.

Weird.

Maybe someone accidentally gave a client my personal cell number instead of my work one.

I answer and put the phone up to my ear. "Hello."

"Hello, is this Samuel Carlyle?" It's a woman's voice, but not one I recognize. Definitely not Lou's.

"That's me."

"Sam, my name is Officer Cindee O'Connell. You were listed as your brother's emergency contact. I'm so sorry to tell you that Jacob was found...."

There's a blaring, high-pitched ringing in my ears, and I don't catch the rest of what she says, but I don't need to. A sinking feeling takes over my body. My stomach is in knots. I can't feel my hands. Anger builds in my core. I can't breathe.

Her voice cuts through the ringing for a second. "Sam, did you hear me?"

I scream at the top of my lungs, my throat shredding, and I throw my phone at the unfinished wall as hard as I can. I hear it crack, and then everything goes black. A searing pain shoots through my knees and palms, and I realize I'm on the ground.

My face is wet, and I know I'm crying, but I can't process it. All I can think is that this can't be happening.

"No. No. NO. NO! NOOOO!"

I slam my fist into the wood floor, and a sensation shoots up my arm that I process as pain, but I barely feel it.

———

LOUISA

It's been two days since Thanksgiving. B and I drove back to the city this morning. Sam hasn't texted me back and I'm starting to worry that my telling him I wanted him to ask me on a second date was too bold. Did I scare him away?

I talked to B about it, and she said I should just text him, but I'm scared. I don't want to seem too clingy. But I'm dying to know what's going on.

After several drafts, I finally get one approved by B. I send the text, but he doesn't respond till an hour later. That was the longest hour of my life.

LOU

> I guess I can be the one to ask you on a second date; this is the 21st century, after all. Want to grab a drink sometime this week?

SAM

> Hey, sorry I've been silent the last couple of days. I've had some family stuff come up and my phone broke. I'm really sorry, but I don't think right now is a good time for me to be dating. It was really nice getting to know you, though.

What just happened? Did I just get dumped by someone I wasn't even dating? I can't decide if this is better or worse than being ghosted.

I'm sick to my stomach. I'm embarrassed.

"B...I think he just ended things with me?"

"What?" she shouts from the other room. In a matter of seconds, she's in my room with a confused look on her face. "He what?"

I hold out my phone to her. "You read it. He doesn't want to see me anymore."

She plops on my bed and grabs my phone. Pepin trots in behind her and jumps up on the bed. He spins in a couple of circles before dropping down and laying his head in my lap. How does he always know when I need him?

"Yeah, he is definitely ending things."

My eyes fill up with tears. "That's not what you're supposed to say."

She looks up from my phone with pity in her eyes. "I'm not trying to hurt your feelings; I'm just telling you what's going on. This shit happens, Lou."

I look up at the ceiling, begging my tears to go away so one doesn't fall. My mom always told me that if a tear doesn't fall, it doesn't count as crying. She mostly says that when we tease her for tearing up at every movie, even comedies. I think that rule applies here as well.

"I will not cry over another boy."

"That's my girl!" B slaps me on the shoulder, causing one of the tears to fall out of the outer corner of my eye and down to my ear. Damn it.

I lower my chin and look at her. I'm sure I look pathetic right now, but I can't help it. I really liked him.

"You know what we're going to do? I'm going to run to the store and get some supplies for a girl's night." She hops off the bed and runs out of my room. "I'll be back soon! Pick out a few movies while I'm gone."

Once I hear the front door slam shut and the lock click, I finally blink and let the rest of the tears fall down my face.

What did I do wrong? I thought everything was going really well. There's no way that some family drama could be so big he can't go grab a drink with me, right? And if something bad happened, he would have said so. No, I'm sure he's just making excuses, trying not to hurt my feelings.

I stroke the top of Pepin's head and scratch behind his ear. "Why do men suck so much, Pep? And why do I even bother crying over them anymore?"

I look down at my phone and reread his message again. "You know what, fuck him. I'm not even going to respond." I lock my phone and shut it in my nightstand. If anyone important tries to get a hold of me, they can contact B to get to me.

————

B MOVED her mattress into the living room and brought out every pillow and blanket we own. When she ran to the store, she brought back ice cream, Oreos, chips with dip, my favorite candies, and several bottles of wine. I know I'm going to throw up later, but I don't care.

It's nearly 4am, and we're on the 4th Harry Potter movie, my favorite one. I had picked out some rom-coms, but B vetoed those and said tonight is not about boys. I'm glad she did that because I've barely thought about Sam. It may be the 2 bottles of wine talking, but I think I'm already over it.

I am perfectly fine without a man. Not like Sam was even "mine" to begin with. I just need to keep reminding myself that I wanted to enjoy being single, and now I have that chance again.

I pull out my phone and turn the brightness all the way down. I open the Messages app and scroll until I find Matt. The last time I saw him was a month ago at his Halloween party.

LOU

Hi

MATT

Hello, princess.

What are you doing up so late?

LOU

Harry Potter marathon with my sister.

What are you doing up?

MATT

I'm always up this late on Saturdays.

LOU

Do you want to grab a drink sometime soon?

MATT

I'm free on Thursday.

LOU

Perfect, I am too. You can pick the place.

MATT

I'll pick you up around 7.

LOU

See you then.

SAM

It's been a week since Thanksgiving, and today is Jacob's funeral. The first few days were a complete blur. If

I'm being honest, I didn't even think about Lou before she texted me. When I saw her message, a flood of thoughts and emotions took over me.

I so badly wanted to confide in her and tell her everything. But the more I thought about it, the more I realized that wouldn't be fair to her. We'd only been talking for less than a month at that point, and this was way too heavy. I knew I would need time to heal before I got back to my old self. She deserves the best version of someone who can give her their all. Not someone who is grieving, going to therapy, and taking sleeping pills every night to cope with nightmares.

It's strange how a person can be so tired yet restless at the same time. I haven't had the energy to work on any of my projects, let alone talk to anyone. And yet, at night, I can't fall asleep because every time I close my eyes, I see Jacob. I see his face through the car window. I see how broken he was, waiting for someone to grab him and pull him out of the darkness he was in.

I saw the look on his face, and I did nothing. Nothing. I just let him drive away. I should have forced him to come to Mom's. I should have put him in my car and drove him there myself. I should have gone and checked on him when he didn't respond to my text. I should have checked on him when he was distancing himself from us all those months prior. I should have gone over to his apartment and hung out with him when he continuously bailed on plans.

My therapist says it's not healthy or productive to think about all the things I could have or should have done. But I can't help it. I'm his brother. He needed me. And I did nothing.

I feel my mom's hand on my arm, and I look down to see that I have completely destroyed the program I was holding.

I throw it to the side and bury my face in my hands as I rest my elbows on my knees. I haven't been listening to a word that's being said. This priest didn't know Jacob, so what could he possibly have to say about his life other than all the clichés?

I'm tired of people telling me how sorry they are for my loss. Don't feel sorry for me; feel sorry for Jacob. Feel sorry that he felt so helpless and alone that he thought complete, dark nothingness was better than being in this world.

At the prayer service last night, some of his classmates and professors came up to my mother and offered their condolences. Where the fuck were they when Jacob needed them? They saw him every day. How could no one notice? Where was the school when he reached out for guidance or asked for extensions?

In the middle of his program, when I still saw Jacob regularly, he always used to tell me how shitty it was there. How everyone was in it for themselves, and everyone was always gatekeeping their secrets to success. He told me how the staff was condescending and always made the students feel stupid in the clinic for not knowing things. He said the patients were often rude to him and would blame him for their problems. He even told me once that there is a high suicide rate among dentists. I guess that's what happens when the general consensus is that everyone hates going to your office, and no one views you as a real doctor.

Fuck, I should have seen it! How could I have been so self-centered that I didn't hear his cry for help? How could I have given my dad grace when he was constantly belittling Jacob and beating up on him?

Speaking of Joel, he's been a total prick this whole week. Barely speaks to anyone except to pay for things. And he thinks just because it's his wallet getting tapped into, he gets to make all the decisions. Fuck that. He probably knows as little about Jacob as this priest does.

Quinn and I tried to talk our mother out of doing the whole church thing. Jacob hated all this stuff. But in the end, the funeral is for the living, not the dead. And our mother needed this. She needed all the bells and whistles to make it real.

If anyone is in more denial than me, it's our mom. With the little energy I have these days, I've been taking care of her. She never remarried, so she lives alone, which meant that Quinn and I have been staying with her since last Friday. The first night, when I was lying awake in bed, I heard her crying hysterically in her room. I went in there to check on her and ended up just holding her in her bed, waiting for her to cry herself to sleep. Quinn came in after an hour and joined us. I felt like a kid again, going to sleep in my parents' room when I had a nightmare. Except this time, the nightmare is real, and my mom can't be the brave one protecting me.

The funeral wraps up, and I only notice because everyone around me stands to walk out. My mom picks up the urn off of the pedestal full of flowers and turns to walk down the aisle, Quinn and I on each side of her.

Joel and Holly walk behind us. I still can't believe he brought her and let her sit in the front row with the family. Hell, Denise deserves a spot up there more than she does. But in her defense, she seems very uncomfortable with this whole thing and is probably going to leave him once he's done grieving. Don't worry, Holly, that won't be long.

Once we're at the back of the church, the priest tells us to head down to the reception hall for the meal. Who started that tradition? For most grieving people, the last thing they want to do is eat cold deli sandwiches in a cold church basement. At least, that's how Quinn and I feel. Once our mom is distracted by friends telling her what an amazing person Jacob was, he and I dip out the back door.

The church is attached to our old elementary school, so there's a playground on the other side of the building. I shrug off my jacket and set it on the pavement. It's chilly out, but I can't stand to have that thing on for another second. The last time I wore it was at my grandpa's funeral. It just reminds me of death and sadness. I might burn it after this.

I didn't notice that Quinn grabbed a basketball out of a bin by the door on our way out. He tosses it to me, and I shoot it in the hoop a few feet away. We continue this for a while, taking turns shooting and not saying anything to each other. He's rarely silent, but when he is, I know not to push him.

"Have you talked to that girl again? The one with the dog?"

"No, I actually ended things with her on Saturday."

He stops mid-shot and puts the ball down between his arm and hip. "What happened? I thought you really liked her?"

"This happened." I spread my arms wide and gesture to the church.

"I don't get it."

"I don't know. It wasn't a great way to start off a relationship. Dead brothers aren't very romantic."

"Whatever. Good luck getting someone as good-looking as her to go out with you again."

That actually makes me laugh. "Ouch."

He smiles back at me and chucks the ball hard at my stomach. Luckily, I catch it, but it still takes a little wind out of me.

"Sadly, I don't think I'll get that lucky again."

"Boys, what are you doing out here? It's freezing." We look behind us to find our mom poking her head out of the door. "Please get back inside. There are people asking for you."

I look to Quinn, hoping he'll tell her off so we can stay out here, but instead, he shrugs. "We'll be right there."

I roll my eyes at him even though I know we should go inside, if not for everyone else, then at least for our mom.

As we talk to everyone there, all I can think about is how exhausted I am. How much I want to go back to my own home and curl up in my bed. As much as I want to be alone right now, having someone to go home with to support me would be comforting. The thought makes my heart ache, knowing I'll be going back to an empty house.

On our way out, I spot my dad talking with someone I don't know. I overhear him telling them, "Jacob and I were really close. It's sad he never found the strength to reach out to me for help."

I snap. "Are you fucking kidding me?"

Everyone looks over at me, shocked by what just came out of my mouth.

Joel is frozen, likely afraid I'll call him out on his bull- shit in front of other people. And he should be afraid; I'm done playing the nice guy.

"Sam, don't talk to me like that. I know you're sad but–"

"You didn't know shit about Jacob, and you are literally the last person he would have ever gone to for help."

His eyes get big, and I can tell he's pissed. "Sam, I think you need to step out for a moment and collect yourself."

"I can't stand by and listen to you pretend you were a perfect dad who cared about his kids. Because you were awful, especially to Jacob. And maybe if you hadn't been such an ass to Jacob all the time, he'd be here to tell you this himself." I swallow and take a second to question what I'm about to say. No, he deserves this. "Fuck you, Joel. I tried to make peace between all of us for years, but I'm done. You're never going to change." I pause again, my breathing ragged and heavy. He just stares at me with a smug look on his face. "I never want to see you again."

I don't hear him try to make things right with me as I walk out, because he doesn't. He never will because he's too prideful to ever admit his faults, and his children have never been worth fighting for.

I glance at my jacket, and I almost grab it but decide to leave it. I don't want anything in my closet to remind me of this day.

"Come on, Quinn, we're leaving."

"You don't have to tell me twice."

We stop and hug Mom briefly before we leave. I'm sure she's embarrassed by my outburst. Only a small part of me feels bad. "I'm sorry about the scene, Mom."

"Don't be. Someone has needed to put that prick in his place for a while now." She reaches up, places her hand on my jaw, and rubs her thumb over my cheek. "Thank you."

Chapter Thirteen

LOUISA

B and I are driving back home again with Pepin for Christmas. My parents love him, and sometimes I'm afraid he'll "go missing" before I have to head back to the city.

Since it's a quick turnaround between the holidays, I haven't spoken to my parents much since Thanksgiving. I'm nervous they're going to ask about Sam. They don't know his name, but I guarantee my mother hasn't forgotten the fact that I was clearly texting someone all day, someone who made me smile a lot.

I'm sure as hell not going to tell her about Matt. My parents are very open-minded, but even that situation would be confusing for them.

Matt and I met up for drinks after Thanksgiving, and it was great. We met at a lounge, and this time, it wasn't one he owns. Afterward, we went back to his place, and he helped me forget all about Sam. Multiple times.

But at the end of the night, I went home alone. Matt has a strict no-sleepover rule, so I went home at 4am and snuggled Pep.

A couple of weeks after that, I went to a club with B and some of her coworkers. It was fun, but I kept looking around, half hoping to run into Sam and half terrified that I would. B kept feeding me shots, and I almost went home with someone. But that didn't work out because I threw up in the bathroom instead. I feel like I'm still recovering from that night.

I don't know how B goes on work trips and does this every night for weeks at a time. She's built differently. I'm not just talking about her iron will to rally; I also wonder how she always seems so strong. More than once in the weeks since Sam ended things, I've cried myself to sleep from loneliness. Some might even call it despair because, late at night, my thoughts tend to spiral. I wonder if I'll ever find someone. The doubts start creeping in about my ability to be loved, and sometimes, I even start to wonder if I'll be capable of achieving my career goals.

These thoughts take over, and I'd do anything to shut them up. Almost anything... I just want to know that everything is going to be okay. Sometimes, it feels like nothing will turn out the way I always planned it would. Sometimes, I just want to give up and start over.

"Do you want to go sledding with some people when we get home?"

I glance over at B, who, for a moment, I forgot was sitting in the passenger seat next to me. "Tonight?"

"No, probably sometime tomorrow. There's a big group chat going on. You're in it, but you obviously can't look at it right now."

I haven't been sledding since I was a kid, and it doesn't sound all that fun, but I have nothing going on, and it wouldn't hurt to see some old friends. "Yeah, sure."

"I'll let them know to count us in."

———

THE NEXT DAY, we get bundled up and head to the big hill behind the high school. I didn't know we still had sleds, but B found some buried in the attic. We brought a thermos full of coffee with Bailey's. It's mostly to help stay warm, but I also need a little liquid courage for the social aspect of this outing. Liam, Evie, and Iris are usually great buffers for this sort of thing, but their family is doing Christmas out of state this year.

B runs ahead to greet a group of friends, leaving me to trail behind.

"Hey, Lou."

I barely recognize the voice; it's familiar but different. I turn around and see my high school boyfriend, Bear. He's still as cute as he was then; he just has more muscle and facial hair now. Sort of like a sexy Paul Bunyan.

It's been a while since I've seen him. The last time was at Evie and Liam's wedding, where he was the best man, but we barely spoke. In theory, it shouldn't be this awkward, but my anxiety is getting the best of me.

"Hey, Bear."

Barrett Michaels was my boyfriend from the end of my freshman year to the winter of my sophomore year. He was a year ahead of me in school, so he was a junior when we ended things. Shortly after, he got together with his now wife, Olivia. They made sense together. He was a star athlete, and she was the class president. They were a power couple.

"I didn't know you'd be here." He has an unsettled energy about him, like he's just as nervous to see me as I am to see him. Why would he be nervous? He's got the dream life. I'm the loser who's single and hasn't reached my career goals.

"B dragged me along." My hands are in my pockets even though my mittens are thick enough to keep them warm. We're standing only a couple of feet apart, so I can see him well, even though this side of the hill is mostly dark.

"How have you been? Are you still living in the city?"

"Good, and yes, I've been there since I graduated last spring. How are you?"

"Well....you know..." He looks down and kicks a snow chunk on the ground with his boot.

I actually don't know, so I just look at him and wait for him to elaborate. I don't keep up with what my high school classmates are doing unless they are someone I see regularly or they post a lot on social media.

"Oh, you didn't hear?"

I shake my head, still confused.

"Olivia and I split up. I guess divorce is the more accurate term."

He's still looking at the ground, clearly uncomfortable.

"No, I hadn't heard. Is it recent?"

"It became official a few weeks ago."

"I'm really sorry to hear that, Bear." Without thinking about it, I reach out and touch his arm, trying to be comforting.

At my touch, he lifts his head and looks at me. I can see that he is holding back tears. It's obvious this is still very fresh for him. It makes my ending with Sam seem like a joke. I can't imagine being divorced at 25.

"Thanks. It's been hard, but life is starting to get back to normal."

"That's—" I'm cut off by a scream coming from over by the hill. It startles me, and I turn around to see where it's coming from before realizing that it's just someone sledding down the hill. Sledding, right. That's what we're here to do.

I use this as a segue to any other topic, but it's because I don't know what else to say to him. I'm curious what happened, but it's none of my business.

"Want to go down the hill with me?" He doesn't appear to have a sled, so I hold mine up. It's small, likely meant for one person, but we could probably fit both of us on it.

His mouth stretches into a smile, and he nods. "Sure."

We walk up the hill, and I realize it's much bigger than I remember. I can't believe I'm getting winded halfway up.

When we get to the top, I try my best to suppress my heavy breathing so he can't see how out of shape I am. I put the sled on the ground where there's an indent in the snow from weeks of kids sledding here. It's packed down, making it slick, so I take my time getting on.

Bear reaches down to hold the sled steady. I sit down and adjust myself as far forward as possible to give him room to sit. This sled is so small I'm honestly not sure he'll fit behind me with his long legs.

I wedge the heel of my boots into the snow to hold the sled steady for him now. He starts to sit and realizes the same thing I did: we're not both going to fit. He kneels down in the snow behind me, legs straddling the sled.

"Here, lift your arms." He leans forward, puts his hands under my arms, and lifts them gently. I'm not entirely sure where he's going with this.

I'm holding my arms up awkwardly with my back to him when I feel the sled shift slightly from his weight. Next, I feel something slide under both my arms. It's his legs. I realize that he's wrapping his legs around me so he can use the small sliver of sled behind me for his butt. He is very close to me right now, and I'm not sure how I'm supposed to feel about this. Why didn't I think this through?

Once he's seated, he scoots his hips forward, close to me, and I can feel his bottom pressed against mine. His arms wrap around my chest, under my upper arms. My elbows are resting on the outside of his arms and thighs.

He leans forward and speaks into my ear. "Is this okay?"

I swallow because the sound of his soft voice in my ear makes me shiver, and not from the cold. To secure myself more, I wrap my hands around his thighs. "Yep. I'm ready if you are."

"Let's go."

I lift my heels out of the snow and tuck my legs as close to my chest as I can with his arms wrapped around me. He unwraps his arms for a brief moment to push us forward onto the downward slope of the hill. He wraps them tightly around me again. I can't tell if the rush in my head and butterflies in my stomach are from flying down the hill or from being so close to him.

The ride down flies by in a blur. My focus is on every point of contact I have with his body. Even though we're both wrapped in layers, I can feel his body heat.

We're getting toward the bottom when the sled starts to turn. We slide sideways for a bit before the edge of the sled catches on a lump of snow, and we flip. Both of us go flying sideways and roll on the ground. After a second of shock, I start laughing uncontrollably. I look around to see where he landed and find him laughing, too.

He makes eye contact with me and says, "That's going to hurt tomorrow."

"It's one and done for me. We're getting too old for this shit." I still can't control my laughter. It has to be partially due to adrenaline.

For the next hour, I walk around mingling with different groups of people. There are about 20 of us here in total, so there's plenty of catching up to do. I don't even get around to everyone before people start to leave. It's getting really cold, and everyone is ready to not be frozen anymore.

A lot of the group will be meeting at someone's house to continue hanging out. B and I promised our mom we would be back tonight to watch Elf with her, so we're going to head home.

I've only chatted with Bear in groups since our adventure down the hill. I see him making his way over to me now as I walk to our car. B notices him heading toward us and pretends to have forgotten something, turning around to run back to where we were standing earlier. I keep walking to my car but slow down so he can catch up to me.

When he reaches me, he walks beside me, close enough for our arms to occasionally graze.

He speaks first. "Are you going with everyone else to keep hanging out?"

"No, B and I are headed home. We promised our mom we would watch Christmas movies with her tonight."

"That's too bad. I was hoping to spend more time with you."

My stomach flutters at the compliment. We've reached my car, and I walk to the passenger side door and lean against it. Bear and I are wedged between my car and someone else's pickup, shielded from the main group.

He steps closer to me and leans in, placing his hands on either side of my head. I can feel my cheeks heating despite the cold. I lick my lips to wet them and look up at him through my frost-covered lashes. One of his hands leaves the car and grabs the back of my neck, pulling me closer to him. Our lips touch, and it's like I'm a teenager again. I open my lips for him and match his rhythm. He was always a really good kisser, and time has only made him better.

Eventually, our lips slow together, and he pulls away from me, lingering for a second before we completely part. As I look at him, I realize that even though this was thrilling, things between him and me couldn't work. He just got out of a marriage, and we live in different places. I would just play into my urges and go further with him, but since our hometown circle is so small, it would only complicate things.

He must read my face because his smile fades. "Something wrong?"

"This probably means nothing, and I'm perfectly fine with that, but I just need to make it perfectly clear that I don't think things would work between us. I want you to know that I don't expect anything from you."

His expression is hard to read. I didn't want him to think I was making assumptions just because he kissed me if this meant nothing to him. But I also don't want him to get the wrong idea. Now, I'm just holding my breath, waiting for him to respond.

"That's perfectly fine. I probably shouldn't be complicating my life more than it already is right now." He gives me a soft smile, and I release my breath. Thank god that didn't make things awkward.

He starts to pull away further, but I grab his arms and put them around my waist, pulling him in close again. "But that doesn't mean we have to stop."

His soft smile widens, and his hand finds the back of my neck again. Our lips lock, and I'm soaking in this feeling, knowing it won't return once I leave this parking lot. Who would have thought I'd be making out with a high school boyfriend in the parking lot at the ripe age of 24? Not me, and probably not him, either. The kiss starts to heat up, and I'm not even thinking about where B is right now and whether she'll return soon.

Turns out it isn't B I should have been worrying about. It's the person who owns the truck behind Bear.

"Woah, what did I walk in on?"

We quickly pull away from each other. At first, my heart starts racing, and I immediately try to act innocent. Then I remember that we're all single adults here, and I can make out with whomever I want, wherever I want.

"Get out of here, Robby. Can't you see I'm busy?" Bear's tone is light-hearted. Robby is a friend of his, so if anything, he's probably glad someone caught us so he can have a witness to what just happened. But luckily, not many people are going to believe Robby when he goes blabbing about this. He's always been a huge gossip with less-than-accurate sources.

"Can't, man; you're blocking my door."

Once Bear realizes that he really is blocking Robby's door, he apologizes. "Sorry, man. Can you just give us two minutes?"

The devilish grin on Robby's face makes me roll my eyes because I know something dumb is about to come out of his mouth.

"Bear, that's a little sad if it only takes you two minutes."

Bear quickly grabs a chunk of snow off the top of my car and throws it at Robby.

"All right, all right! I'll get out of here."

Robby leaves, and Bear leans back into me, resting his hands on the car behind me. I can't help but chuckle, and I lean into his chest to suppress it. I know he's laughing too, by the way his chest shakes.

I pull myself off of him and lean against my car. "I really should get going."

"Alright, if you must." He leans in and places one soft yet firm kiss on my lips, and I kiss him back. "I'm glad I ran into you, Lou."

Smiling up at him, I admit, "Me too. And who knows, maybe if we're both still single at Christmas next year, things may play out a little differently."

———

THE BED CREAKS as I roll over on my side and sling my arm around Pepin. I haven't been able to fall asleep yet. My mind keeps shuffling through a rolodex of worries that have been accumulating over the past six months. Since my life got flipped upside down, I don't recognize myself. I like this new version of me, but it's still unfamiliar territory, and I worry if I'm doing the right thing by straying so far from my original path.

Kissing Bear tonight only made me question things more. It was nice to feel desired by someone again, but it didn't feel the way I know it should. I keep comparing it to how I felt when Sam kissed me. I did the same thing when I met up with Matt, though I was able to deny it since I know things will never go anywhere with him.

Why do I let these men have such control over my emotions? I need to focus on what I can control. And right now, that's my career. I need to study my butt off for my licensure exams so I can achieve my dream of becoming a licensed architect. That I'm good at. That I can do. Then I'll know that not all hope is lost, that I may actually have a chance at being happy someday.

———

SAM

"Can you pass me the salt, honey?"

I reach over and pass her the salt grinder. My mom and I are in the kitchen cooking dinner. This year, Mom, Quinn, and I decided to celebrate Christmas at my house, just the three of us. Understandably, Mom didn't want to host our extended family this year, so I offered to have it here.

I figured having it at her house would bring up too many memories of Jacob. She got our childhood home in the divorce, so all of our Christmases have been spent there since we were kids. That's the home where, for 28 years, Jacob opened presents, ate Mom's cooking, and watched Christmas movies with us.

She's been struggling a lot since Jacob died. Quinn and I have been trying our best to help her, but it's been hard with her living on the complete opposite side of the city. She's been staying with me all week, and I told her I would do all the cooking, but she insisted on helping. Quinn isn't the best cook in the world, but he's good at baking, so we put him on dessert duty. I'm in charge of the ham, and Mom is working on the sides.

For a moment, it almost feels normal. For a moment, I can just pretend that Jacob is in the other room and that the rest of our family is on their way over.

The snow is ruthless outside. I'll have to get up early tomorrow to complete a few jobs, so I'm enjoying my time with my family now while no one else needs me.

I check the meat thermometer and turn off the oven. "Ham just needs to rest for a bit, and then we're ready." Mom is just finishing up mashing the potatoes while Quinn sets the table.

After the ham rests, I pour everyone a glass of wine, and we sit down to eat. I take a moment to look around. The fireplace is roaring, Christmas music plays in the background, snow falls outside the big window in the dining room, and my family is here. All the family I need.

I feel a sense of peace in the simplicity of our meal. No stress, no fuss, no chaos. I don't know why we didn't start doing holidays like this sooner, and I think my Mom is feeling the same way. I can tell by the way she smiles at me, like this is the first time in a month that she has felt at peace.

She mouths to me, "I love you," and I say it back.

The Christmas playlist I have on starts playing 'Holiday' by Lil Nas X. After about 30 seconds when the song really gets going, Mom looks at me very confused.

"What kind of Christmas song is this?"

Quinn and I look at each other and crack up; a few seconds later, we are all belly laughing, almost in tears. To be fair, it came on right after 'I'll Be Home For Christmas' by Amy Grant, so it was quite the contrast.

We haven't laughed like this in a long time, and it feels good. Sad...but good.

Later tonight, we'll open presents and watch a Christmas movie. Mom's favorite one is Elf, so of course, we'll watch that one. Quinn won rock paper scissors to pick the second movie and chose Love Actually. He and I debated back and forth over whether or not it was a Christmas movie. In the end, Mom sided with him, and I lost. Honestly, it was just nice to have some normalcy, so I don't care what we watch. Plus, that movie is actually pretty good. But I would never admit that to Quinn.

Chapter Fourteen

SAM

It's New Year's Eve, and Quinn is DJing a big event at a club downtown. I haven't been out in a while, so being around people will be nice. I'll mostly be hanging out with Quinn's newest plaything, Brian, since Quinn will be up in the DJ booth most of the night.

He was able to get us a booth with bottle service, which I've never experienced before. Unless you count one time on family vacation when my dad snuck me and my brothers into a club, that experience was not fun at all. He told us to hide out in the corner and keep our mouths shut. Jacob was twelve, I was ten, and Quinn was eight, so we just drank the mixers all night and tried to talk amongst ourselves while Joel flirted with younger women, even though my parents were still married at that time. I'm guessing this bottle service experience will be much better than that.

I'm meeting Quinn and Brian at the club because I had to do some work. When I get to the door, a bouncer with a clipboard asks my name and checks the list to make sure I'm on it. Last time Quinn worked a party was on Halloween, and he forgot to put my name on the list, so I was stuck in the lobby of the apartment building, trying to convince the doorman to let me up to the penthouse. Eventually, he got the host to put my name on the list, and I got in.

Once the bouncer finds my name, he unhooks the rope blocking the door and lets me in. A young woman dressed in a lacy top and leather mini skirt directs me toward a hallway where you access the bottle service area and takes my coat from me. She walks back down the hall, and I can't help but stare at her butt in that skirt. I haven't thought about sex in a while, but something about the lights, music, and atmosphere here is making me think about it again.

I walk to the booth, where I see Quinn and Brian. As I get closer, I can see they already have a row of shot glasses lined up and filled with a clear liquid. Please don't let it be tequila.

"Hey, we have some tequila shots for you!" Quinn doesn't get drunk before his gigs, so I'm lucky I don't have to play major catch-up.

"Quinn, you know I can't do tequila."

"No, you *can* do tequila. You just don't like to because you become too fun when you drink it."

I look at Brian to clarify for him. "By "too fun," he means I get feral and usually end up making decisions I regret the next day."

Brian laughs and raises his eyebrows. "I think that sounds like the best way to ring in the new year!"

"Come on, Sam. This is your first night out in a while. Don't be old and lame."

"Old? I'm only two years older than you. And I am *not* lame."

Quinn picks up a shot glass and holds it out to me. "Then prove it."

I reluctantly grab it from him. I look around the table, spot a small cup with lime wedges, and pick one up. "I hope you know you're responsible for whatever comes of this." I throw back the shot, suck on the lime. I shiver as it burns down my throat.

———

LOUISA

"Hurry up, we're going to be late," B shouts at me from the bathroom.

"Are you seriously worried about being late for once?" I walk down the hall and peer through the bathroom door to see her still doing her makeup. "And you're not even ready."

She puts down her brush and looks over at me with a cheeky grin. "I just wanted to see what you would say."

"You are so dumb, you know that!"

She goes back to fixing her eyebrows in the mirror. "But you love me anyway."

I roll my eyes and walk to the kitchen to feed Pepin before we leave.

"Here ya go, buddy." I lean down, which is difficult in my tight, short dress, and fill his food bowl. When he hears the clinking of kibble hitting the metal, he jumps off his chair and trots over. I pet his back while he eats because I feel bad that we are going to be out all night. He's completely fine when we're gone, but I always end up missing him. He's sort of become my security blanket.

B walks out into the living room, where I'm waiting for her, and I notice her new outfit. "You changed *again?*"

"The other one was riding up my ass too much."

"That's never seemed to be a problem for you in the past."

"Well, Daniel has a DJ for tonight, and I plan to be shaking my ass all over that dance floor. I can't have it hanging out all night at a work party." She looks at me and crosses her arms like I should be taking her seriously right now. But I can't. I know her too well.

She orders the ride, and I pour us some shots to take before we leave. We throw them back, wince at the burn, then grab our purses and head out.

———

SAM

There are still a couple of hours until midnight, and I'm already drunk. But I'm self-aware enough to realize I should probably switch to water for a bit. Quinn is up at the DJ booth killing it, so Brian and I have been hanging out in the bottle service area. Brian made friends with the groups on either side of us, and we've all started to mingle back and forth between our three areas.

To our right was a group of five men dressed in what I can only describe as frat boy clothing. They're all in their 50s, with the exception of one young guy who looks like he's maybe 19 and clearly got snuck in here somehow. I believe he's one of their sons, and he is wasted. The kid looks like he's having the time of his life and getting attention from some hot girls though, so good for him.

The group to our left is made up of a mix of men and women, all in their mid-20s and all incredibly attractive. You can tell they do this sort of thing often and are used to getting a lot of attention here.

Once we all started mingling together, the older men were hitting on the younger girls so hard. Most got rejected, but some of the girls sought out the better-looking ones and have been flirting with them. It occasionally reminds me of my dad and his young girlfriends, but I try to shake that thought from my mind any time it pops up. I am not letting the thought of him ruin my night.

Brian is flirting with one of the guys from the younger group who says he has a wife, but Brian whispered to me earlier that he's for sure a closeted gay man. My brother and Brian aren't in a serious, committed relationship, so I'm not bothered by the fact that he clearly wants to get in that man's pants, but I do feel bad for his girlfriend. I think her new year might start off on the wrong foot if Brian gets what he wants.

A few girls have flirted with me, and I've flirted back, but they all were too drunk for it to go anywhere. I'm not above a one-night stand, but I do not fool around with super drunk girls who likely won't remember it the next day.

I have to admit that I feel sort of strange up here, separated from the rest of the club. Don't get me wrong, it's nice to have the space to walk around without getting drinks spilled on you and not have to wait in line at a bar. But something about it feels elitist, and sometimes I like being smashed body to body on a dance floor. There are fewer eyes on me down there. Up here, I feel like I'm in a fishbowl being observed by everyone.

I tell Brian I'm going to step out for a second, but he doesn't seem to care. I walk around the booth and into the back hallway where the bathrooms are, but I keep walking past them. I reach the end of the hallway, which leads out to the main area of the club. I want to go say hey to Quinn and see if he needs anything. I know there are workers who check in on him, but I wanted an excuse to walk around the club for a bit.

I maneuver my way through the crowds and up to the

DJ booth. I wave to get Quinn's attention. Once he sees me, I step around toward the back and wait for him. He'll likely play a couple more songs and then put on a long track that he uses when he takes breaks.

While I'm waiting, someone bumps into me from behind, and I feel cold liquid running down my back. See, this is what I was talking about. Right as I'm whirling around to see who spilled their drink on me, I hear a barely audible female voice, "Oh my god, I am so sorry!"

When I'm fully turned around, I see a gorgeous woman picking up an empty plastic cup off the ground. She stands up once she retrieves her cup and looks at me with a guilty look on her face. "Someone ran by me and shoved me into you; I am so sorry." She grabs my arm and turns me around so she can take a look at the damage she did to the back of my shirt. I'm wearing white shirt, so you can see the full contents of her pink drink soaked into my back.

"It's all good. This place is crowded." I have to yell so she can hear me since we're right by a set of speakers.

"Follow me; I'll help you clean it up." That's really not necessary, but if I don't have to live with a sticky back for the rest of the night, that would be great.

I look up at where Quinn is and consider letting him know I'm leaving, but he'll figure it out when he doesn't see me standing here anymore.

We walk through the crowd, and she leads the way. When we get to a packed section, she reaches back and grabs my hand so we don't lose each other. We weave in and out of groups and make our way toward the front. Once we get out of the crowd, she goes to turn left toward the public bathrooms, but I tug her arm over to the right.

I nod my head toward the private area of the club. "Let's go this way."

She gives me a skeptical look like she knows we're not allowed back there. Well, she doesn't know yet that *I'm* allowed back there. She lets up on her resistance and allows me to guide her to the ropes that block off that area.

The security guard recognizes me and lets us in, not even questioning the fact that I came back with another person I didn't leave this area with. Men must bring back women from the crowd all the time. That makes me feel a little sleazy, but I figured the bathrooms would be way less crowded back here.

Her eyes get wide when he lets us through without question. I feel like I need to explain so she doesn't think I'm some super-rich guy who does this all the time.

"My brother is the DJ; that's why I was standing over there by the booth. I was waiting for him to go on a break. The club gave him a booth, so I'm just here with him."

I can't help but notice the slight look of disappointment that crosses her face, but I don't care. I don't want to get women to like me by deceiving them.

I realize I'm still holding her hand and let go since there's no need to be guiding her in an empty hallway.

When we get to the bathroom door, I open it and let her in first. The bathrooms back here are single rooms with locked doors, so I shut the door behind us but don't lock it. I don't want her to feel trapped in here with me since she probably didn't know we were going to be shut in a room together.

"Here, it'll be easier if you take it off." She walks toward me and grabs the hem of my shirt, lifting it up. She's much shorter than me, so I have to help her get it over my head. Once my shirt is off, she grabs it, turns towards the sink, and turns on the water. She pumps a handful of soap, and before she puts my shirt under the water, she looks at me in the mirror and asks, "This isn't some super expensive fabric that I'm going to completely ruin with hand soap, is it?"

"Not that I'm aware of."

She runs it under the water and gently scrubs the soap in. The pink stain immediately starts to lift, and I just stand there, watching her. I feel a little bit like an idiot because I didn't really need her help with this. But I guess subconsciously, I liked the idea of having the company of a beautiful woman.

At some point, she must feel me staring at her because she looks up at me in the mirror and smiles. Her eyes travel from mine down to my bare chest, and it's my turn to smile at her for clearly checking me out.

I step closer to her and press my bare front to her back. I pull her hair off her shoulder and lean forward to press my lips to her neck. She sinks back into me and rubs her ass into my jeans. One of her arms lifts up and wraps around my neck, holding me close. I continue kissing her down her neck and across her bare shoulder. She drops the shirt and turns around to face me, leaving the water running. I reach around her to turn it off, making her giggle.

I brace my hands on the counter on either side of her and lean into her. Her wet, soapy hands wrap around my neck and pull me even closer until our lips meet. The tension between us has been building since she grabbed my hand on the dance floor, so at this point, we both snap.

I grab her hips and lift her onto the counter. Her hands explore my chest, my stomach, my back. Our lips devour each other. I can't remember if she had lipstick on, but I don't care right now. If she did, then it's all over my face because her lips run wild over me. I slip my hand under the skirt of her dress and touch her.

I'm so caught up in the moment that I forgot my

manners. Stopping, I pull back and remove my hand. She looks confused and annoyed, but I have to ask. "Are you sure you're okay with this?" She nods. "If you want me to stop at any point, I will." Her eyes soften, and I think she can tell I'm being genuine.

"I don't have a condom on me, so unless you do, I'd like to stop before we get to that point." She looks a bit nervous. Like she thinks I'll get mad or want to just stop right now.

Damn it. I hadn't even gotten that far in my head yet.

"I don't have one either. I'll make sure I can stop before then."

She smiles. "Okay."

We resume right where we left off as if we never stopped. If anything, she seems even more turned on right now. Her lips are all over my face and neck. I run both hands up her thighs and under her skirt. It's loose enough that I can easily maneuver around and lift it up above her hips. When I realize she's not wearing any underwear, I feel my dick pulse against my stomach, restricted by the waist-band of my jeans.

I get on my knees and lift her legs over my shoulders. She braces one hand behind her, and the other clutches my hair. I dive into her and hear her moans echo through the room. I lick up her center and suck on her clit. She's so wet, and I can feel her starting to tense. After a few minutes, my jaw starts getting tired, but I don't stop until I feel her pull my hair and her legs start to shake.

I can tell she's trying to be as quiet as possible, but there's no way anyone can hear her over the loud music, even in the empty hallway outside.

She slides off the counter, and I stand as she wraps her arms around my waist. I wipe my face and lean in, giving her the option to kiss me or not. She lifts herself up on her tiptoes and sticks out her tongue to lick across my lips before locking hers with mine. She's so hot, and even though I want to fuck her so bad, I'm fine just kissing her.

We make out for a little bit before parting. She turns around with a smirk on her face but doesn't say anything. She simply grabs my soaking wet shirt out of the sink, rinses out all the soap, and wrings out the excess water. Then she walks over to the hand dryer and turns it on to dry off the shirt.

I finally break the silence. "Are you here with a group?"

"Yeah, I'm here with a group of girlfriends."

My shirt is drying surprisingly quickly, so I take it from her even though it's still slightly damp. I throw it over my head, and the cool fabric feels good on my sweaty skin.

"I'll walk you back if you want."

"That would be great. They were over by the DJ booth when we left. So you can finally talk to your brother like you were trying to do when I so rudely interrupted you."

I smile and lean down, hovering my lips right over hers. "It was a very worthwhile interruption."

"I'm glad you think so too." She presses her lips to mine for one more brief kiss before we head back into the empty hallway.

I lead her back to the other side of the club, where we find her friends and say goodbye.

As I'm walking over to see Quinn, I realize that I never even asked her name, and she never asked mine. I smile and chuckle to myself. What a wild night.

Chapter Fifteen

LOUISA

It's after midnight, and everything has gone wild here. The bass is pounding in my chest, and I'm covered in sweat. The dance floor is packed, so I can barely tell whose hands are on me at any given moment.

B and I spot each other through the strobe lights and dance over to each other. We grab hands, lacing our fingers together, and dance. I feel untouchable in this moment. Just B and I against the world with nothing stopping us.

That's likely the Molly talking. I guess that's a thing I do now. When we first arrived here, B's coworker offered us some, and at first, I said no. After thinking about it, I thought maybe it would help me feel something that I've been missing. Lately, I've been in a dark place that I can't seem to get out of. I thought the holiday would cheer me up, but I just felt a whole lot of nothing. Tonight is a fresh start —a new year—and I'm hoping it brings with it a new Lou.

David throws wild parties that only escalate as the night goes on. I've never stayed at one this late, so this is a new experience for me. I don't think I could do this regularly, but once or twice a year is enough to scratch the itch of my very tame wild side.

B always says I'm boring, and I'm here to prove her wrong.

She yells over the music to get my attention. "Are you having a good time?"

"The best!"

I let go of her hands and run mine down my body as I sway back and forth to the music. Every sensation is heightened. I can feel beads of sweat running down my neck, I can feel the music vibrate the floor and up through my body, and I can smell all the perfume and cologne of everyone around me mingling together.

It's so blissful until all of a sudden, I feel sick. I need to find some fresh air, asap. I've been to Daniel's place before, and I remember there being a rooftop. Where were those stairs? I spin around to scan the room, and I spot them in the back corner near the balcony.

I spin around to find B again. When I spot her, I grab her arm and pull her close. "I'm going to go to the roof for a bit to get some fresh air. Do you want to come with me?"

She can't hear me over the music this time. "What?"

"I said, I'm...never mind. I'LL BE RIGHT BACK!"

She nods to confirm she heard me that time and gives me a thumbs up.

I walk toward the stairs and look back to find B spinning in circles by herself, dancing without a care in the world. I smile to myself because I wish I could be that happy. I mean, I'm happy in this moment, but I want to be that happy a majority of the time. B seems to have cracked that code, but I can't seem to figure it out. These days, there seem to be more bad days than good.

When I reach the stairs, I have to dodge a few people

coming down as I make my way up to the roof. At the top is a steel door labeled "Roof Access. Please no jumping; you can't fly." I laugh even though that is a horribly morbid thing to be laughing about. For a split second, I think about how freeing it would feel to fall from that high. I bet all my worries would go away in that freefall.

Jesus Christ, Lou!

I open the door and instantly feel the cool air freeze the sweat on my skin. Fuck, I should have brought my jacket up here. Where is my jacket anyway? Whatever, I won't stay out here that long. Wouldn't want to get tempted by the ledge.

Daniel's rooftop has a bunch of heaters for people to gather around. Thank god. I needed some fresh air, not to catch hypothermia. I go to stand by the one that is the least occupied since I'm pretty high and don't want to have to converse with anyone. A man stands there alone, someone I don't recognize. I stand on the opposite side, trying not to be awkward.

"Aren't you freezing in that tiny little dress?"

I look down at myself and see pebbles all over my bare legs, and acknowledge that my mid-thigh length dress is doing absolutely nothing to keep me warm. "I couldn't find my jacket. I'm just getting some fresh air for a second, and then I'll head back in to warm up." I didn't want to sound stupid and admit that I didn't think to bring it.

He sets his drink down on the ledge of the heater and starts to shrug off his suit coat.

"Oh no, you really don't have to do that."

He pauses and looks at me, confused. "I was just taking it off because I was getting warm."

My skin heats as I realize he wasn't about to offer it to me. I'm an idiot. I close my eyes and scrunch my face, nodding. That ledge sounds pretty tempting right about now.

He laughs, and I open my eyes to confirm he's laughing at me. Then, he holds out his jacket. "I'm just messing with you. I insist you wear it as long as you're standing out here."

I want to be polite and pretend to refuse it, but I am freezing and don't want to risk him rescinding his offer, so I reach out and take it from him. I throw it over my shoulders and wrap it around me. I pull it tight near my neck, which brings it close enough for me to smell his cologne. It smells so good and reminds me of...Sam. My heart sinks, and I'm worried about how the drugs are going to make me react to something that has repeatedly made me sad.

Before I think about it for too long, I make eye contact with the stranger again and get a good look at him. He's tall and handsome, probably in his early 30s. The attraction is there, but I can't quite get a read on him. I would definitely go home with a stranger tonight. What better way to round out my wild evening than a one-night stand?

Just as I'm about to get the courage to move closer to him, another man walks up to us. He puts his arm around the stranger who gave me his jacket and kisses him on the cheek. "Honey, are you already taking your clothes off? It's only 1:00am."

Oh my god. I can't believe I was just about to hit on a gay man. That rejection would have had me digging a hole and burying myself alive in it or maybe jumping off the roof. I am so grateful his partner walked up and saved me from that shame. The first man smiles and laughs at his partner, gesturing toward me. "The poor thing was about to turn into a popsicle."

"Honey, that jacket is not going to save you. Your legs are turning purple; get back inside."

He points at my legs, and I look down again to see that my legs really are turning purple. I really should go back inside. I take off the man's jacket and hand it back to him. My arms are frozen again, and I can't get inside soon enough.

"Thank you for lending it to me."

I don't even wait for a reply; I sprint for the door as best as I can in these heels. The door flings open right before I get to it, and someone else steps outside. I wait for them to pass through the door and then step inside. The heat hits me like a wall of fire, and I feel myself starting to thaw. But I'm afraid I am so frozen to my core that it'll take a miracle to fully warm up here.

My head starts to ache, and I can tell the drugs are starting to wear off. I need to go home and go to bed before this wonderful evening starts going downhill.

Before going back down the stairs, I use my vantage point to search for B. I spot her grinding between a guy and a girl. I can't make out who it is, but I'm assuming I don't know them since I don't know most of the people here.

I mark her location in my brain and make my way down the stairs. The dance floor is way too packed for anyone to get through, so I cut my losses and decide to just text her. I let her know I'm heading home and to let me know if she plans to crash here for the night so I'm not waiting up for her. I send it and try to track down my coat.

———

WHEN I UNLOCK the apartment door and open it, Pepin is there to greet me. I bend down and pet him, giving him a big hug.

"What are you still doing up? I thought you would be passed out in my bed by now."

I shut the door behind me and lock it. B texted me saying she has already claimed one of Daniel's spare bedrooms for the night and will be staying there, so I don't bother leaving it unlocked for her. That also means I won't feel obligated to stay up and wait for her.

I'm still really cold, so I walk to the bathroom and turn on the shower. I strip out of my dress and thong and step under the hot water. I release a big sigh at the warmth I feel running through my body. Again, this is probably the drug talking, but this feels amazing. It feels like a big, warm body wrapping around me and keeping me warm. I, oddly, start to get a little horny.

I have an idea! I jump out of the shower and quickly run naked and soaking wet to my room to grab something. I return merely seconds later with my silicone vibrator that I remember is waterproof. I select the setting I like and hop back in the shower. I got a little cold running to my room and back, so the hot water warms me up again, feeling like an embrace.

You know you're lonely when warm water turns you on. It's an all-time low for me. I push those thoughts aside because I need to take care of myself right now, and I can't have that kind of negative talk in my head if I want to get off.

I bend over slightly so my forehead rests on the shower wall, and the stream of water is hitting my back. I place the vibrator between my legs and glide it back and forth in my wetness until it's spread all over me. Making small circles around the apex, I start to shudder.

. . .

155

Emma Pathy

I FANTASIZE *about a man standing behind me, a warm body pressed against mine, kissing my neck. He's holding the toy for me, so eager to make me come. He puts his other hand on my breast and massages it. He takes the vibrator and presses it against my center, toying with my entrance. I move my hips so I'm grinding against it, and it slips in. I whimper and feel a shiver run through my body. He flips me around so my back is against the shower wall and touches all over my front, running his finger down past my naval all the way to my clit. He slowly rubs in circles, all while he pulls the vibrator out of me just to push it back in. I'm starting to orgasm when I look up and see his face. I see it's Sam, and my legs give out from under me with the amount of pleasure surging from my center.*

I CATCH myself on the ledge of the tub and am able to right myself once the buzzing stops. My heavy panting makes water spray from my mouth as it runs down my face. I finally admit that it's usually Sam I fantasize about when I'm touching myself. In addition to getting out of my funk, maybe my New Year's resolution will be to stop doing that.

Then again, I've never had a successful New Year's resolution in my life.

Chapter Sixteen

LOUISA

I'm lying in bed studying for my exams when I get the urge to open the dating app. I haven't been on it in a while, and the last time I touched a guy was when I made out with Bear over Christmas.

I open it up and realize it's been so long that I first need to update the app, so I do that. Once it's finished, I open it up and go to my messages. I go to click on messages from Sam because I want to read back through some of them, but I realize that they're gone. I click on the toggle that says "View Unmatched Messages." It will show you previous messages to and from people, even after they unmatch with you...or delete their account.

Sam deleted his account.

Right at the bottom of our chat, it says, "This user no longer has an active account." That means he could have just paused his account or he could have completely deleted it. There's no way for me to know.

I have conflicting emotions running through my brain. I can't decide if I'm happy because he may have been telling the truth and really did take a break from dating. Or it could mean he met someone else and deleted his account because they're dating now.

Whatever. I can't think about that for too long, so I get out of messages and start swiping.

A few hours later, I start messaging back and forth with a guy named Cameron. He goes by Cam; he's 6'5", has blonde hair, and blue eyes. I can tell he isn't looking for anything serious, but neither am I. We agree to go out for drinks next weekend.

————

CAM and I are sitting at a bar, a couple of drinks deep, and I can tell this is going to end with him in my pants. He's funny and very confident in himself, verging on being cocky. But something about him just tells me it's going to be worth my time. I've gotten better at being able to tell, and when I think back to my first hook-up after Jay, I cringe at all the signs I missed, or chose to ignore.

The bartender comes over and asks if we want another round.

Cam looks at me and shrugs, leaving the decision up to me. I stare back at him, wanting him to decide. The stare-off continues until he decides for us. "We'll take the check, thanks." He turns back to me. "You want to come back to my place? I just live a few blocks down."

I nod. "Sure."

The bartender comes back over with our checks, and Cam picks them both up and hands them back to her with his card. I like it when I don't have to play chicken with a guy over the check. It can get awkward. So I like that he just does it without saying anything.

I stop the bartender before she walks away. "Can I ask you a favor?"

The bartender turns back around to face me. "Of course, what can I do for you?"

"Do you work tomorrow?"

Both Cam and the bartender are now staring at me, confused. They probably think I'm hitting on the bartender right in front of my date. She hesitantly replies, "Yeah, I work the morning shift for brunch. Why?"

"Perfect! Can I see your phone really quick?" I've seen it in her back pocket all night, so I know she has it on her.

She puts our checks in one hand and reaches around her back with the other, pulling out her phone and handing it to me.

"Thank you!"

I reach over and grab Cam's wallet out of his hand and fish through it until I find what I'm looking for. I open the camera on the girl's phone and take a photo of Cam's ID. I hand Cam his wallet and ID back, then reach out and give the bartender back her phone, along with my ID.

"If I don't come back tomorrow morning to retrieve that, you know who to blame my murder on." I point my thumb at Cam.

They both look at me like I'm joking, and when they realize I'm not, they both start laughing.

She grabs both her phone and my ID from me. "That is probably one of the strangest things I've witnessed in a long time. I will absolutely be waiting for you and would gladly help convict a felon if need be." She bats her eyelashes at him. Probably in hopes of still getting a good tip despite just threatening him.

I look at him and giggle.

Of course, I will also let B know where I'm going, and

we have our locations shared. But I've been listening to a lot of true crime podcasts on my walks with Pepin. I've learned that you can never be too safe.

———

WE GET BACK to his place, and it's actually pretty nice. He's only 22, so I was expecting a poor guy's college apartment. His family must have money and help him out.

"Your place is nice."

"Nice enough to commit murder in." He glances over at me with a smirk on his face.

I choke on a laugh and play punch him in the shoulder.

As soon as he locks the door, he starts slowly making his way toward me, looking at me with a hunger in his eyes. I'm backed against a wall, and he comes closer. He hooks his fingers through my belt loops, tugging me close, and whispers in my ear, "Shall we?"

I run my hands up his arms to his strong shoulders and up to his face. I pull it down toward mine, but he really has to bend over to get to me. I help him out by standing on my tiptoes, but he just scoops me up and wraps my legs around him. He pins me against the wall and kisses me, biting my lower lip.

After a moment, he pulls me off the wall and walks us to the bedroom, where he tosses me on the bed with some force. So he likes to play rough, does he?

I already knew this from the dirty talk he was messaging me earlier this week. I'm a bit nervous but mostly excited. No one has ever been that rough with me before. But I've fantasized about it when touching myself, so I have high hopes that I'll like it.

He starts taking off his shirt while he's still standing at

the edge of the bed, staring down at me. "What's your safe word?"

"I've never had one."

"I don't plan on being too rough with you, so I don't think we'll need one, but I like to be safe. Let's just use yellow and red. Like a stoplight. Yellow when you're getting uncomfortable, and red means full stop."

My breathing picks up. "Easy enough." I swallow hard.

He gets on all fours, straddling me. He's so tall that there's a lot of space between us right now.

"Roll over." It comes out firm and assertive, which turns me on.

I roll over onto my stomach and rest my hands under my chest, head turned to the side. His hands grip my hips and pull my ass up to meet him. I can feel how hard he is when I'm pressed up to him like this. And especially when he grinds on me.

"Mmmm, Lou, you are going to be such a good girl for me." I can see the grin on his face out of the corner of my eye. He reaches around to my front and undoes my pants. Once he gets them undone, he pulls them down to my knees. He sighs right before I feel a sharp sting on my ass coupled with a smacking sound.

He just spanked me, and I liked it. He does it a second time. Yeah, I really like that.

I feel his hot breath near my center, and then he licks me from behind. I arch my back at the sensation. His tongue works its way around my folds, and I can feel something building.

I let out a whimper and my body shivers.

He keeps licking me until I'm shaking. He pulls back and slaps my wet center. Oh, that felt good. My body tries to fall to the bed, but his hands hold my hips up.

He lets go with one hand, and I can hear it jostling with his belt and pants. Then we both move slightly as he leans over and digs through the drawer for a condom. After he gets it on, he pulls my pants completely off and spreads my knees wider. I gasp when I feel his hard cock thrust into me. He's big and rough and oh so good at what he's doing.

I'm moaning and losing control of myself when I cry out, "Oh, Sam!"

Oh my god, did I just call him Sam?

I did, didn't I?

I go quiet, waiting for a response that he never gives. Either he thought I said "Cam," or he's choosing to ignore the fact that I just called out another man's name in his bed. I move on and keep moaning, making a note not to call him the wrong name again.

I was slightly worried about not being in control, but I really like it.

He stops slamming me from behind and rolls us over so I'm lying on my back on top of him. His body moves under mine so his cock is thrusting in and out while I brace myself with my legs spread on either side of him with my feet on the bed. My hands reach over my head and touch his chest.

I feel like my body can't go any longer, but he pulls out of me and moves me to his side so my back is now on his bed. He moves around so he's kneeling straight up between my legs, facing me. His big hands wrap around my ankles and lift my legs in the air, spread apart. He enters me again and pumps hard and fast, making me come again.

He pulls out of me, whips the condom off, and strokes himself until he comes all over my stomach.

I'm exhausted, and my body feels like it can't even move. I am going to be so sore tomorrow, but it felt so good that I don't care.

He gets up, grabs a towel from his attached bathroom, and cleans me up. I get dressed and order my ride. He offers to let me stay the night, but it's still relatively early, and I'm afraid if I stay the night, we'll end up going for round two, and I know I couldn't handle that.

He walks me out and kisses me on the forehead. "Text me any time you want to hang, okay? I had fun with you."

I'm not sure what he means by that because I was a rag-doll the whole time while he took charge, but I'll take the compliment and consider texting him again.

"Will do. Night Cam, thanks for the drinks...and the sex."

He winks at me before shutting the door.

———

THE NEXT MORNING, I almost forget to return to the bar.

Thank god I didn't; that could have turned out so bad!

When I get there, the bartender from the night before hands me back my ID with a big smile. "I'm glad you didn't get murdered."

I laugh. "Me too."

I grab my ID, but she holds it for a second longer. "So, was he as good as he looked?"

I lean over the bar and whisper to her, "Better."

We both laugh, and she lets go of my ID. I turn and leave with a huge smile on my face. So why do I still feel empty inside?

Chapter Seventeen

SAM

I step out of the elevator and into the hallway. I can never remember if it's a right or a left, so I go left and check a few door numbers to see if I'm going the correct way. I'm not. I turn around and start heading the other way.

My head has been in a fog all week in anticipation of this. I've been putting it off for over four months, and I finally feel ready for it. Not that I'll ever truly be ready, but I was not in the right head space to do it prior to now.

I fumble with the keys and try them in the lock, one by one, until I find the right one. The latch clicks, and I pause with my hand on the knob for a moment before opening the door. A smell hits me square in the face. I know I shouldn't have waited this long. I'm sure everything in the fridge is rotten, and if the garbage wasn't taken out, that would definitely explain the smell.

I step into Jacob's dark apartment, and the creek of the floor startles me. I don't know why, but I'm a little skittish being here. It feels eerie, like a time capsule from before he was gone. Everything that Jacob saw during his last days.

I look around for a light switch and flick it on. I've been paying the bills since it got passed to me, so I know the electricity still works.

The light flickers on, and I walk to the kitchen first, hoping to get rid of the smell so I can tolerate being here long enough to sort through his things. I put my sweatshirt over my nose and open the garbage.

Yep, that is definitely where the smell is coming from. I take it out and tie up the bag as quickly as I can, then take it down the hall and throw it in the garbage shoot. When I get back, I locate some Lysol spray and air freshener, spraying a generous amount of both in the garbage bin.

Next, I take an empty garbage bag and throw out everything in the fridge, repeating the Lysol and air freshener combo. After I finish, I open up a couple windows to get some fresh air in here.

Now that the smell is taken care of, I can move on to the fun part. Going through his things feels wrong, and I don't know what I'm going to find. Thankfully, Jacob has always been neat, so there aren't drawers and boxes full of junk.

I start with the closet because that seems the most straightforward. I promised Mom I would save some items for her, and Quinn laid claim to most of his shoes since they had the same size feet.

There's only one thing I want to keep for myself, so I look for that first. I sift through the section of sweatshirts hanging up and find it there—Jacob's high school football sweatshirt. I tried to steal this from him so many times, but he always noticed and stole it back. I don't know what it was about this particular sweatshirt that made me want it so bad. Probably just because, in high school, I idolized Jacob; I wanted to be just like him. I wonder if her ever knew that?

I slip it off the hanger and hug it to my chest, taking in

the scent of it. Jacob's scent. I don't even realize I've been crying until I feel a tear fall down my cheek, then another. Soon, I can't control them; they keep falling, and my chest starts to tighten. I walk backwards until my shoulder blades hit the wall and slide down it till I'm on the floor.

I sob into his sweatshirt. My eyes burn, my throat feels like it's closing in, and my chest hurts from my quick, shallow breathing. I miss him, but I'm mostly angry that such a promising life got thrown away. And I can't shake the could haves and should haves from my mind.

"I'm so sorry, Jacob. I'm so sorry." My voice is muffled by the fabric, but it doesn't matter. There's no one there to hear me anyway.

———

AFTER I ALLOWED myself to have a good cry, I finished cleaning out the closet and started on his desk. The desk was harder to go through than I thought it would be. I had to stop and take a break to cool off.

I want to burn every textbook that ever caused Jacob distress, shred every assignment that he gave up sleep to finish, and tear apart every notebook full of information he didn't even care about but felt pressured to learn. In the end, I recycled what could be recycled and threw what couldn't.

After I go through all his school stuff, I move on to his personal effects. Medical information, student loan mail, banking information, and cards that he kept.

I glance through the cards to see if there's anything my mom may want to look at and notice a piece of loose leaf paper stuffed into an envelope that was way too small for the letter it contained.

My heart stops.

We never found a letter from Jacob, and at first, I hope that this is it, that maybe we can get some answers, even though we think we already know most of his reasons. I drop the cards and open up the unsealed envelope, pulling out the letter.

I suck in a big breath and brace myself for more tears when I realize it's not a letter that Jacob left for us; it's a letter that I wrote Jacob years ago. He kept it. I remember writing it when I was a freshman in college. Mom had sent me envelopes and stamps because she thought sending mail was still as big of a thing as it was when she was in college. I never used them until one day, I got bored and wrote a few letters to send, just for fun. I wrote one to my mom, one to Quinn, who was still living at home, and one to Jacob, who was off at a different college.

The letter isn't anything special. No grand secrets or exciting information were revealed. It was just a simple letter written on notebook paper, telling my brother how much I was enjoying my first year of college. I told him about the first party I went to, the first girl I hooked up with, and a lot of other firsts. At that age, Jacob and I didn't share many details of our lives with each other, so this was probably more than I told him in person in an entire year.

I'm surprised he kept it this long. It likely was just something he forgot existed in the back of his drawer, but he didn't throw it away after he read it like I assumed he would.

———

IT TOOK me a whole week to get through Jacob's apartment.

Quinn came over one day to help me move all the big

items. We barely talked the whole time. We just moved the items and closed it up. He offered to help me sort through everything earlier, but I told him that I could handle it myself. In hindsight, I'm really glad I did because it allowed me to grieve him.

To truly grieve him.

The landlord is taking back the keys today and reimbursing me for the last couple of months of rent, likely out of pity. I told her she didn't need to do that, but when I arrived today, there was an envelope shoved in the door with a check written for two months' worth of rent.

She told me that Jacob was always so kind to her seven-year-old daughter, who often comes to the building after school while she finishes up her work. In the envelope with the check is a drawing made by her daughter.

It's a picture of what I'm assuming is her and Jacob playing chess or maybe checkers; she's seven, so it's hard to tell. I put the picture in the box I'm taking to Mom's house; she would want to see that.

I take one more look around and make sure I didn't leave anything in the cabinets or closets. Once everything is checked over, I put the last few boxes on my dolly and lock up.

On my way out of the building, I drop the keys off in the main office with a note thanking the landlord for the check and head out.

I never found a letter from him. There likely isn't one, and that's okay. He doesn't owe us anything.

Chapter Eighteen

LOUISA

It's finally getting warm outside, and B is meeting up with some friends from college for a bonfire. She invited me to go with, and I have nothing else to do, so I tag along.

The party is at someone called Big Mike's house. When I questioned B about his name, she just shrugged and said it's what everyone has called him as long as she's known him. Big Mike was B's weed dealer in college, and I'm pretty sure he still is because I've seen his name pop up on her phone from time to time.

We Uber there because B told me to be prepared to get super fucked up. That's not my plan, but I don't want to stop myself from letting go and having a good time.

When we pull up, I'm slightly surprised by the place. I was expecting a total dump, but it's actually really cute and looks well taken care of. Maybe he still lives with his parents.

I grab the case of beer, and B grabs the case of seltzers we brought. We hate showing up empty-handed. I follow B up the driveway, and she heads straight around the house to the backyard. I can hear people laughing, and when we round the corner, I see a big group in lawn chairs around a bonfire. I love bonfires but don't get them often since moving to the city.

B walks right up to someone I don't recognize and throws her arm over their shoulder, startling them.

"Hey losers, the party has arrived!"

Everyone greets us, and B introduces me to the people I haven't met. There is no way I'm going to remember anyone's name.

I hear noises coming from the house, and when I turn to check it out, I realize there are a lot more people here than I thought. A group is walking out of the house, and through a window, I can see more people mingling inside. I honestly like big groups because then I can just blend in and observe. Parties with B's friends have always made for great people-watching.

Someone brings out some more lawn chairs, and we take a seat near a guy smoking.

"Want some?"

B reaches over to take it from him. "Yes please!" She takes a hit and offers it to me.

"No, I'm good for now; I'll probably smoke something later. I don't trust myself to get high this early in the night."

The guy takes it back from B and takes another hit. "Fair enough. At least you have keen self-awareness."

I laugh because I'm not sure I would say that, but he's not totally wrong.

The group around the fire starts playing a drinking game, so I crack myself a seltzer. The game is more luck than skill, and the universe is not on my side tonight. I fly through my four-pack of seltzers quickly, and I'm not in the mood for beer, so I sit out a round.

B tells me to go inside and grab a drink. When I give her a skeptical look, she reassures me that the drinks in there are for everyone and that it wouldn't be weird. I'm not sure why she doesn't just offer to go in and grab one for me since they're her friends, but she doesn't. She's pretty into this game and pretty into the guy sitting next to her.

Although I'm uncomfortable walking into a stranger's house and helping myself to their alcohol, I do need to pee. I don't bother to ask her to come with me because she'd just tell me to be a big girl.

I walk up to the back door and let myself in. Most of the people have migrated outside to the bonfire, so the house is pretty quiet. I look around and locate the kitchen off to the left. I walk in and see a bunch of coolers on the floor, and I sheepishly start opening them.

Rummaging through other people's things feels wrong, but B swore it wasn't an issue and told me to grab her one, too. I brought the beer in here with me to put in the coolers, which makes me feel a little better.

I eventually locate a cooler with more seltzers in it and dig through the ice for a flavor I like. My hand is freezing by the time I pull out a pineapple for B and a lime for myself. I shake off the ice stuck to them and find a dish towel to dry them off. Then, I run my hand under warm water to warm it up.

With the sink running, I don't even hear someone walk into the kitchen behind me.

"Hey, how's it going?"

"Jesus!" I jump about a foot in the air, so startled by the sudden voice behind me. "Oh, you scared me so bad." My back is now to the counter, and my hand is keeping my heart from pounding out of my chest. I let out a little laugh because now I'm embarrassed by my reaction when I see that it's a really cute guy behind me.

He laughs too. "Sorry, I didn't mean to startle you. Just came in here to grab a lighter." He fishes through one of the drawers and grabs one out without taking his eyes off me.

"It's all good. Do you, by chance, know where the bathroom is?"

He smiles; I'm not really sure why, though. He leans through the entrance to the kitchen and points to a hallway to the right. "It's down that hall, the door straight ahead of you."

"Thanks." I grab our drinks off the counter and squeeze by him to head to the bathroom. It's a pretty small bathroom with no counter to set the drinks on, so I just hold them while I pee, and now my hands are freezing again.

I finish up and walk out, heading for the back door. I spot that same guy sitting in the living room, packing a bong. He looks up and catches me staring at him.

"You want some?"

I honestly don't want to go back outside just yet, so I figure, why not?

"Sure."

I walk into the living room and sit on the couch next to him. "My name is Lou, by the way; I'm B's sister." I guess I just assume that everyone knows B without even thinking if he knows her or not.

He smiles. "Yeah? You're the big sister?"

I scrunch my eyebrows together, confused. So he does know B. Does she talk about me to her friends? "I hope the fact that you know who I am isn't a bad thing..."

"Nah. B only says good things about you. She says you used to have fun when you were in college, but now you are a lot more tame. A "mature" adult, as some would say."

I laugh at the idea of B telling people I'm mature. But, I guess up until this summer when Jay dumped me, I had gotten pretty boring and didn't do anything that wasn't good for my future.

"Did she also tell you that I've recently learned to let loose again?"

"She may have mentioned that."

I smile at him, and he hands me the bong. I take a hit and inhale the cool, smooth smoke, letting it out after a couple seconds. I almost instantly feel it since it's been so long since I've smoked.

I turn to hand it to him and realize something. "Sorry, I didn't catch your name."

"I'm Mikey."

"Mikey? As in Big Mike? Or are there two of you?"

He chuckles. "No, that's me. I prefer Mikey, but everyone calls me Big Mike for some reason. I honestly can't even remember how it started."

I look him over, and it truly doesn't compute. This man is not what I expected someone called Big Mike to look like at all. This guy is clean-cut, handsome, and has clear, bright eyes. He doesn't look like any dealer I ever met in college.

"Do you live here alone?" This is my attempt at subtly finding out if he lives with his mom or if he really just isn't the stereotype at all.

"No, I have a couple roommates. I own the house, but I rent out rooms to friends who need cheap rent. It helps pay the mortgage." I look at him, and my face must ask the question because he answers it. "I bought the house with money from my college adventures, but I don't do that anymore. I work at a bank in the next suburb over."

My eyes widen, and I can't help but giggle. It's likely the weed, but that seems really funny to me for some reason. A college dealer is now working at a bank. Why not, I guess. I used to smoke in college, but now I have a very respectable, professional job.

In my head, people who did this a lot only had fun, crazy jobs like B or worked in the service industry. But Mikey surprises me and reminds me that I shouldn't subscribe to stereotypes.

My body feels lighter, and my brain feels clear. I need to do this more often. I forgot how nice it is to escape all the anxiety that clutters my thoughts and affects my everyday life. I lean into the euphoric feeling and sink back into the couch.

"Hey, Mikey?"

He leans back onto the couch alongside me and looks over. "Yeah?"

"Do you have any snacks?"

He laughs. "I think most of them are out by the bonfire."

I grumble. "I don't want to talk to people right now."

"There's a gas station just down the street. We could walk there and get some new snacks."

I look over at him, and I can feel my eyes light up. "Can we?" Oh my god, I probably sound like a little kid whose parents told them they could go out for ice cream.

"Let's go." He stands up and grabs my hands to help lift me off the couch. My purse has been strung over my chest all night, and I'm thankful I don't have to run outside to grab it.

He walks to the front door, and I follow him. We make our way down the sidewalk, side by side, and I can see the lights of the gas station up ahead. Wow, he wasn't kidding. It is really close.

The fresh air feels good on my skin, and I breathe it in, filling my lungs.

We walk in silence for a while, which I don't mind at all. But he eventually strikes up a conversation.

"What do you do for work?"

"I'm an architect," I say, but I quickly correct myself. "Well, not quite yet. I graduated with my degree, but before I'm officially licensed, I need to complete a certain amount of hours and then pass six licensure exams."

"That sounds pretty intense."

"It is. I have my first exam coming up this summer, and I'm super nervous about it."

"Well, if you're half as smart as B is, then I'm sure you'll do just fine."

I know how smart B is, but I didn't know that her friends knew. She never really shows that side of her, especially when she's partying. People usually think she's all personality and no brains. But she landed the job with Daniel Perez for a reason. And it's not just because of her knowledge of designer jackets.

"Are you and B pretty close?"

He shrugs. "Yeah, I'd like to think so. We took some classes together in college and would study together."

"Did you guys ever...you know, hook up?"

He laughs and shakes his head. "No, it wasn't like that. I honestly thought she was a lesbian, so I never tried. It's probably best we didn't, though."

"Why's that?"

He shrugs and then turns his head toward me. I look back at him, and he's giving me that look. I narrow my eyes and smile at him, then roll them.

Is he hitting on me?

We get to the gas station after what seems like hours. But it was more than likely a five-minute walk in total. I grab some chips, a bag of sour candy, and a hot dog. Man, I'm hungry. We check out and walk back to the house.

I finish my hot dog before we even make it a block away, and I catch him staring at me while I lick ketchup off my fingers. I stare at him with a blank face until he looks away, smiling.

The walk back is mostly silent because we're both stuffing our faces. But every now and then, I feel the bare skin of his arm brush against mine, sending a tingle up to my shoulder. I look over at him and catch him staring again.

"You have really pretty eyes."

"They're brown," I say. I've always hated my brown eyes.

"Yeah, but they're a light caramel-colored brown."

My cheeks heat up, likely turning red. Sam called my eyes caramel brown when we first started talking. I don't know how to respond, so I look back down at my feet and continue walking.

When we get to his house, he opens the front door and lets me in first. I immediately go to the sink to wash the chip residue off my hands and the crumbs off my face. That had to be attractive.

I dry my hands and face on the kitchen towel and turn to look for Mikey, but I don't see him.

I hear the toilet flush and realize he went to use the bathroom. While the sink runs, I only have a minute to make a decision: go back outside or...

I quickly walk down the hall to the bathroom and get there right as he's opening the door. He's surprised to see me at first but then gets this cheeky grin on his face as if he already knows what I'm about to do because he was thinking it, too.

I walk into him, push him back into the bathroom, and shut the door behind me. He had already shut off the light when he was coming out, and I don't bother turning it back on. I grab his shirt in my fists and pull him toward me.

Our lips lock, and we start wildly kissing, tongues flying everywhere. He reaches behind me and turns the lock. Then his hands rest on my ass and squeeze. I frantically start pulling his belt off and unbuttoning his pants. As I do that, he starts to undo mine, our arms fighting each other for the space between us.

Once we get each other undone, we each pull down our own pants before reconnecting. He must have grabbed a condom from somewhere before going to the bathroom because he pulls one out of the pocket of his pants on the floor. He tears it open and puts it on.

I'm already so wet and ready for him, but he doesn't know that, so he runs his fingers along my center and quickly finds out for himself. He groans when he feels me and lifts one of my legs up over his hip. He continues to hold my leg up for me as he grabs the base of his already solid cock in his other hand. He pushes into me, and I involuntarily whimper. It echoes through the bathroom, and he cups his now free hand over my mouth and whispers in my ear, "Shhhh."

His breath on my neck sends chills down my spine as he thrusts in and out of me. He releases his hand from my mouth and grips my jaw instead, tilting my head away from him to give him better access to my neck.

He trails his tongue up the length of my neck, then sucks his way back down that same path to my collarbone. That's definitely going to leave a mark.

He starts pumping faster, and I can tell he's not going to last much longer. And thank goodness for that because a few seconds later, the knob rattles, and then there's a knock at the door.

A female voice calls out, "Is anyone in here?"

He stops moving and replies to her, "Uh yeah. Be out in a second."

"Oh, sorry! Take your time."

He looks at me, and I can see the disappointment on his face.

I can't help but laugh. "We should hurry up and finish so that poor girl can pee."

We both laugh at how awkward and ridiculous of a situation we put ourselves in. Especially since he has a bedroom we could be in right now. We clearly didn't think this through.

He starts pumping again, and I pull him in to kiss me. His movements get fast and wild. My mouth hangs open as I pant, and he sucks on my lower lip, biting it gently. He thrusts hard one last time, and his body tenses under my hands as he comes.

By the end, we're both breathing heavily and have to collect ourselves before we leave the bathroom. I'm not sure why we bother; she's going to assume we were fucking in here anyway. Knowing she's waiting on us made it impossible for me to come. But whatever, he didn't seem to care and neither do I. I think.

He opens the door, and I follow behind him. The girl had the courtesy of at least waiting in the living room rather than the hallway. As soon as she sees us, her face turns red. She definitely knows what she intruded on. "Sorry, Big Mike. I really have to pee, and your bedroom was locked."

"Don't worry about it. It's all yours now." He gestures down the hallway to the now unoccupied bathroom. She jumps up from the couch and sprints, slamming the door behind her.

He turns to me and drops my hand. I didn't even realize

he was holding my hand when we left the bathroom. "Well, that did not go as planned."

I lean against the wall, trying to act super casual. "You planned this?" I tease.

"No, I definitely didn't. I mean, once I saw you, it was on my mind, but not the way it happened. I thought I'd have you spread out on my bed upstairs."

A smile spreads across my face, and I can feel my cheeks heating up. I'm not sure why that makes me blush when he literally just had his dick in me. I shrug. "What can I say? When I see something I like, I've gotta have it."

He laughs and shakes his head. "You Blake women and your jokes." He reaches out and tucks my hair behind my ear. "Want to go out to the bonfire? I'm sure B is wondering where you ran off to."

"I doubt it. But yeah, let's go."

He doesn't grab my hand this time, and that's fine because I don't think I want to give anyone the wrong idea. After all, this was just for fun. I've learned to stop falling so fast because that only gets me hurt. So I'm just living my life in little moments and trying not to look too far into the future, but that's easier said than done.

Chapter Nineteen

LOUISA

It's the end of spring, and I've been on a couple of dates with guys I met on the dating app, but none of them were all that interesting, and none went past a first date. Life has been pretty uneventful. I mostly work, walk Pepin, and work some more.

I'm sitting at my desk working when my phone buzzes. I try not to check my phone at work, but I've been bad about that recently. I reach over just to see who it's from.

Matt's name pops up on the screen. I haven't heard from him in a while, so I'm intrigued. I thought maybe he had moved on to the next girl and forgotten about me. I unlock my phone and go to messages.

MATT

> Hello, gorgeous. How would you like to accompany me to a charity ball in a few weeks? It always looks better to investors when a gentleman has a beautiful woman on his arm.

LOU

What's the date? I'll check my calendar.

I don't have to check my calendar; I know I have nothing going on for months.

MATT

Second Saturday in June.

LOU

I'm available. What should I wear?

MATT

I'll have a gown and shoes sent over to your apartment next week. Let me know if any alterations need to be made, and I'll send someone.

LOU

That works for me. See you in a few weeks.

I throw my head back and my hands on my face. I let out a little scream, but not loud enough for my upstairs neighbor, Sarah, to feel the need to come check on me. I was really trying to play it cool, but I'm freaking out! A ball? A gown? My mind is running wild with ideas about what it's going to be like. I never thought I'd be someone who goes to an event like that. I likely never will again, so I'm going to fully enjoy it while I have the opportunity.

———

I⊤'s the night of the charity ball, and I have to get ready by myself because B is traveling for work. I'm fully capable of doing it by myself, but I just enjoy having her around for stuff like this. She always hypes me up and makes me feel sexy, though it would be really hard not to feel sexy in this dress.

True to his word, Matt had a dress sent to my apartment the week after he invited me. And he didn't just send one; he sent *three*. One is a deep red A-line sequence gown. The second is a plum-colored silk sheath gown. The third is a long black gown that hugs my top and midsection, then falls loosely on the floor with black straps tied in neat bows on both shoulders with a slit all the way up to my hip.

I tried them all on multiple times and finally chose the black one. He also sent over several pairs of shoes in my size. I bend over and lace up the red velvet strappy heels I picked out, wrapping the velvet ribbon twice around my ankle before tying it off in a bow in the back.

I stand up and check myself out in the mirror one more time before heading out to meet the car.

"How do I look, Pepin?"

I turn to him sitting on the bed and do a slow twirl. Pepin starts panting with his mouth open, so it looks like he's smiling at me.

"Thank you. I think so too."

I kiss him on the forehead and grab my clutch.

———

ON THE DRIVE OVER, I start getting nervous. I'm not sure why it hasn't fully hit me till now. I'm going to be surrounded by hundreds of millionaires, and I'll have to blend in with them. I hope Matt doesn't ever leave me hanging by myself, but I also don't want to seem clingy. I take in a deep breath, trying to calm my nerves. My dress is tight, and it slightly restricts my breathing, so I take another one.

The car pulls up to a large, beautiful building, and the front steps are littered with people. Camera flashes go off, and people greet each other with side hugs in an attempt to avoid wrinkling their outfits. I spot Matt waiting by the curb for me, and I am so grateful that I don't have to go in alone and try to find him.

When I step out of the car, his chest rises with a deep breath, and a grin spreads across his face. I first step out with the leg that has the high slit in the dress, and Matt's face goes from a grin to pure animalistic hunger. I can see it in his eyes, and it gives me a sick satisfaction knowing that I did that to him. He cocks his neck side to side and rolls his shoulders as if trying to get comfortable in his own skin. I have rarely seen him flustered, so this is very amusing for me.

"I was secretly hoping you'd pick that one." I walk up to him, and he grabs my hand, directing me into a full spin to show him all sides of me. "You are stunning. I'm going to have every investor in the palm of my hands tonight, solely because they will be so captivated by you."

"And what will the wives think of that?"

"My guess is they'll be eyeing the sight of you too." He winks at me.

I roll my eyes and link my arm in his as we walk up the stairs to the main entrance. Matt doesn't bother to stop and talk to anyone on the way in. He is a man on a mission right now. I don't know exactly what that mission is, but I guess I'm along for the ride.

We get checked in, and someone escorts us to our table. The table seats 10 people, and I start to wonder who we will be seated with and if I'll know them. We don't sit just yet, though. Matt takes my hand and starts heading for a hallway tucked away on the side of the main event area.

I'm starting to realize what his mission was, and I can't hold back my smile. I look around as we get further down the hall, checking to see if anyone is down there or if anyone might have seen us come over here.

He quickly pulls me to the side, which throws me slightly off balance, and I grab his arm to stabilize myself. He wraps a hand around each of my wrists, lifts them above my head, and pins me to a wall behind a large pillar.

His face is so close to mine that I can feel his breath on my lips. My body is racing with adrenaline for so many reasons; I wasn't expecting this part of the night to happen so soon, so it takes me by surprise, as does the thrill of someone finding us. I've learned that Matt has a thing for doing sexual activities in places where other people might catch us.

He doesn't press his lips to mine yet, and they are aching for the touch of his.

"I don't want to ruin your makeup before the evening even begins."

He moves his head so my lips are right by his ear and his by mine. He switches his grip on my wrists, so now both of them are in only one of his hands. With the other, he feels across my hip until he finds the top of the slit. His hand enters my dress and runs along my inner thigh until he reaches my center. He wastes no time and pulls my panties down with one hand so they are now stretched around my thighs.

He inserts two fingers because he knows well enough now that I can take it. I gasp into his ear and press my face to his cheek. I'm trying not to smudge my makeup, but I need to be pressed against him.

His fingers move in me and find that sweet spot. I moan at the feel of his forceful hand shaking violently, pulling me toward release. I'm so horny at this point that it doesn't take long for me to come all over his hand.

"Good girl," he whispers into my ear, and it makes my body shake in the aftermath of pleasure.

He removes his fingers and releases my wrists from above my head. He pulls out his pocket square and neatly unfolds it to wipe me off of his hand, then folds it back up. I should be grossed out, but I'm not. Part of me likes the idea of him talking to people all night without them knowing that his pocket square, mere feet from their faces, is wet with my cum. And I know that is exactly why he did that.

I reach down to pull my panties up when he stops me with his hand.

"Take those off."

I look into his eyes as I slowly bend over, pull them down my legs, and step out of them. When I'm leaning forward, I quickly glance down the hallway to make sure no one can see me.

"Those are mine."

He reaches out for them, and I hand them over to him. He stuffs it into his inside jacket pocket and then pats it from the outside, giving me a wink.

He takes my hand and walks us to the nearest restroom, where I go in and clean myself up as best as I can. It's a good thing this dress is black, so hopefully, there won't be an obvious wet spot where I came on my dress. After I'm finished in the stall, I wash my hands in the sink. As I'm reaching for the stack of clean hand towels, someone gets my attention.

"I love your shoes."

I look down at my feet as if I'm not aware of what shoes I'm wearing, then back up at her.

"Thank you. They are actually very comfortable as well."

I don't know who this woman is, but she is gorgeous. She's maybe in her mid-50s but has definitely had some work done to make her look like she's in her 30s. No matter how hard people work or how much money they pay, you can usually tell when a woman is desperately trying to hide the fact that she's aging. But this woman has been pretty successful in staying youthful without looking fake.

"Love that even more."

I don't know what else to say, and it seems a bit awkward to do a formal introduction in the bathroom, so I just smile and dry my hands. She is on the same wavelength as me and doesn't say anything else before ducking into a stall.

I exit the bathroom and spot Matt waiting for me on the opposite wall with two drinks in his hand. I grab my drink from him and tuck my clutch under one arm so I can link the other around Matt's. He walks us back to our table, where several other people are now seated.

My stomach flips, and the nerves I forgot about when Matt was finger-banging me in the hallway have suddenly returned. Before we sit down, Matt takes a moment to introduce everyone seated around the table. Most of them are people who work alongside Matt or are friends from some other facet of Matt's life I know nothing about.

Sometimes, I forget that Matt and I know very little about each other. I always tell myself it's better that way, and I stand by that. If I knew more, it might ruin the essence of intrigue and mystery that comes with Matt.

We eat dinner, which is one of the most amazing meals I have ever had in my life. I am shocked when one of the men at the table complains about theirs, saying it's just mediocre and that last year, the Wagyu beef seemed fresher. I pull out my phone and Google what Wagyu means and was shocked by the average prices I see listed.

It makes me wonder how much Matt paid for these tickets. He probably doesn't even know since it was likely an insignificant amount to him. But out of curiosity and knowing Matt won't be offended, I ask, "How much does a ticket to this event cost?" To make it more humorous and emphasize that I'm not trying to be rude, I add, "I may buy a ticket next year just so I can taste beef better than this, according to that guy." I raise my eyebrows and tilt my head toward the man who, earlier, was complaining about his meal.

Matt laughs quietly. "Do you really want to know?"

I nod. I'm pretty sure I want to know.

"I can't exactly remember," I knew it, "but I think it was somewhere around four or five thousand dollars."

I chose the wrong time to take a bite of my cheesecake and nearly choke.

He laughs again, this time at my expense. "Whatever is left over after paying for the event all goes to charity."

That makes me feel a little better, but I can not imagine spending that much money to get all dressed up and eat a meal. There isn't even any entertainment other than a few speeches, mostly thanking people for the donations they made in addition to their tickets.

After dessert, Matt leans over and whispers in my ear, "There's someone I want you to meet."

"Who?"

"Come with me."

I have no idea where this is going, so I'm, yet again, anxious. My nerves are going to be completely shot by the end of the night from all this excitement. I take his hand and follow him to a small group of people standing together just a few tables away.

Matt lets go of my hand and touches the shoulder of a woman whose dress I recognize, even from the back. She turns around and confirms that it's the woman who complimented my shoes in the bathroom. I can't believe this is who he wanted to introduce me to. So ironic. And now I'm really dying to know who she is.

Matt greets her with a hug, and they exchange brief pleasantries. Then she looks over at me. "Matthew, you have a woman here with quite some taste. I complimented her shoes in the bathroom." I didn't notice her accent in the bathroom, but now I can hear that she's English, like Matt.

Matt smiles and looks between us. "I knew you two would hit it off."

We all giggle, and Matt finally introduces us. "Louisa, this is Erin Freid. She—" I cut him off.

"You're the UK's most renowned female architect. You were featured in Architectural Digest last year. I'm so embarrassed I didn't recognize you at first. It's so nice to meet you." I reach out and shake her hand.

"I'm just glad to hear that someone knows of me for my work and not my face. Every now and then, I have a hard time getting people to take me seriously in this business because I'm just a beautiful woman to them." I love her confidence, but I'm sad that she has to deal with that. Such bullshit.

"Erin, this is Louisa Blake. Louisa is working toward getting licensed right now."

I nod, not able to calm the giddy excitement I feel about meeting someone whose work I have admired for years. "I'm about to take my first licensure exam in a week. I'm very nervous."

"That first one is tough when you don't know exactly what to expect, and you still have all the nerves. It's a very important exam to pass. It can set the tone for all the rest of your exams. I know a few colleagues who took over 3 years to complete all their exams because they failed the first one and had so much fear about failing exams two through six that they put it off for so long."

I was already extremely nervous, but now I feel even more pressure, hearing from her just how important this is. I feel my hands go clammy, and I'm glad Matt isn't holding one right now.

"I'm sure you'll be just fine, though." But I'm not sure I will be fine. "If you were smart enough to take advantage of this buffoon, then I have the utmost faith in you." She points her finger at Matt and laughs at her own joke.

I fake a laugh because, in other circumstances, I would find that very funny. Most people would see me as a gold digger if they didn't know the situation. But Erin sees it for exactly what it is: a young girl enjoying the spoils of having an occasional sugar daddy, taking advantage of our youth and beauty. I like her. But I can't get out of my head right now. I don't even realize that she's asked me a question until I notice them both staring at me, waiting for an answer.

"I'm sorry, can you repeat that? My mind was somewhere else for a second."

"I asked what your preferred architectural style is if you had full creative freedom."

Erin and I talk for over an hour, mostly about architecture but occasionally about other things if the conversation flowed there. At first, I was trying to impress her, but eventually, I settled in, and it was like talking to a colleague or a friend who has the same interests as you.

"Well, I should be getting back to my wife. I have no

idea where she ran off to." She goes up on her tiptoes to scan the room. "Ah, she's over by the bar. Perfect, because I need another drink. It was very nice to meet you, Louisa."

I'm bummed that our conversation is ending, but I'm just glad I made it through without saying something stupid.

She reaches into her clutch, pulls out a small rectangular card, and offers it to me. "Here is my business card. You contact me when you're done with your exams, and we can see if there's a position that might suit you."

I clench my teeth together; otherwise, my jaw would likely be on the floor right now. When I pictured how tonight would go, it was not at all like this.

I take the card from her. It's made of very thick paper and is so well designed. For a moment, I imagine having *my* name on a card like this.

"Thank you so much. I will absolutely reach out. It was so great chatting with you."

We both stand to leave, and she surprises me with a quick hug. I was expecting a handshake. "It was great chatting with you as well."

I turn around, looking for Matt, and spot him at a bar different from where Erin's wife is. I walk over there and wait by his side, slightly behind him, until he finishes his conversation. He doesn't notice me, but I don't want to be rude and interrupt. He says his farewells, shakes hands, and turns around. He lightly bumps into me because I am standing so close to him, like a weirdo. Why was I doing that?

"Sorry!"

"Lou, how long have you been standing there?"

"Not long, maybe five minutes."

"You could have gotten my attention." He smiles because what I did was pretty strange, and I realize that.

I shrug my shoulders and give him a lazy smile. "I'm not sure what I was thinking."

He puts a hand on my shoulder and runs it down my arm.

"How was your conversation with Erin? I was hoping she would be here tonight so I could give you an introduction. I didn't want to tell you ahead of time because I didn't want to get your hopes up."

"Thank you so much for that. We had a great chat, and she actually gave me her card and told me to contact her when I get my license."

"That's great, Lou. I'm happy for you."

He touches me again; this time, his hands slide around my waist, and he pulls me in, kissing me gently. I look around, slightly uncomfortable doing this in front of so many people.

"Don't worry about them. I hope they're watching and that now they know you belong to me tonight."

I throw my arms around his neck. "And what exactly do you plan to do with your plaything tonight, Matt?

He gives me a devilish grin, and I feel a tingle between my legs. All of a sudden, I remember that I'm not wearing underwear.

"Want to get out of here and find out?"

I nod. "Thought you'd never ask."

Chapter Twenty

SAM

"Ouch, you got glitter in my eye!" I rub my eye with my fist for one second before Quinn slaps my hand away from my face.

"Don't touch your eyes; you'll smear my masterpiece!"

I look behind him to check myself in the mirror and see that I didn't even touch the rainbow going across my face. "It's fine."

Quinn is painting my face for a day full of Pride festival activities. June is always an exciting month for him, and he's constantly busy with his friends. I've been going to the festival with him ever since he came out to me at age 13.

Every year, I let him paint my face and pick out my outfit. Though I do have ultimate veto power in case he tries to put me in fish nets and booty shorts like he did a couple years ago. I put a hard stop to that.

I'm all about supporting him and going all out, but I do have boundaries. This year, he put me in a crop top that says, 'Ask me about my brother. He's fabulous,' and jorts with little rainbows embroidered on them. Now, he's painting a large rainbow stripe across my face and insists on using glitter. I'm not against wearing glitter; I just hate how messy it is.

"Are you almost done?"

"Yes, you big whiny baby." He finishes it by wiping off the excess glitter.

I look at myself in the mirror and have to admit that it looks pretty cool. He did a good job.

"Who is all meeting us there?"

"Just some friends from the club and a few guys from work."

"You convinced the guys from work to come? I hope for your sake they finished up the Anderson project and didn't just leave it half finished to go to this."

I'm a pretty chill boss, but I hate disappointing clients, so I'm strict with promised deadlines.

"Don't worry, they finished it up yesterday afternoon."

"And you signed off on it?" I recently started letting Quinn do final checks and sign off on projects. It's been a big help, especially during the busy season.

"It looked really good. Now quit fussing; today is about fun!"

———

It's hot as hell out, and I'm regretting the face paint. We spent the last hour mingling in the beer garden area, and now we're just walking around and checking out the different vendor booths. We walk past a drag show and stop to watch the contestants for a bit, getting brief relief in the shade. A drag king takes the stage and dances. At the end of their performance, we cheer, and they run backstage. Up next is a drag queen in a large gown. I have no idea how she isn't passing out from the heat in that outfit. Her performance is very entertaining, and one of Quinn's friends runs up and throws some money on the stage for her.

We keep walking around and stop to buy some pottery from the booth of a local studio. I don't have many mugs at my place, so I buy one that has a curvy female figure etched on it. All of this artist's pieces have nudity on them, and I respect the commitment.

Our group is constantly changing as we lose people and gain new friends, so I can't keep track of who's in our group and who isn't. I know Brian from New Year's Eve, the guys from work, and a few of Quinn's other friends, but Quinn is currently flirting with someone I don't recognize.

He waves me over, and I go to join them.

"Sam, this is Daniel. Daniel, this is my brother Sam." We shake hands, and Quinn points a finger at me while whispering to Daniel. "I know he's adorable, but he's horribly straight, so don't get any ideas."

I never get tired of him introducing me like that at these events, where I am clearly in the minority.

"I've DJ'd a few of Daniel's parties. Tonight, he's throwing a big one, and we're all invited. I turned down his request to work it because I plan on being completely wasted."

I scoff at him. "Shocker. I guess that puts me on babysitting duty then."

"Oh shut up. I want to see you having fun tonight, too. I want you to be so in the moment that you question your sexuality."

I roll my eyes because we've been over this before. Just like he can't picture sleeping with a girl, I can't picture it with a guy. It's that simple; I'm very straight. All I can do now is shake my head at him and laugh along. I love Quinn, and I hope he never changes.

I look to Daniel, who is also rolling his eyes at Quinn. "Thanks for inviting us, sounds like it'll be a fun time."

———

WE JUST ARRIVED at Daniel's party. I wanted to swing by the house to wash my face paint off, but Quinn was in too big of a rush to get here, so it's somehow still on my face. With all the sweating I did today, I'm shocked it's still in as good of shape as it is. Quinn better not have used anything that is permanent or stains skin. I can't imagine showing up to a project on Monday with a slightly faded rainbow across my face. Though I'm sure Quinn would piss himself laughing if that happened.

We mingle for a while near the bar before I wander off and find a quieter spot to sip my drink and chat with Brian. I guess he needed a little social breather as well. We're talking about all sorts of random things, and then the conversation takes a turn to the spicy side.

"Have you ever hooked up in public?"

I choke on my drink, and his eyes get big.

"You have! Tell me!"

"I hooked up with a girl in the private bottle service bathrooms on New Year's Eve."

"What?"

The shock on his face tells me that he probably didn't even notice I left long enough for something like that to happen.

"When I went to say hi to Quinn, a girl spilled her drink on me, and we went to the bathroom to clean it. One thing led to another, I was shirtless. I don't know, it just happened." I shrug and take another sip of my drink.

"Quinn said you were boring, but boy, was he wrong. What else have you done, Mr. Dirty Pants?"

"First off, it was my shirt that got dirty." I wink at him in an attempt to cover up my bad joke. Thankfully, he laughs. "What do you want to know? A few more of these, and I may be spilling all my secrets to you." I lift my drink up. The drinks here are strong, and I am definitely not driving home tonight.

Right as he's about to say something to me, Quinn walks up to us and sits on the arm of Brian's chair. "What are we talking about over here?"

"Your brother was just telling me how he fucked a girl in the bathroom on New Year's Eve."

Quinn's jaw drops, and his eyes get big. "You did *not* tell me that."

"We didn't *fuck*, we just fooled around. And I didn't tell you because it never came up."

Brian leans in like he's going to tell me a secret. "Honey, fooling around, fucking, sex, whatever you want to call it. It's all the same to gay people. That's a very hetero thing to say."

I hadn't really thought about it like that. But I guess what we did would be considered sex if we were both women.

"Then, in that case, yes, I had sex in the bathroom. But not the public one with stalls. It was a private one."

Quinn puts his hand over his mouth to fake a gasp. "You dirty dog. I'm so proud of you. But I'm still mad you didn't tell me."

He crosses his arms over his chest and leans onto Brian's shoulder.

"Was that the first girl after *her*?" He puts emphasis on 'her' as if I'm supposed to know who he's talking about.

But the truth is, I do know. He means Lou.

Brian perks up at the sound of more potential tea about to be spilled.

"Yeah it was." I nod slowly, my face neutral.

"You've gotten some since then, right?" Brian asks it like he's concerned for my well-being.

I run my hand over the back of my neck because I know they're going to freak out at my answer.

"Actually, no. I haven't."

Shock and confusion are written all over both their faces. But it's Quinn who pipes up. "So you're telling me that you just 'fooled around" with that girl in the bathroom, which means you haven't gotten your dick wet in over six months!"

"Seven, actually."

They both obnoxiously gasp as if I just told them I never brush my teeth.

"Seriously, guys. That's not that long." I'm ready to move on from this conversation.

Brian leans over and puts his hand on my knee. "Sam, we need to get you laid."

"No, you don't. But you can get me another drink." I lift my drink up and rattle the ice in my empty glass.

Brian and Quinn look at each other, having a stare-off. Eventually, Brian gets up, grabs all our empty glasses, and heads toward the bar. I didn't actually expect him to get me one, but I appreciate it.

"Thank you, Brian."

Quinn plops down into the chair Brian was previously occupying and looks at me. "Sam, I'm worried about you."

This time, there is a little less joking in his tone and a dash of actual concern.

"Quinn, I promise you I'm fine. With Jacob and everything, I just really haven't been prioritizing that part of my life. Plus, I went a whole year without sex prior to *her*. So it's not anything new. You know I've been busy."

"I know, I know. I just don't want you to blink, and you're a 30-year-old born-again virgin."

I laugh so hard my eyes start to water, and Quinn laughs right along with me.

"I promise I won't let that happen."

"Good."

Brian is back already with our drinks, and I thank him again as I take mine out of his hand.

"What did I miss?"

Quinn takes a sip of his drink and rests an ankle on his knee. "Sam here has promised to get laid tonight."

I glare at him. "I did *not* promise that," I say sternly.

Brian turns to Quinn and says, "And how the hell is he supposed to find a girl at this party who likes straight men?"

We look around, suddenly remembering we're at a Pride party. The odds of that happening are very slim. We all burst out laughing, and again, my eyes are watering.

Not long after, Quinn and Brian hit the dance floor. I chose to hang out here for a while longer. Every now and then, a new person sits down to relax for a second, then leaves to go dance or mingle again.

One person sits down that I recognize as Daniel, the host of the party. I lean closer to him and yell over the music, "Great party. Thanks again for the invite."

He looks over and recognizes me. He stands up and moves over a few seats to sit next to me so we can hear each other better.

"It turned out great, didn't it? Quinn seems to be having a fun time. It's funny to see him on the dance floor instead of behind his table."

I nod. Those are two different versions of Quinn. He takes his DJing very seriously and doesn't drink much when he's working. He gets really zoned in on what he's doing, and it's like the dance floor doesn't even exist. He's not one of those DJs who is constantly talking on the mic and getting people hyped up. His mixes do that for him.

"So what do you do for work, Sam."

We still have to talk loudly to hear each other, but at least we don't have to scream. "I run a small landscaping business. Quinn actually works for me during the busy season, which is most of the warm months."

"I didn't know that." He eyes Quinn, scanning him up and down as he moves around the dance floor. "Say, I need someone to redo the landscaping around one of my vacation homes. Send me your portfolio, and I'll consider you for the job." He reaches into the inside pocket of his neon pink suit jacket and pulls out a business card.

"That would be great. I'll send it over right away. I'd be happy to come out any time and give you a bid for the project." I take it from him, my hand shaking a little with excitement. Getting a client like him is an incredible opportunity; it would open so many doors for me.

He smiles, and as he's about to say something, we're interrupted by a girl. She runs up to Daniel and puts her hand on his shoulder. He looks back and says, "Hello, darling."

She leans down and says something in his ear. I don't think she's trying to be secretive; it's just really loud in here. When she pulls her face away, I hear him say, "Yeah, that's fine, just lock it up when you're done."

I immediately recognized her purple hair. It's B, Lou's little sister.

She runs off without acknowledging me. I don't think she knows who I am then I remember I have a giant rainbow painted on my face, making my features a little harder to see.

My heart races, and I glance around, looking for Lou. She has to be here, right? They do everything together. I want to throw up from feeling so many emotions right now. Do I go look for her? Should I just sit here and hope she comes over?

Then, the most obvious choice dawns on me. I lean over and ask Daniel, "That girl, was that Briella Blake?"

"Sure was. She's my assistant and a damn good one. Do you know her? That was rude of her not to say hello if you do." He turns, looking to where B just ran off to, but she's long gone.

"No, I've never met her, but I know her sister, Lou. Do you know if she's here tonight?"

"I don't think so. B didn't have me put her on the list. I think she's studying or something responsible like that."

My heart sinks, and I sag back into my chair.

"Gotcha. Just curious." I smile at him to hide the fact that I'm dying on the inside.

I go round and round with myself, debating if I should find B and ask how Lou's doing. I also debate just texting Lou and asking myself. I can use seeing B at this party as my excuse to check in.

No, Sam, stop that. That's not fair to her.

I ended things pretty abruptly, and the more I think about it, the more I realize she may have been hurt by it. Because I know I am.

I'm sure she's moved on by now, and hearing from me would likely just annoy her. Plus, if I talked to her again, I'd feel like I owe her more of an explanation, and I don't want to tell her about Jacob.

People get really weird when you tell them your sibling died, and even more so when you tell them he did it to himself.

I try to wipe away the thoughts of Lou because there's no use dwelling on it. What's done is done. I screwed up my chances and have no one else to blame but myself.

———

LOUISA

I open up a snap from B, and it's of her dancing with Daniel at his Pride party. B begged me to go, but I honestly wasn't feeling up to it. I used studying for my licensure exam as an excuse since that should be what I'm doing. The date of the exam is quickly approaching, and I have really been slacking on studying.

I thought this year was supposed to be a fresh start for me and that things would start looking up again. Unfortunately, over the past several months, I've done quite the opposite. B's been gone for work a lot, and I've been extremely lonely. It's made studying, or any task for that matter very difficult.

I forced myself to stay home tonight in hopes that I would get through the study material. I'm only about a quarter of the way through and have a long way to go, so I pour myself another cup of coffee in hopes that it'll help.

Once my exam is over, I can relax. That is until I start studying for the next one. At this point, it seems like I'm never going to get to the finish line, and I'm already so exhausted. I already feel like a failure.

I send back a picture of me studying. I lock my phone again and shove it to the other side of my desk so I'm not tempted to check it.

Chapter Twenty-One

LOUISA

I walk out of the exam room, and everything is a blur.

What just happened?

The lady at the desk asks for my name and logs it into her computer that I am checking out. I grab my phone out of my designated locker and call B.

She answers after the first ring. "How did it go?"

My eyes start to fill with tears as I walk out to the parking lot. "Not good, B. That was awful."

"Lou, you always feel that way when you take exams. If I had a dollar for every time you thought you failed an exam and you actually didn't, I'd be able to pay off my student loans."

I let out a tiny laugh that sounds more like a whimper. "I know, but this one felt particularly bad."

"Come home, and I'll have a drink ready for you."

"Okay." I hang up and get in my car.

The whole drive home, I'm in my head, thinking about all the things that'll go wrong if I fail that exam. By the time

I walk through the apartment door, I've gone completely mad.

"There she is! How's my smart, amazing—" She stops in her tracks when she sees my face. "No, no, no, no. No crying in this apartment." She shakes her finger at me and walks the rest of the way over to me. She puts her hands on my cheeks, squishing my face. "Stop it. I will not allow you to stew about this until you get your results." She squishes my cheeks harder, giving me fish lips. I know I look ridiculous right now, and I think that's her intention. "You will have fun tonight. And you will have fun at Evie's cabin this weekend. You hear me? I will not take no for an answer."

Her voice is so theatrical, pretending to be serious and grumpy. I can't take it any longer, and I crack, my chest shaking with laughter. She cracks a smile too, giving up her ruse, and wraps me in a hug.

"Alright. Now it's time for drinks!"

Chapter Twenty-Two

LOUISA

It's the 4th of July weekend. B and I were invited up to Evie's parents' cabin. Evie, Liam, and Iris arrived yesterday, but B and I are just getting here. Iris's boyfriend was supposed to be joining us, but he ended up taking a job as a camp counselor, so now they are doing long-distance for the summer. From what B tells me, it's not going very well. I've been warned not to bring it up.

Liam runs out to help us carry our bags and shows us our rooms. B and Iris are sharing one of the guest rooms, so I get a room all to myself. There's another room full of bunk beds that I'm told will be filled throughout the weekend as different people come and go.

After I unpack and change into my swimsuit, I make my way down the stairs and follow the sound of laughter. I've been here a few times before, so I know my way around, and I know that Evie's parents want everyone to make themselves at home. So before heading out to the yard, where everyone is hanging out, I grab a seltzer out of the fridge and crack it open.

I promised B I wouldn't talk or think about my exam until I got my results back. This weekend is a great way to get my mind off of it.

Outside, everyone is playing yard games, so I join the girls in a game of cornhole. I'm partners with Evie, and we are absolutely destroying B and Iris. By the time we're finished, a few more guys have arrived. All four of them are Liam and Evie's friends from college. I've never met any of them, but from what I've gathered, two are dating each other, and the other two are single. This should make for an interesting weekend.

Evie's dad and Liam are grilling dinner, and the rest of us are playing flip cup around a table in the yard. B is giving a demonstration and making sure everyone is familiar with the rules. I've played this several times, so I tune her out. Iris is on my right, and one of Liam's single friends is on my left. I still haven't gotten everyone's name down, and I can't remember which one he is.

The game starts, and B is first for our team, followed by Iris. It takes Iris several attempts to get her cup flipped. She's starting to sway, so I steady her with my hand on her back. Most of us have been drinking all day, so we're already pretty tipsy. Iris finally makes it, but the other team is already on their fourth and final person; it's one of the college friends. He is struggling just as much as Iris.

Once Iris successfully flips her cup, it's my turn. I chug my drink and successfully flip my cup in one try.

The guy to my left starts chugging his drink. Everyone is screaming as it's down to the last person on each team. Whoever flips their cup over first wins. I watch as our guy's Adam's apple bobs up and down with each gulp. Beer is pouring out the sides of his mouth and running down his shirtless chest. I know I'm staring, but he looks so hot right now. He slams his cup down and lines up, taking his time.

"Hurry!" B yells from the other end of the table.

He flicks his finger, and with one 180-degree rotation, the cup lands upside down, and everyone on our side of the table jumps up and screams. The guy to my left turns to me in celebration and gives me a high five that I'm pretty sure is going to bruise, then wraps me in a quick hug. I don't even mind that his chest is sticky from sweat and beer.

Through the celebration, I can hear Liam call for us. "Dinner's ready!"

Everyone calms down and quickly picks up the game so the cups don't go flying across the yard in the wind.

"That was very impressive."

I look over at the guy and smile. "Thanks. You as well. That was super clutch at the end. Once Iris got stuck, I totally thought we were going to lose."

One of the other guys yells from the house, "Hey Tony, can you grab me another beer on your way in?"

Tony, that's his name! Okay, I am now committing that to memory. Tony. Tony. Tony.

We all go into the house and scarf down food like we've been starving for days. Drinking all day will do that to you. I took down two brats and a burger myself.

After dinner, most of us go out on the pontoon for a midnight stroll. Out of the four guys who arrived later today, only Tony comes out with us. The other three were sicker than dogs and went to bed early.

Liam drives the boat to the sandbar and throws the anchor in. There are no cabins on the water over here, creating a private pocket of the lake. We brought a cooler of drinks along and plan to hang out here for a while. We all crack open a new drink and find seats in a circle.

"Alright, what are we playing first?" Evie looks around at us with a mischievous look on her face and sips her drink.

"My vote is for Truth or Dare," B pipes up before anyone else.

I roll my eyes; B would suggest that. She has loved that game ever since she realized the kind of power you can wield as the person giving out a dare.

Iris gives her opinion, "I want to play Never Have I Ever."

"Oh, I like that one." Tony smiles and takes a sip of his drink.

"Let's warm up with Never Have I Ever, then switch to Truth or Dare once our drinks have kicked in a little more."

Everyone agrees with Liam, and Iris starts since she is the one who made the suggestion. The agreed-upon number of fingers was five so we can at least all have one turn.

We all put up five fingers, and the game begins.

"Never have I ever...done cocaine." Iris looks around at us all.

Tony puts a finger down and drinks.

Liam immediately calls him out for the rule break. "Take another drink! Tony, you know you have to clap any time you put a finger down. No cowards on my boat."

Evie looks at Liam, annoyed. "This is not your boat."

Everyone laughs, and Liam whispers to Evie, "You know what I meant."

Tony claps once, then drinks again. "My bad, I forgot about that stupid rule you guys added."

Evie and Liam have a house rule that whenever you *have* done the thing, not only do you need to drink and put a finger down, but you also have to clap to own up to the thing you've done. Otherwise, people will sneakily put down a finger when no one is watching. Iris, B, and I have also adopted this rule and taught it to several other people. It's a crowd favorite.

B chimes in through the laughter, "Alright, it's my turn. Never have I ever...dated someone I wanted to marry. Like it never crossed my mind once during the relationship."

Evie and Liam obviously put a finger down since they *are* married. Iris and I put a finger down as well. Tony does not. That's a bit of a red flag if you ask me, and yes, that includes B.

Liam's turn. "Never have I ever...totaled a car."

Iris glares at him as she claps and puts a finger down. "You can't target people."

"It's not targeting when anyone else could have also done that."

Iris sticks her tongue out at Liam. And now, it's Evie's turn.

"Never have I ever...had to go to detox."

Iris, B, and Liam all clap and put a finger down.

Tony is up next; he doesn't even hesitate. "Never have I ever...spent the night with a one-night stand."

This one is hard for me to answer because I spent the night with Sam, but I'm not sure that counts as a one-night stand. Sure, we only had sex once, but we were talking for a long time. Since it's borderline and I'm a rule follower, I clap and put down a finger, as does B.

It's my turn, and I start with one of my go-to answers. "Never have I ever...fucked a teacher/professor."

Tony claps and puts a finger down.

We're now back to Iris. "Never have I ever...had sex on the water." Everyone looks at her, waiting for clarification. "I mean, like on a boat, jet ski, I guess that could mean *in* the water too."

Evie and Liam clap—no surprises there since she has a

lake cabin. I'm sure they've had sex on this boat in this exact spot several times. I know I would have.

B must have had the same idea because she looks at the seat she's sitting on with disgust and pretends she's catching cooties. Once she gets everyone laughing, she sits back down. "Okay, okay. Settle down. Never have I ever...been in a long-term relationship. Let's say more than a year."

Iris, Liam, Evie, and I all clap.

Liam looks around the circle, contemplating what he should say next. "Never have I ever...injured myself during sex."

B and Evie both clap. Now, *that* is a funny story. One time, when hooking up with a guy, B got a concussion. He was on top of her on the bed, and with every thrust, he scooted her a little further off the bed until, eventually, she fell off and smacked her head on the floor. She even claims to have blacked out temporarily.

Evie follows up her lost finger with, "Despite all my efforts, never have I ever...had sex on a plane."

She looks over at Liam like he should feel guilty. And he does. Everyone laughs because this is pretty typical. Evie is definitely the more adventurous one who pushes Liam out of his comfort zone. "Tried to, but my husband here left me to wait in the bathroom for 20 minutes.

"I got nervous, okay." He throws up his hands in defense.

I laugh super hard because I can imagine the earful Liam got when Evie returned to her seat after waiting.

Everyone agrees that joining the Mile High Club would be super cool, but no one claps, and we move on to Tony.

"Never have I ever...had a dad."

Umm, that was dark. But everyone still laughs to mask the awkwardness in the boat.

The rest of us clap.

That leaves Iris, Liam, Evie, and I all with one finger left. Tony and B both have two. I'm shocked B is doing so well. Usually, she's the first one out by a long shot.

It's my turn, so I say another one I always use. "Never have I ever...had a threesome."

B claps, which is only a little shocking to me since she hasn't mentioned it. The bigger shock is both Liam and Evie clapping and losing the game.

Iris looks over at her brother and sister-in-law, shocked by this revelation. "Excuse me? Tell!"

Evie and Liam look at each other, trying to hold back their grins and laughter, failing miserably.

"We'll let you use your imagination."

All of us stare at them with wide eyes and our mouths open. They smile and shrug.

Breaking the silence, Iris chimes in. "B, tell us your story! I know you're dying to share the details. Was it recent?"

"It was on New Year's Eve with this gorgeous man and another bi girl. It was very steamy."

Iris leans in. "More details, please. Do I know either of them?"

"I don't think you do. The guy was named Cam, and I honestly don't remember the girl's name. I only remember his because she kept moaning it over and over. But god, I don't blame her; he was so hot."

B goes on to describe the guy in detail. Realization slowly creeps in, and I burst out laughing. All eyes are on me, questioning.

I finally get enough air in my lungs to speak. "B, I'm pretty sure we hooked up with the same guy."

"No fucking way. Are you serious?"

"Yeah, I met a guy named Cam on a dating app a few months after New Year's. Oh my god, this is hilarious."

Luckily, everyone else on the boat also finds it very funny. Some sisters might be grossed out by that, but I'm honestly not. We have very different tastes in men, so I never thought this would happen. But Cam is one of those people with a universally attractive face and a hot body, so it makes sense.

After we all calm down over the threesome, we remember that Liam and Evie both lost the game. They finish their drinks as punishment and crack another one for the next game.

Next, we move on to Truth or Dare. This game makes me nervous, but I'm tipsy, which helps.

B starts off by asking Liam, and he picks truth. Safe way to start.

"What is the kinkiest thing you and Evie have ever done?"

He thinks about it for a moment. "I guess maybe that ropes course we took last year." He's looking at Evie, waiting for her to correct him if there's something else he's missed. She doesn't correct him. "Yeah, probably that. We went to a local adult store and took a little course on how to tie people up. It was actually really fun." Evie nods in agreement.

Liam turns to me and asks, and I pick dare. Why not spice things up a bit?

"I dare you to kiss Tony."

I look over at Tony, and he nods, indicating that he's fine with it if I am. I crawl across the cushioned seat and grab the side of his face, angling it toward me. I brush my lips on his, and he kisses me back. It's brief but long enough for me to realize that I didn't feel a spark at all. You know when you kiss someone, and it just feels wrong? Or when they touch you, and it almost annoys you instead of making your skin feel like it's on fire?

I'm not sure if some of the things I've learned about him tonight are causing it, but I have officially decided that I'm not going to pursue him in any way. I can't tell how he feels about it.

I ask Iris, and she chooses dare.

"I dare you to shotgun a beer."

She obliges and downs it faster than I was expecting her to, and everyone is impressed. Especially Liam. "Where the hell did you learn to do it like that?"

"I learned from the best."

At first, Liam thinks she's talking about him since she's looking his way. "Awww, thanks, sis; I'm glad I could be such a great role model for you."

"Not you." She smirks and turns her head to her left. "I was talking about B."

Liam puts his hand on his chest, acting as if the insult were a dagger to his heart.

Iris asks Tony, and he picks dare.

"I dare you to take a body shot off of B."

After B agrees to let him do it, she lays on her back and lifts up her shirt to expose her navel. Iris fills her belly button with cinnamon whiskey since it's the only hard liquor we brought on the boat. Tony bends over her and sucks it up, then licks her a little more than what I would deem necessary.

Next, Tony asks Evie, and she chooses dare.

"I dare you to show us with your hands how big the biggest dick you've sucked was."

"First off, I'm not telling you who it is. For all you guys

know, it could be Liam." He gives her a side eye and holds back a smile.

Evie adjusts her hands until she's satisfied with the eyeballed measurement. "He's about this long." She leaves both hands up and makes a circle with her fingers overlapping. "And about this thick."

B starts clapping. "Bravo, Evie. Good for you."

Evie asks B, and she chooses dare.

"I dare all the girls to go skinny dipping; no boys allowed!"

Tony raises his hands in the air to question her. "Hey, that's not fair; you can't dare the entire group and then exclude people. I want to come."

"My boat, my rules. If you don't like that, then you can swim back to the dock."

The dock is a long way away, so Tony keeps his mouth shut.

As we girls run around the boat all giddy, taking off our outer layers, Liam gets up and joins Tony on the back of the boat.

Once we're stripped down to our swimsuits, we all jump off the front of the boat together. We opted to wait and take our swimsuits off once we got in the water. So now I'm treading water while undoing the back of my swimsuit top and sliding off my bottoms.

There's something so freeing about being naked in the water when no one can see you, the cool water running over your skin, uninterrupted. I can only see vague outlines of the other girls, but I can hear them. It sounds like B is trying to drown Iris, but Iris is putting up a good fight.

We all laugh and float for a while until I hear Liam. "Hey Tony, don't do that."

Before Liam can stop him, Tony pops his head over the edge of the boat and shines his phone flashlight at us.

"Hey!" we all scream.

Liam grabs Tony's phone, and the light goes away. "What the fuck, Tony?"

"I just wanted to see some hot naked chicks."

"One of those hot naked chicks is my *sister,* and another is my *wife,* you pig. They clearly don't want to be seen, or they would have invited you."

Tony tries to save himself from Liam's wrath with a fruitless excuse. "Sorry, man, beers went to my head."

"Uh-huh." Liam doesn't change his stance.

I can't see Evie, but I hear her. "Liam, can you put some towels on the edge for us so we can get out."

I hear towels slap the floor of the pontoon, and we start making our way to the edge. The boat is visible only from the moonlight reflecting off the metal, but I make it there with no problem. The other girls beat me there, so I'm the last one out. I grab a towel when I'm halfway up the ladder and wrap it around my chest, letting it slide over my butt, and I climb up the rest of the way.

We locate our wet swimsuits and put them on. The mood has definitely shifted, and we use the excuse of being wet and cold to go back to the cabin.

Liam turns the boat lights on, pulls up the anchor, and makes his way back to the dock.

Since I was the last one up, I sit in the only remaining seat, which is next to Tony. It's not where I would have chosen to sit, but the dock is only a few minutes away. I don't want to make a scene, and I'm too drunk to try and stand while we're moving. So next to Tony it is.

Chapter Twenty-Three

LOUISA

We get to the dock, and I'm standing up to get out when I feel a hand on my ass. My towel is still wrapped around me, but I can feel it. I choose not to say anything because I'm exhausted, and I just want to shower and go to bed.

Liam stays to secure the boat and ensure everything is put away before he comes up to the cabin. The rest of us walk through the grass and enter through the sliding glass door.

B and Iris go to their bedroom on the right. Evie goes down the hall to where her and Liam's room is. Tony and I trail behind, and we both start to go upstairs to where the extra guest rooms are.

I'm about halfway up the stairs when I feel hands grab my waist and pull me down a step. I slip on the step and fall backwards into Tony, dropping my towel. He wraps his arms around me from behind and nuzzles his face into my neck.

I try to pull away from him, but he has me in a tight grip.

"Tony, get off me," I whisper because I don't want to wake up Evie's parents or the other guys.

"What, you change your mind now?" He starts kissing across my shoulder and up my neck.

I try to pry his arms apart, but he's too strong.

"What are you talking about?"

"Don't act like you haven't been after me all day," he says between kisses.

He reaches one arm up while still maintaining a tight grip around my waist and grabs my jaw, turning my face around toward him. He starts kissing my cheek, past my ear, and down my neck. I try to turn my head away, but his grip holds me where he wants me. When he gets to the base of my neck, I feel my skin get hot and feel a tight pressure where his mouth is.

"Ow!" I think he's biting me. "Tony, stop." It comes out a little louder this time, but still not loud enough for anyone else to hear.

"You kissed me on the boat."

"That was a dare."

"And then you sat next to me on the ride home." I can tell he's starting to get angry at my resistance. He takes his hand off my jaw and moves it down to my chest, cupping my breast and squeezing it too hard.

"Tony, I don't know what you're talking about. Please let me go."

"You can't let a guy grab your ass and talk about all the dirty things you've done in front of him, then expect him to not get his hopes up."

I try to pry off his arm around my waist, but again, it doesn't budge. So this time, I dig my fingernails into his arm as deep and hard as I can.

"Oh, you like it rough, do you? I'd prefer those claw marks on my back."

His hand that's cupping my breast trails down my stomach. He puts his palm over my bikini bottoms and curls his fingers under me, between my legs.

My mind is racing, and I can't think straight long enough to come up with a way to get out of this. Tears are running down my face, and my body is shaking.

"Please, Tony, let me go." I'm gasping for breath as his grip tightens on my waist, cutting off my air.

"No, I think I'll—"

He's cut off by a man's voice that I barely hear over the ringing in my ears. I didn't comprehend what they said or who it even was. I vaguely hear the sliding door slam shut and footsteps rushing across the kitchen toward the stairs.

The next thing I know, Tony lets me go, and I fall down onto the stairs, gulping down air. My knees sting when they hit the carpet.

I hear commotion on the stairs behind me. I whip around to see what's happening, but my eyes are full of tears, so it's all a blur.

"What the hell is going on in here?" Evie. That's Evie's voice. "Liam!"

I blink away the tears, and before new ones can replace them, I see what's going on. Liam has Tony pinned to the ground at the bottom of the stairs, hand around his throat.

Evie rushes over to them and pries Liam off of Tony. "Liam, I said what the fuck is going on!"

Liam turns around to look up at me. His face is filled with rage, and at first, I'm nervous he's mad at me. Then his face softens. "Are you okay, Lou?"

I nod because I just want this to be over. I can't believe this is all happening because of me. And it only gets worse when B and Iris come running out, B with shampoo in her hair and a towel wrapped around her chest. Then, as if this couldn't get more devastating, Evie's parents run out of their bedroom to find this shitshow.

Everyone is stunned in silence until Evie's mother speaks. "Can someone please explain to me what's going on?"

Liam looks around. "Everyone go back to bed. I've got this handled."

I look around to find that a large vase that was once next to the stairs has fallen over and shattered.

Evie gently slaps Liam's shoulder. "Clearly you don't if you're beating up your friends."

My stomach is twisting in knots. I don't want him to tell everyone what he more than likely saw through the windows. Liam looks back at me again, and I subtly shake my head.

No, please, no.

Before he can speak, I run up the stairs to my room. I can't sit there any longer. I can't have any of them looking at me with confusion and pity in their eyes.

I can hear footsteps following me up the stairs, and it only spikes my panic.

When I get to my door, I shut it behind me. Shortly after, I hear the locked doorknob rattle, and then I hear B on the other side. "Lou, open up. What happened?"

"Go away."

"Lou, come on, talk to me."

"B, please. I'm begging you, leave me alone. I promise I'll talk to you tomorrow."

There's a long stretch of silence, and I hope that she's left.

"Okay, I love you, and I'm just downstairs or a text away if you need me."

I know I'm going to have to do some explaining tomorrow, and the thought of that makes me want to throw up. But for now, I'm grateful to B for giving me space when I asked for it.

With my back still up against the door, I can hear voices coming up the stairs. Male voices.

"Get the fuck out of this cabin. Right now. You can grab your things, but then you're out."

"Liam, come on. You don't even know what was going on."

"All I know is that she clearly didn't want you touching her, and you were. That's all the information I need to stand here and tell you to get the fuck out."

"I didn't drive here."

"Then wake up the other guys, and whoever drove can give you a ride home. They'll be sober by now."

"Come on, Liam. You're just drunk and overreacting."

"Being drunk is *not* an excuse for anything. Now go before I drag you out."

I can't listen to this any longer, so I walk over to the attached bathroom. I take a long hot shower and use that as an opportunity to cry without anyone being able to hear me.

When I'm finished, I dry off and get dressed in my sweats and baggy T-shirt. I'm not sure I'll even be able to sleep after that, but I have to go through the motions.

Shortly after I crawl into bed, I hear a soft knock on the door. Although it was barely loud enough for me to hear, I startle. I don't want to talk to anyone right now, but I also don't want anyone to worry. It's probably B coming to check on me, and if I don't answer, she'll just come in anyway.

I crawl out of bed and walk over to the door, opening it

slowly. I see Liam standing in the hallway. He's wearing a different shirt and sweats than he was before, and his hair looks wet from showering.

I don't say anything because there's nothing to say. I ruined his 4th of July weekend, along with everyone else's.

"I'm sorry to bother you. I'm sure you want to be alone right now."

I just stare at him through the cracked door.

With my silence, he continues. "I'm so sorry that happened to you, Lou. I just want you to know that I didn't tell anyone what I saw. If you want to tell them, that's your call. I just needed to tell you that so you wouldn't worry about it all night. And I wanted to tell you that Tony and the rest of the guys are gone."

I still don't know what to say. Tony is probably feeding them all lies on the ride home. Telling them I asked for it or that I came onto him first.

Liam bends down to catch my eyes, which I didn't even realize had been staring at the floor.

"I feel responsible for what happened to you."

I cut him off. "Liam, no. You had nothing to do with what happened."

"He was my friend that I invited here. I was never close with Tony because I don't like the way he treats women, and Evie has never liked him. But I still invited him here with that group. I brought him into a house with my wife, sister, and two other women I care for very much."

His eyes are full of tears, one escaping down his cheek, and he quickly wipes it away.

"That was irresponsible of me, and I won't forgive myself for what he did to you."

"Nothing happened, Liam. I'm fine."

"I'm okay with everyone else believing that if you'd like,

but I don't ever want you to think that what happened was nothing. I sure as hell don't."

His words hit me in a way I wasn't expecting, and my eyes are wet again. I want him to leave. I don't want to talk about this anymore. I want him and everyone else to forget what happened and move on.

"Goodnight, Lou. Please let Evie or me know if you need anything."

He turns and walks away. I lock the door and lay back down in bed, thinking about what Liam said.

———

THE NEXT MORNING, I wake up, unsure of when I fell asleep. The last time I remember checking my phone was around four in the morning.

I walk to the bathroom and look at myself in the mirror. My eyes are bloodshot from crying, and I spot a hickey on my neck from where Tony was biting me. I shiver and push that memory away, deep down.

I splash my face with water and throw on a sweatshirt to go downstairs. I can hear everyone eating breakfast in the kitchen. The last thing I want to do is go down there and face everyone and answer their questions. But I know that the longer I stay up here, the bigger a deal it becomes, which is exactly what I don't need.

I get down to the kitchen, and everyone watches me as I descend the stairs. I'm grateful when no one asks any questions, but I can still feel the tension thick in the air. I sit down at the table and pour myself a bowl of cereal. I keep telling myself nothing happened, everything is going to be fine, and that I just made a big deal about it in my head.

Chapter Twenty-Four

LOUISA

The rest of the cabin weekend should have been fun. We lit fireworks, played more yard games, and went out on the water, but I couldn't shake the ghost of what happened that night with Tony and Liam. No one has brought up the incident except B. She came up to my room the following night while I was getting ready for bed. She curled up on top of my sheets, and we talked.

I told her what happened in as little detail as possible. She could tell I was uncomfortable, and she repeatedly told me that I had nothing to be ashamed of and that Tony was the only one to blame. But I can't help but be embarrassed and hold back, which is something I've never done with B before. It makes me feel a little guilty, but what she doesn't know won't hurt her.

B and I picked up Pepin from our parents' house and are now on our way home. I'm driving faster than usual because B has a quick turnaround today. She's heading to Paris with Daniel for a week, and she'll be back the day before my birthday. She made Daniel reschedule the trip so that she could be on time for it. I told her that was overkill, but she insisted.

Once we get home, she unpacks her lake clothes and repacks with her Paris clothes. I'm driving her to the airport in an hour, and I'm starting to think we might not make it.

"B, hurry up. You know we have to be there earlier for international flights. Do you want my help with anything?"

"No, I'm fine. I'll be ready to go on time."

I sit down on the couch and turn on a show. I mindlessly check my email like I have been for the past two weeks since taking my exam. I scroll through and delete all the junk mail and open a few bills to make sure the payments look correct.

Then I see it—the email with my test results.

"Hey, B, get in here."

"What?" She walks into the living room and leans over the arm of the couch to look at my phone screen. "Holy shit! Did you open it yet?"

"No. I'm too scared." My heart is racing, and my palms are clammy.

"Well open it. We can celebrate while I finish packing."

I look up at her and hand her my phone. "You do it."

She snatches the phone out of my hand with no hesitation. I see her click the link, and I hold my breath. Her face is blank, so I can't read her.

"It says you need a password."

"Right, I forgot about that. Here, let me put it in." I grab the phone back from her briefly to type in my password, then hand it back before pressing submit.

She clicks it, and I think she's waiting for it to load until I see her face turn white.

"B, quit playing games with me. What does it say?"

She looks up, expression blank but slightly grave.

"I knew it. I didn't pass, did I?"

Her head shakes so slightly that you can barely detect it. But I know. I knew deep down that it didn't go well. She doesn't need to say it.

My mind starts racing with a million thoughts, wondering which questions I got wrong. My stomach turns, and I'm about to throw up. My lower jaw quivers, and I can feel my throat closing.

B climbs over the armrest and onto the couch. She throws the phone on the floor, wraps her arms around me, and whispers into my shoulder, "I'm so sorry, Lou."

The confirmation is all the permission I needed to let go. The sobs roll out of me, and I can't believe this is happening. Pepin comes over and nudges my arm with his nose. When I don't respond to it, he simply lays his head on my lap.

B gently rubs my back and tries to soothe me. "Shhhhh, breathe. Breathe. It'll be okay. You can always take it over again; remember, there are no penalties for trying again." The sobs continue, and I'm not sure how much time passes before she lets me go.

"Do you want me to cancel my trip? Daniel can take one of the other assistants; it's really no problem."

"No, please go. I think I just want to be alone for a few days, anyway."

"You sure?"

I sniffle and wipe my nose. "Positive."

"Okay, well then, I'm going to continue packing so we're not late."

I nod and give her a soft smile to try and convince her I'm going to be fine. That look on her face tells me she doesn't buy it for one second.

The next 30 minutes are a mad dash to finish getting her packed and all her bags in the car. For how often she travels, you'd think she would be better at packing light, but she's not. During the drive to the airport, she runs through her mental checklist to make sure she didn't forget anything, even though the odds of us turning back now are very slim. As long as she has her passport, the rest she can buy in Paris.

Once we get to the airport, I help B get her bags out of the trunk and give her one last hug. "Be safe. And remember not to go in the catacomb." She giggles and rolls her eyes. "I'm very serious, B. You saw those videos I sent you; people die down there."

"I promise I won't go down there, or get kidnapped, or get hit by a train, or..."

I wrap her in one more hug. "I love you."

She pulls back and looks at me. "Are you *sure* you don't want me to stay?"

"I'm sure."

"I'll see you in a week, and then we're celebrating the shit out of your birthday." She starts wheeling her bag away, and I get back in my car. She turns around and yells so I can hear her through my closed car window, "I love you!"

I blow her a kiss, and then she disappears through the doors.

———

B HAS BEEN GONE for two days now, and I have never been so low. I've barely been getting through work.

A few people have asked if I got my results back over the long weekend, and I have to fight back the tears and lie. I regret telling anyone I took it. If I hadn't, then I would have been able to retake it, and no one would have known I failed it the first time.

I can't decide what's worse, the thought of telling people I failed or the fact that I have to study and take that exam all over again. And then I have to do that all over again, at least five more times, assuming I don't fail any more.

The odds of me failing more along the way seem so much higher now. Any time I get caught up thinking about it, I have to shake myself out of a funk. I try to avoid the topic if I can. I'll tell them eventually; I have to. I'm just not ready to tell them now. It's too fresh.

I'm off work now, and I'm just lying on the couch, snuggling Pepin, and watching a movie. It's one of my favorites, but as I sit here, I feel nothing. Not sadness, not joy, not confusion. I feel numb. Not in the way where my limbs are tingly, but inside.

An ad for food delivery pops up on the screen, and it reminds me that I haven't eaten yet today. In fact, I think the last time I ate was yesterday morning.

I pull out my phone to order some food for delivery. As I scroll through my options, nothing sounds good, and I don't even think I'm that hungry. I lock my phone and throw it back on the coffee table. I lean my head back on the couch and slump down into an uncomfortable position. I stay there for a while before my back muscles spasm, and I have to readjust myself.

I'm so exhausted. It's only six in the evening, but I already want to go to bed. I barely managed to take Pepin on his daily walk yesterday. I convinced myself the fresh air would do me some good, but I still felt the same.

I haven't taken him on a walk today, and I'm surprised he hasn't reminded me. Usually, when it's getting late and he hasn't been on a walk, he reminds me with one precious bark. Pepin *never* barks, only when he wants to go on his walk. And even then, it's one soft, deep bark, and he's done.

I look at him and debate on getting up and taking him; I just can't.

I pick up my phone again and start scrolling through social media. Almost right away, I notice a notification. I haven't posted anything recently, so I'm confused as to what it could be. Maybe one of the girls posted about the weekend and tagged me. I click on the notification and see that someone liked a photo of mine. I don't recognize the username, so I click on them. My profile is public, so anyone can view my feed. But it's not often that strangers like my posts.

When the profile loads, I freeze. It's Tony. I quickly click to see if he's following me; he's not. So he had to go out of his way to go to my profile and like a photo of mine. Maybe he was just creeping and accidentally liked one.

That still doesn't sit well with me.

I go back to notifications to see which photo he liked. I click to make the image pop up and see that it's an old picture of me in a bikini with friends.

The thought of him in his home looking at my page makes me sick. I always knew that people would do that if I had my profile public, but it has never felt this gross. I quickly go into settings and change my profile to private.

I'm breathing heavily, and my heart races, but at least now he can't see them anymore.

I get another notification. Tony has requested to follow me. I shake because that means he has been looking at my profile a lot to notice that I just went private. He liked the picture sometime yesterday. How many times has he looked at my pictures?

I take deep breaths to calm myself. Why am I reacting

like this? If it were a boy I liked, I'd be thrilled if I knew he looked at my page a lot. But all of a sudden, I can feel his breath on my neck. I can feel the crushing weight on his arm around my waist. I can feel his skin under my fingernails and his hushed voice in my ear.

I jump up from the couch and run to the bathroom. I can feel tears streaming down my face, but I can't feel the emotion of it. I just feel physically ill, like my brain can't process everything that's happened in the last few days, so my body is trying to do it. I get to the bathroom and have no clue why I came in here.

My body is on autopilot.

I rip the shower curtain open. I grab the handle and flip the shower on, getting into the tub fully clothed. I let the water hit my face, and I can't tell if it stings because it's too cold or too hot. Either way, I don't care.

I reach out my foot and step on the drain to plug it, allowing the water to start pooling up in the bottom of the tub. I sit down under the stream and let the water crash over me.

As an unknown amount of time passes, the water gets higher and higher. I stare at the wall the whole time, stuck in my head with all my thoughts.

You failed.

You're not smart enough.

So much wasted time.

You're in too deep.

Only one way out.

You're almost 25.

What have you accomplished?

Nothing.

You're in too deep.

Only one way out.

You're a tease.
A slut.
You'll always be alone.
You're in too deep.
Only one way out.
Only one way to make it all stop.

I slowly sink down into the water, the same way I sunk into the couch, moments, minutes, hours ago.

Before my lips reach the surface of the water, I take one deep breath.

Fully submerged, I feel the weight of the water around me.

If I quit now before anyone finds out I've truly failed at everything, then those who are left behind can make up a happy ending for me. They can dream up a fantasy of what could have been.

And that is much better than what they will witness if I don't.

I slowly let out my breath, hearing the air bubbles break as they reach the surface. After the last of my breath has escaped me, I pause. But pausing only leads to doubts, and I don't have time to wrestle with doubts.

Not now. I'm too tired.

I just want to rest.

Although my eyes are closed under the water and all I see is darkness, I feel a different kind of darkness washing over me. And it feels good. It feels safe from those who would harm me. It feels free of the burdens that plague me. It feels so far from time.

My lungs start to ache, and I fight it. My body is so tired, but I can win this last battle with myself. I can fight for me. I can fight for the end.

That darkness gets thicker and thicker as it takes over me.

I focus on the sound of the water falling and hitting the surface above me.

It's calming...

Suddenly, I'm jerked from my euphoric trance by a bark. One single soft, deep bark.

My body betrays me, and I jolt out of the water, gasping for air and choking.

After a moment, my vision becomes less blurry, and I am fully aware of my surroundings.

The tub is overflowing into the bathroom. The shower is still on. My skin is white, and now I can tell it's from the water being too cold.

I look to my right and see Pepin sitting by the edge of the tub, just staring at me. No judgment in his eyes, just sadness. Unfazed by my coughing or the pool of overflowing water that he sits in.

I slowly reach over, turn the shower off, and pull the plug, draining the tub. I just sit there for a moment, catching my breath. I can't even think about what just happened because I truly don't know.

Eventually, once the tub is completely drained, I crawl out and grab my towel off the hook. I usher Pepin out into the hallway and grab more towels from the closet. Throwing them on the ground, I begin to mop up my mess.

Pepin sits outside the open door, monitoring me.

After I've cleaned up my mess, I walk to my bedroom and strip out of my wet clothes. I put on new underwear and an oversized shirt. Pepin and I snuggle on the couch for the rest of the evening and finish the movie.

The events that played out tonight will forever be me

and Pepin's secret. The secret of how he quite literally saved my life.

He licks the tear that falls down my cheek, and I kiss him on top of his head. "I love you, Pepin." I snuggle him even closer and rest my head on his neck, whispering, "Thank you."

Chapter Twenty-Five

LOUISA

I wake up to the smell of bacon. With heavy eyelids, I step out of my bedroom and walk to the kitchen to find B cooking breakfast.

"Good morning, birthday girl!"

I yawn and stretch my arms high above my head. "Morning."

"I have the whole day planned out for us. First, we eat this delicious breakfast. I almost burned the apartment down trying to make it, so it better be fucking delicious. Then we're spending the morning at the spa. And then tonight we're going out dancing."

She turns from where she's flipping pancakes on the stove to look at me and gives me a soft smile. "Does that all sound good?"

She still feels bad about leaving me right after I found out my test results. I was able to convince her that I was just fine and that it was not that big of a deal. But she still is trying extra hard to make my birthday special.

For her birthday earlier this year, I was able to get her backstage passes to Grumpy Old Bear, courtesy of Matt. She's been talking about my birthday ever since and thinking of how she's going to make my birthday just as special.

A day at the spa is exactly what I need, and somehow, she knows that, despite my best efforts to fake being okay.

"That sounds perfect." I walk over, wrap my arms around her from behind, and rest my head on her shoulder as she continues to flip pancakes.

"You've been extremely affectionate since I got back yesterday. Did you miss me?" She says it in a sort of mocking way because she has no idea just how much I did.

I lift my chin off her shoulder and kiss her on the cheek. "Don't flatter yourself too much."

She giggles and shoves me off. "You need to give the master chef space to work. If you mess me up, we're going to have to eat bagels from the coffee shop down the street."

"I like bagels," I tease her with a wink.

"Oh, you're so lucky it's your birthday, so I can't say what I really want to say to you right now."

I pour myself a cup of coffee and go snuggle with Pepin on the couch while I wait for breakfast to be ready. I slept in today, and I heard B slip Pepin out of my room this morning. I'm assuming it was to feed him and take him on a walk since we will be gone most of the day.

A few minutes later, B walks out of the kitchen with two plates full of food. I take in the delicious smell, and I'm relieved that my appetite is back. I take the plate from her and eat almost every bite until I'm about to throw up.

B DROVE us to the spa, and we are currently getting massages. She joked about scheduling a couples massage, and I told her to do it. Typically, I'd want a room to myself for some peace and quiet, but I've been alone in silence all week, and I just want to have her near, even if that means listening to her flirt with her masseuse for an hour.

We finish up and put our robes on to walk to our next treatment, which I believe is pedicures. An employee walks us through some hallways until we get to a set of frosted glass doors leading to the nail salon.

They sit us next to each other and bring us drinks.

I take a sip of my mimosa and look over at B. "This is really great, B. Thank you."

She reaches her glass over and clinks it against mine. "Anything for you, my darling."

"Anything?" I raise my eyebrows in question.

"Nope, I take that back. *Almost* anything."

"Where are we going out tonight?"

"I thought it would be fun to go to that club we went to for Iris's 21st. Except this time, I'm not leaving you alone with strange men until I vet them myself."

"Sounds good to me." I laugh and take another sip of my drink.

B tells me all about her trip to Paris, how she met a girl there and they spent three straight days together. The girl even went with B to gallery viewings for work.

I don't get how she can fully embrace a romance like that for such a short time, then leave and be just fine. Some part of me would always be sad and wonder what could have been. But not B; she seems entirely unfazed.

"How do you do it?"

"Do what?"

"How are you so into people one minute and then are able to just move past it the next."

"Because I'm a heartless bitch." She says it a little too loud, and people turn their heads to look at us. "Sorry," she whispers.

I roll my eyes at her. "No seriously, B. How?"

She adjusts in her seat, careful not to move her feet and mess up the nail tech. "I guess I always just go into things knowing they won't last. I live in the moment and enjoy the time I have with each person, and then I move on because I knew that's what the ending would be. Does that make sense?"

"But what happens when you meet the person you're supposed to be with?"

"I don't know, I've never been ready for or wanted that. I guess when my circumstances change, I'll have to change my mindset along with it."

I lean back in my big chair and watch the tech work on my nails, thinking about what B just said.

I'm really glad that works for her, but I'm not sure where I'm at in life or what I want. For so long, there wasn't a difference between what people expected me to do and what I actually wanted to do. I guess a good place to start is figuring that out first.

We sit in silence for a while, and I almost fall asleep.

Someone taps my legs. "You're all done, Ms. Blake."

I sit up straighter and blink the sleep out of my eyes. Once they clear, I look down at my soft pink toenails. "They look great, thank you so much."

I turn to B, who is also finished. "What's next?"

"Manicures, of course. You can't get the paws done and not the claws."

"You're so extra."

A spa employee walks us to the front of the room, where all the tables are set up for manicures, and we take seats next to each other. Then, we discuss what color and shape we want with each of our nail techs.

B chooses ballerina-shaped black nails, and I choose almond-shaped, the same soft pink to match my toes.

B leans over to see what I chose. "You're so predictable."

My eyes narrow into slits, and I glare at her. "You better shut up, or you're not invited to my birthday party."

B bursts out laughing, and it becomes contagious to me as well. She's laughing so hard that her nail tech has to ask her to hold still; how embarrassing.

The frosted glass doors open with a faint creek, and I look over instinctively, as if I'm going to know whoever is walking in. I think that's a small-town habit still engrained in me.

But this time, I do know them. It's Sam.

My heart stops for a moment, and my eyes get as wide as they can stretch before I duck my head down.

He's with a woman. Who is she? Why do I care?

I keep my head ducked, pretending to be interested in what's happening with my nails.

"Louisa?"

Fuck.

I look up slowly, trying to put on my best face like I'm noticing him for the first time. He's stopped in front of our table. The woman he's with is over by the wall, looking at nail polish colors.

"Hey, Sam."

I look over at B and see that she's just as stunned as I am. But unlike me, she's not even trying to hide her shock.

I look back, and he's still there.

"How are you?"

He stutters a bit. Is he nervous? "I'm good. How are you?"

"Same."

Oh my god, could this be more awkward? I'm sitting here in a damn robe, and I'm sure my hair is greasy from the massage oil.

It dawns on me that I'm in a nail salon at a spa. What is he doing here?

"You here to get your nails done too?"

"I'm here with my mom." He gestures to the woman that he walked in with.

"That's sweet of you."

There's a pause filled with silence as we just stare at each other, unsure of what to say next.

His mom walks up behind him and hooks her arm in his. "Alright, I picked out my color."

He turns to walk away with her; she clearly was unaware he was even talking to me. Before he gets too far, he turns back around. "It was good to see you."

I respond with a forced smile. And then he's gone.

They seat him way in the back, and with the pony wall between the two sections, he's blocked from view. A small blessing. If I had to attempt not to stare at him for the rest of this appointment, I fear my head would explode.

B leans in and whispers, "Was that *the* Sam?"

I nod and keep focused on my nails.

"Damn, he's attractive."

"I know."

"Sorry, that was a dumb thing to say."

I just shrug as I look over at her. "Let's not talk about him."

"Okay. But fuck that was awkward."

I glare over at her again; this time, it's less of a joke.

She successfully steers the conversation away from what just happened, and we go the rest of the appointment without mentioning Sam. When we finish, we're walked back to the locker room to change out of our robes.

My mind wanders back to Sam and the night we spent together. He looked really good today, and now all I can think about is the feel of his soft lips in my skin. My nipples harden, and I shake the thoughts away.

You're being stupid, Lou. He doesn't want you, so stop wanting him.

I try, but I can't.

———

B and I are at the club about to meet up with some friends. The music is too loud, just like last time, but I don't care as much because I don't plan on taking anyone home. I want to go into 25 with just myself and me.

When we got back from the spa earlier, B and I ordered my favorite takeout and ate while we got ready.

I chose to wear a tight-fitting black dress that is twisted between the breasts to look like a bow with a slit under to expose my sternum. The straps are thin, and the bottom only comes down to my upper thigh. My hair is slicked up into a low bun, and I chose black stilettos to go with the dress.

I have to admit, I look pretty hot.

Our friends arrive, and we all head to the bar to get drinks. B begged me to wear an "it's my birthday" sash so I could get free drinks, but I refused. So, I will be paying for

Emma Pathy

all my drinks tonight, which is worth not having to wear that damn thing.

I order my new regular, which is a Malibu Diet. I've learned that the lower alcohol percentage allows me to pace myself better. But that strategy only works if people aren't buying you shots all night long, which is exactly what our friends are doing.

First, Evie bought me a lemon drop shot, then Liam bought me a tequila shot, and not long after, B bought me a couple shots of fireball. All of this is an absolute recipe for disaster, but you can't say no when someone buys you a shot on your birthday.

I'm feeling pretty tipsy right now, so I drag B and Iris out to the dance floor. The lights are flashing, and the bass is vibrating the floor. B grabs my hands, and we spin in a circle, singing along to the song that's playing. I only know half the words, but I'm at that point in the night where I'm really good at making up the other lyrics, or at least I think I am.

The song changes, and it's the kind of song you want to bend over and shake your ass to, so that's exactly what we do. My hair is falling out of its bun, so I get rid of it and shake it out. I'm sandwiched in the middle of our grind train, and in this moment, it's hard to believe that less than a week ago, I tried to give up on it all.

A few songs later, B yells in my ear that she has to go to the bathroom, so Iris and I follow her there. As we're waiting in line, all I can think about is the last time I was here and how that night ended.

I think about how the last nine months of my life have played out. How many new people I've met. The things I've done that I have either never done or hadn't done for a long time. I'm trying not to think about the bad, so I focus on the good.

I think about my favorite moments. Then Sam pops in my head.

I think about running into him today and how my body reacted to seeing him. It was a tornado of conflicting emotions: anger, excitement, sadness, desire, discomfort, and curiosity. As the line slowly moves forward, he's all I can think about.

———

SAM

I'm sitting on my couch watching a documentary about serial killers. I don't know why I watch this stuff so late at night; I'll be the first to admit that it gives me the creeps. But my curiosity always gets the best of me, and I can't stop watching.

I jump when my phone starts ringing. I must have accidentally turned the sound on because it's usually on vibrate.

After getting that phone call about Jacob, anxiety takes over whenever I get an unexpected call. It draws up all these negative and fearful emotions from deep inside me, where I shoved them down long ago.

But I have been going to therapy, and I'm slowly starting to work through some of the demons that haunt me.

I dig for my phone in the blanket draped over my legs for a while before it falls on the floor. I pick it up, and I'm shocked by the name on the screen.

It's Lou.

I was really taken aback by seeing her today. I've been thinking about her a lot since I saw B at Daniel's Pride party, but I always shut down any thoughts of contacting her.

Being that close to her was such a tease. I wanted so badly to hug her and take in her scent that I still have memorized, but not only were we physically separated by a table, time and my actions have separated us emotionally.

By the poor performance I put on today, I'm assuming she has to know I still feel something toward her. I kept telling myself that she was nervous too, but if she was, that doesn't mean it's for the reasons I hope it is.

I answer and put the phone up to my ear. At first, all I can hear is music that is way too loud.

"Hello? Lou, are you there?"

Maybe she called me by accident. No, how could she do that if she hasn't called me in months? She had to intention-ally call me, right?

Her voice is faint and muffled, so I can barely make out what she's saying. "Sam, can you hear me?"

"I can barely hear you. Are you at a bar?"

"Club. One second."

There's some shuffling on the other end, and then the music fades slightly. Her voice comes in only slightly more clear.

"How about now?"

"Better."

I can't tell if she's not saying anything or if I just can't hear her.

"Lou, do you need something?" Shit, that came out harsher than I intended.

"Do you ever think about me? Like, *think think* about me?"

I can tell by her slurred words that she's drunk.

"Lou, I don't want you to take this the wrong way, but are you okay?"

"I'll take that as a no. Okay, I'm embarrassed now. Goodbye."

"No, wait! Don't hang up."

"So you *do* think about me?"

"Of course I do."

I can't tell if she heard me or not.

"Did you know it's my birthday?"

I remember her telling me it was sometime in July, but it didn't even cross my mind today when I saw her at the spa. It makes sense.

"I did not...Happy birthday."

"Thank you."

"Lou, are you with B right now?"

"No, she's in the bathroom. I got tired of waiting, so I went to find our friends again."

"Did you find them?"

She laughs. "No, I did not. Those sneaky bastards keep hiding from me."

"So you're by yourself right now at a club, lost?"

"I guess you could say that. Oh, look, I found the entrance! See, I'm not lost."

"Lou, I want you to find a bouncer and stay put. Please. I'm going to come get you, okay? Can you tell me the name of the club you're at?"

I quickly put my shoes on, grab my keys, and head out the door. I would just call B, but I don't have her number. And I'm not sure Lou is capable of giving me her number at the moment.

"Excuse me, sir, my friend said to find you and stay put."

There's rustling on the other end.

"Are you looking for a very intoxicated brunette?" It's a man's voice.

"Yes, can you tell me what club she's at? And can you please watch her until I get there? I'm on my way there right now."

"Yeah, but hurry, the club closes in an hour." He tells me the name of the club, and I punch it into my GPS. I think I know how to get there without it, but I'm not risking taking a wrong exit and delaying my arrival by any amount of time.

It eases my mind to know that a bouncer is watching her. But that's not his job, so who knows how committed he'll be if she tries to bolt.

———

Fifteen minutes later, I'm getting out of my car and headed for the elevator in the parking ramp. GPS said it was supposed to take 25 minutes, but I sped the whole way here, within reason, of course.

I get to the street level and jog down the block until I see the neon sign for the club. I get inside and talk to the first worker I see. They don't seem to know what I'm talking about, and I start to get nervous. Then I spot her. She's sitting on the floor, against the wall, with her head hanging down. Next to her stands a large man in a security shirt. I pay the cover charge and run over to them.

When I get there, I kneel down and lift her chin up so she's looking at me. "Hey, I'm here."

"Heeeey yooooou." She smiles, but her eyes are blank.

I look up at the bouncer. "Thank you for watching her. I really appreciate it."

"No problem, man. I have a little sister, too."

Well. Nope, I'm not going to correct him. It's better for him to think I'm her brother. Otherwise, he might get leery and not let me take her with me. I nod and smile.

"Come on, Lou, let's get you home."

"But what about my friends?"

"We can text them from your phone when we get to the car. You need to go home."

She sighs but stands when I grab her hands and help her up. I put one of her arms around my waist and grab her heels out of her other hand. She leans into me, resting her head on my chest, and wraps her other arm around me.

She's basically dead weight, but I don't feel comfortable carrying her in public with how short her dress is, so this will have to do.

It takes us a while to get back to the car, but we eventually make it. The first thing I do is grab her phone and have her unlock it. There are 12 missed calls from B and several other texts and missed calls from people I don't know.

Without looking at her messages, I start texting B, letting her know that it's Sam and that I'm taking her home. I text her my number so she can call me if she wants.

B

Omg, thank you! We've been looking for her!

LOU (SAM TEXTING)

Do you want me to wait and give you a ride home as well?

B

No, you should get her home. It'll take me a while to wrangle all our friends and get everyone to close their tabs.

LOU (SAM TEXTING)

Okay. I'll let you know when she's home safe.

B:

I have her location, but that would be great.

Part of me wonders if B mentioned the location sharing in an attempt to disincentivize me from kidnapping Lou. Either way, I know I'm not going to do that, so I have nothing to worry about.

I drive out of the parking lot to Lou's apartment. It's a good thing I still remember where she lives because she is not capable of telling me how to get there. She falls asleep against the window, and I don't wake her until we get to her apartment building. She opens her eyes enough for me to walk her to her front door.

I grab her purse and hesitantly open it, not wanting to be intrusive. "Where are your keys?"

"In my purse, look in the inside pocket."

I look all over and can't find her keys anywhere.

"I must have dropped them at the club."

"Why would they have been out of your purse?"

"I don't know, but they're clearly not here."

Shit.

I try to call B, but she doesn't answer, so I call her again. When she doesn't pick up after the third time, I start to get nervous. Lou needs to get to a bed or a toilet right now. How long is B going to take? I don't think Lou should wait that long; she needs to sleep.

"How about you just take me to your place?"

"Lou, we should wait for B."

She starts to sniffle and stick out her bottom lip in a cute, pouty way. "B has never been on time for anything in

246

her life. She's not going to be here any time soon." She's stumbling over her words a bit, but she still knows what she's saying.

"Are you sure?"

"Yes, I just want to wash my face and go to sleep."

I debate back and forth about what to do. I remind myself that I know she's going to be safe with me, but I worry about how it's going to look to B when I take her sister to my house instead.

"Pleeeeeeeeeeeaase. It's my birthday wish."

"That's quite a strange birthday request, if you ask me."

She slowly blinks her thick lashes at me.

"Okay, fine, but you're calling B on the way to tell her yourself where you asked me to take you."

"Deal."

We get back to my car, and she calls B, who again doesn't answer. I tell her to leave a voicemail, and she does. I would pay a lot of money to watch Lou listen to that voicemail when she's sober. She would die. She called me "the sexy man" several times.

I pull into my driveway, get Lou out of the car, and carry her into my house. She stumbles on the stairs, but I catch her. I take her straight to the guest bathroom because during the whole car ride, she looked like she was going to yak.

I get her situated on the floor by the toilet and run to grab her some water, electrolytes, and crackers. While I'm in the kitchen, I hear her yell from the bathroom, "Why did you stop talking to me?"

I hesitate because I wasn't expecting the question.

"What's the real reason, not the fake one? Did you just not like me anymore?"

I don't answer; I just gather the items and go back to the bathroom.

"Here, drink this." She takes the glass from me and starts sipping on it. While she does that, I squat down behind her and reach in the pocket of my sweatpants for the elastic band I grabbed.

Gathering her hair up on top of her head, I give my best attempt at a bun. It's clearly awful. She knows that without even having to see it, and she laughs at me.

"Hey, quit making fun of me. It's just meant to keep your hair out of the toilet; it doesn't need to look great." I attempt it again, and it's a little better.

She never ends up throwing up, which is a pleasant surprise. I give her a pair of my shorts and a shirt to change into since I'm assuming she doesn't want to sleep in her dress.

I get her all tucked into the guest bed with a glass of water and some painkillers on the nightstand for whenever she wakes up. As I'm about to leave, she stops me by grabbing my wrist. "Thank you."

"Of course." I start to leave again, but she keeps her hold on me.

"You never answered my question."

"Which one?" I know which one she's referring to, but I'm hoping I'm wrong.

"Why you stopped talking to me."

"Let's talk about that in the morning. I'm guessing sober you will prefer that."

Her eyebrows scrunch together like she's contemplating it. "Mmmmmmmmm, fine."

"Goodnight, Lou."

"Night."

I walk back to my room and shut the door. This night

took a completely unexpected turn, and now I have a girl–who I once really liked but fucked it up with–in my house.

I brush my teeth and crawl into bed, exhausted. I plug my phone in and set it on my nightstand. I lay in bed staring at the ceiling for a while, wondering what I'm going to tell Lou when she asks again tomorrow. I guess the only right answer is to tell her the truth. But how much detail do I go into?

This is likely just a chance encounter with Lou, but if, for some reason, the universe is handing me a second chance with her, I don't want to screw it up.

Chapter Twenty-Six

LOUISA

I wake up to the sound of birds chirping, which is unusual since my apartment is downtown. Typically, I only hear pigeons outside my window.

I rub my eyes and reach over to my nightstand to grab my phone. I feel around for it and bump into a glass, weird. I blink a few more times and realize I'm not in my room.

Fuck. Where am I?

I start to panic and look for my phone. It's plugged in next to a glass of water and some pills. I notice a sticky note on top of my phone that reads, 'B knows where you are. Text me when you're up. - Sam'.

I look around and see that I'm in a small bedroom that's very tidy and decorated in warm, neutral tones. I'm in a queen-size bed, and I can't tell if the other side has been slept in or if I just messed up the sheets while sleeping.

So many questions race through my mind. Is this Sam's room? Did he sleep in here with me? Where is he? How the hell did I get here?

I look over at the nightstand again, pick up the glass of water, and take the pills. I only have a slight headache, which is shocking since I don't remember most of the night. Sam must have taken care of me and made sure I was hydrated before I fell asleep. I unlock my phone to read through my messages and look at my call history.

After piecing everything together, I guess that I called Sam while very drunk, and he came to pick me up. My keys were missing, so he brought me here, keeping B updated every step of the way.

I get out of bed and realize that I'm wearing an oversized shirt and shorts that are staying around my waist only due to the tightened and knotted drawstrings. I unplug my phone and walk to the door. I need to find a bathroom; my bladder is so full right now. I step out into the hallway and look around. I find the bathroom, relieve myself, and brush my teeth with a toothbrush he left out for me before going back out into the hallway.

I hear music playing from somewhere, so I follow it to the kitchen, where I find Sam making breakfast. He doesn't hear me walk in, so I clear my throat.

"Morning."

He whips around, slightly startled by my silent entrance. "Morning. How are you feeling?"

"Surprisingly, not too bad. Thanks for taking care of me last night. I'm really sorry I called you."

He gives me a questioning look. "Do you remember much from last night?"

"No, I don't even remember calling you, but I checked my messages when I woke up and put two and two together."

He nods and turns back to the stove.

"I hope I didn't embarrass myself too much." To be honest, I am mortified. I have no idea what I said or did.

"No, you were fine. Just drunk. " I don't know how, but I can tell he's lying.

I walk over to get closer and hop up on the counter next to him. I just sit there and watch him make eggs.

He takes his eyes off the pan and looks over at me.

"You hungry?"

"Starving."

He gives me that adorable soft smile that melts me. "Good."

"So why were you at the spa with your mom yesterday?"

"She was having a bad week, so we spent the day together."

"That's so sweet. Did Quinn and Jacob join you guys, or are you the favorite son?"

He hesitates. "Quinn joined us later for lunch and a movie."

"Well, your mom is very lucky to have sons who will spend the day with her when she's having a hard time."

He just shrugs, and the corners of his mouth lift, but the smile doesn't reach his eyes.

When he finishes, he hands me a plate, and I dish up some eggs, bacon, and toast. He walks over to the stools by the island, and I follow, taking a seat next to him. I could have left an empty stool between us, but I don't.

I feel like I should be more nervous than I am, but after he saw me in such a drunken state last night, the ice has already been broken again. We eat, and he fills me in on the details I'm missing about how last night played out.

I just laugh because what else can I do at this point? He doesn't appear to be annoyed by any of it, which is a slight relief. I would say I forgot how kind and understanding he is, but I didn't.

Sam is the type of friend you call when your car breaks down because you know he'll drop everything to help. Maybe that's why I called him last night. Then again, it likely has more to do with the fact that I still have feelings for him and had just run into him that morning.

His arm is close to brushing mine, and I can feel the static between us. I want to touch him so badly, but I still don't know how he feels.

I glance over at him and catch him looking at me. At first, he looks away, embarrassed, but then he looks back at me, and I stare into those eyes.

They're a mixture of blue, green, and brown. Not the kind that change color, but the kind where there are patches of each color speckled around his iris. They're like an abstract painting or a patchwork quilt.

So unique and so mesmerizing.

I break the tension by speaking. "This hit the spot, thank you."

He nods, still keeping eye contact with me. "It's no problem."

I'm the one to finally break the stare. I look down at the clothes that I'm assuming are his.

"Would you mind if I rinsed off before I leave?"

"Yeah, that's no problem at all. The bathroom is across the hall from the room you slept in, and the towels are in the hall closet next to my room."

I didn't sleep in his bed after all; that's a relief.

I go to grab my plate to bring it to the sink, but he beats me to it. I walk back to the hallway to grab a towel out of the closet. Most of the doors are shut, so it's a bit of a guessing game, but I eventually find the right door.

I go to reach up for a towel but stop when I spot a shelf full of games, and right up front, I see a little red box. It's the question game that we played together when we first started talking.

I smile to myself and grab it off the shelf. Fond memories flood my brain, and I want to read a few cards to bring me back there, back when I thought I was falling for Sam and that he was falling for me.

We talked about so many things and didn't just stop at the questions. We often got lost on tangents, talking about things that related to the cards but going way deeper, sharing way more. I look over my shoulder to make sure he can't see me. I turn back to the box and open it, taking out a few cards from the Level 2 section.

My brows scrunch together in confusion.

What is this?

The cards I picked up have writing on them. I grab out a few more cards and realize that almost all of them are covered in black Sharpie. I read the slightly messy handwriting and realize that it's answers to the questions. My answers.

He had been writing down my answers to the questions. My heart starts to ache, and water pools in my eyes, making my vision blurry. I blink them away, and one falls on the card I was reading.

"Did you find it?"

I startle and turn to see Sam standing at the other end of the hallway, near the kitchen. He looks at me with that sweet face, standing there in his blue shirt and grey sweatpants.

He looks so good.

He must notice my tears because his face turns, and he

looks concerned. His eyes wander to the box and the cards I'm holding.

My voice is slightly hoarse from choking back tears, but I manage to ask, "You wrote down my answers?"

He slowly nods his head, and he looks hesitant. "I didn't want to forget anything about you."

My chin quivers, and I focus all my effort on not letting any more tears fall. How did it go from this to ending so fast? I don't get it, and I'm even more confused now than I have been in the past eight months.

I can see his chest rising and falling, his breathing labored. He takes a couple steps down the hall, closing the distance between us, but stops with a few feet remaining. I can see his face better now, and it looks just as pained as my body feels.

I drop the cards on the floor and lunge forward the last few feet to close the gap. His arms reach out and catch me, pulling me in close to him. My arms wrap around his neck, and I plant my lips on his.

Our lips move wildly across each other's, and my hands work their way through his curls, pulling him even closer and pressing our lips even tighter together. My heart is racing, and I can feel his against my chest, keeping pace with mine. His hands slide down my back to my thighs, and he picks me up, wrapping my legs around him.

His tongue sweeps into my mouth and brushes up against mine. I moan and move my hips against him, unable to control myself. The next thing I know, he's carrying me down the hallway and into his bedroom. He walks blindly all the way to his bed without a single misstep. He puts one knee on the bed to stabilize himself and lays me down.

My legs are still wrapped around him, and I hold them

firm when he tries to pull away. I want to keep him close to me; I don't want to let go. His full weight is on me, and I take pleasure in the compression of him. His hands, no longer needing to support my weight, still linger on my thighs. He runs them up and down, finally resting them on my ass.

He lets go and lifts himself up; this time, I release him. He kneels on the bed between my legs, and I lift myself up on my elbows, waiting for his next move. He lifts up his shirt that I'm wearing, enough to expose my stomach. He bends over and runs his lips across my skin, kissing from my sternum, across my naval, and lower to the waistband of the shorts. I run a hand through his hair and lay back, closing my eyes, soaking in every ounce of his touch.

He teases at the waistband, pulling it down only slightly and running his tongue along the sensitive skin on my hip. My body is begging for him, so ready to feel him again.

He stops, and I look down at him to see why he stopped. I find him looking at me, a question in his eyes. I nod. "Yes...please."

He continues, pulling down the shorts painfully slow and thoroughly kissing each new section of skin that gets uncovered. Finally, he's where I want him. He grabs the shorts, pulls them the rest of the way down, and throws them behind him.

For whatever reason, I chose not to keep my underwear on when I changed last night, and I'm glad I didn't. I can't take any more of this slow torture.

He licks up my already wet center and moans into me, sending a shiver up my spine. I echo his moans as he devours me like he's been starving for days. I'm so worked up that it doesn't take long for me to come all over his tongue. He didn't even have a chance to use his fingers this time.

I sit up slightly and lean forward to grab his chin, pulling it up toward my face. I kiss him while he's still got my come all over his lips, and I taste myself on him.

He looks winded in the best way. I bite my bottom lip, and he reaches one hand up to cup my cheek, running his thumb across my wet, swollen lip. I playfully bite the tip of his thumb, and he smiles at me, eyes hungry for the promise of more.

I wiggle out from under him, and he waits for my queue. I push gently on his shoulders, coaxing him up on his knees and then further onto his back. He swings his legs around and adjusts himself so he's more centered on the bed and takes off his shirt.

When I finally have him where I want him. I spread his legs and crawl between them. Then, with both hands, I grab his sweats and tug them down. He lifts up his hips to help me as I pull them all the way off, tossing them on the floor.

He's also not wearing any underwear under his sweats, which was a bold move, knowing he'd be seeing me in the morning. It just proves that he wasn't expecting this at all, and that thought turns me on even more.

I run my hand up and down his rock-solid shaft and bend forward to position myself. I keep my eyes on his face because I like watching how much I can drive him crazy.

When I run my tongue up his length, his mouth falls open, his eyes close, and his head tilts back into his pillow. I put as much of him as I can in my mouth, bobbing my head up and down, completely soaking him. From this view, I see his abs flexing with every bit of pleasure I'm giving to him.

He reaches down and puts his hand on the back of my head, gently grabbing my hair. "Lou, you're going to make me come before I even get inside you."

I feel a flutter between my legs at his plea. I lift my head up to look at him, his cock slipping out from between my lips. He's panting even harder now with his eyes still closed. He opens them and huffs out a laugh. "Sorry, it's been a while."

I smirk at him to let him know it didn't bother me. "Where are your condoms?"

He sits himself up, and I move out from between his legs so he can swing his over the edge of the bed. He stands up and walks over to his dresser, opens a drawer, and pulls one out, but he doesn't open it yet.

He walks back over to the bed where I'm sitting up on my heels waiting for him and tosses it next to me. He grabs both sides of my face with his hands and lifts me off my heels to an upright kneeling position.

His eyes wander down to my lips and back up to my eyes, then he pulls me in to kiss me. It's soft and slow this time, not hurried and frantic like it was in the hallway. His hands leave my face, and I feel my shirt start to lift, so I raise my arms up as he pulls it over my head.

We're both completely rid of our clothes, and I'm pressed up against him, his hard length wedged between us. My hands on his chest move to his hair when he leans over and starts kissing my neck.

A large hand cups my breast, and his thumb grazes over my stiff peak. His lips travel further south until they're over my nipple. He sucks gently and runs his tongue over it, then moves to the other side and repeats it.

I need him inside of me, now.

I reach over, grab the condom, and unwrap it. He stands up straight and gently runs his fingertips up and down my arms as I roll it onto him.

Once it's on all the way, he guides me onto my back again and positions himself above me. He reaches over and grabs a pillow, placing it under my hips. He runs a finger against my center and slides it in, making sure I'm still ready for him.

He confirms I am and looks into my eyes, asking that same question. I put my hand on the back of his neck, pulling his lips right over mine, and whisper, "Please just fuck me, Sam." He leans his head forward, resting his forehead on mine, then lifts his head and takes a deep breath.

He reaches down to grab the base of his cock and eases it into me. The stretch has me focusing on my breathing until I've adjusted to him. Once he's fully seated, he starts to thrust his hips, and I moan into his ear.

He continues to move his hips as I run my hands all over him, across his chest, down his arms, over his abs, and around to his back. When my arms are around him, he picks up the pace, and I sink my nails into him, moaning his name.

"Fuck...Sam."

He reaches a hand down and gently guides one of my legs up and over his shoulder. This allows him to enter me even deeper and at a slightly different angle that sends me through the roof. I'm moaning and panting, and his thrusts get faster and harder. My pelvic muscles clamp around his cock, and it makes him come with me.

As we both finish, he grabs the back of my neck and presses his lips into mine, opening for me. As we fight for breath between kisses, he stays fully seated in me for a moment.

He pulls his lips from mine and looks at me. His hand comes up to brush the loose hair out of my face. He leaves me with one final, soft kiss before pulling out of me and lowering my leg that was over his shoulder.

He sits back and removes the condom while I lay there,

still catching my breath. He lays down next to me and props his head in his hand, smiling down at me. A big grin stretches across my face; I can't believe this is happening.

I roll onto my side, facing him, and he puts his arm over me, rolling onto his back so I can comfortably lay my head on his chest. The hand that was holding his head now wraps around me, securing me to him. And his other hand gently strokes my side.

I close my eyes and take in his scent and the feel of him. We lay there for a while. I'm afraid to move, to ruin it, to lose him again.

I feel his chest vibrate under my head as he finally talks. "It's taking you an especially long time to find that towel. Do you need my help?"

I laugh and bury my face into him. "Yes please."

We sit up, and he walks into the hallway, still naked, and returns with two towels. He walks over to the other door that leads to his attached bathroom and stops in the doorway to look back at me.

"You coming?"

I crawl off the bed to follow him into the bathroom.

It's gorgeous in here, just like the rest of the house. He told me about all the renovations he was currently working on last fall and the ones he had planned. From what I've seen of the house, pretty much everything he mentioned looks finished. He must have been working overtime this winter and spring to have finished it all.

The shower is tiled with no doors or curtains. The whole bathroom is tiled off as one big wet room, including a large soaker tub.

He sets the towels on the counter, walks over to the shower, and turns it on. I walk over to him and wrap my arms around him.

"It looks great in here. The last time we talked, you were in the middle of this and your bedroom. When did you finish it all up?"

He pivots us so I'm under the stream of water and runs his hands over my head to push the now wet hair out of my face.

"I finished it in February. I actually finished the whole house."

"It looks really great."

"Yeah, but now I get kind of bored with no projects to work on."

I laugh, and he leans down to kiss my mouth.

"Well, if you need something to fill your free time, I know a girl." I wink at him.

"Oh yeah? What's she like?"

He reaches behind me, and I hear plastic bottles rustling. His hands go to my scalp, and I can feel him massaging shampoo through my wet hair. It feels so good my eyes roll back, and I moan.

It's a good thing I still have my arms around his waist to steady me because I think my knees are about to give out. The only person who has washed my hair for me is my hair-dresser, and it's not nearly as sexy as this.

"Well, she really likes whatever the fuck you're doing right now."

He boops my nose with his finger, leaving suds on the tip. I lean my head back into the water again and rinse it off. When my head comes back up, I have to blink away the extra water as it runs down my lashes.

"Well, she's incredibly sexy, and it makes me want to do things for her."

He runs his hands through my hair to rinse out the shampoo. I turn around and find the conditioner. I'm a little particular about my conditioner routine, so I put it in myself and tie my hair up to let it sit for a minute.

I take that time to fill my palm with body wash and turn back toward him. I rub it all over him in a more sexual way than necessary, but I can't help myself. I love watching him when he's turned on.

He never got fully soft after we finished, but now he's starting to get hard again.

He grabs the body wash and returns the favor, also lingering in places that don't need that much special attention in a normal shower.

Before things escalate too far, I rinse out my conditioner. When he sees I'm done, he backs me into the shower wall. The tile is cold on my back, but my body is a furnace right now, so I appreciate the temporary relief. I'm curious where he's going with this. My hips are significantly lower than his, so doing this standing is going to be nearly impossible. He must read the hesitation on my face.

"Do you trust me?"

Now I'm really curious.

"I do."

"I'm going to grab another condom, don't go anywhere."

I lift one eyebrow. "And where exactly would I go?"

He narrows his eyes at me in annoyance. "You know what I mean." He walks out of the bathroom and returns shortly with a condom.

He gets close to me again and rolls the condom over this thick length. Then he grabs my shoulders and turns me around so I'm facing the wall. I'm still curious as to where he's going with this because I don't see the solution yet.

He lifts me up under my arms, and when he sets me back down. I'm about half a foot higher than I was before. I look down to see I'm standing on a small ledge cut out in the wall. I didn't see it there before because I didn't look down.

I look behind me, and he gives me a cheeky grin.

"It's meant as a footrest for when women shave their legs, but it can serve alternate purposes."

My jaw drops, and I go back to facing the wall. He presses up behind me to support me, I suppose from slipping off the ledge. He reaches his hands between my thighs, and I part them as wide as the ledge will allow me.

His hand moves across my clit, and he sticks a finger in. When he knows I'm ready for him, he slides his cock into me from the back.

It's not nearly as deep as when I'm facing him, but it's a new angle that hits a sweet spot, making my legs shake. He thrusts hard but controlled, trying not to let my knees bang on the wall. My calves are burning, but the pleasure is overtaking me, and I know I won't have to hold myself up much longer.

When I start to climax, I lean back into him, and he wraps his arms around me, kissing my neck. My whole body lights up with sparks, and I can't hold myself up any longer.

He eases me down from the ledge and turns me toward him, supporting my weight by throwing my arms around his neck. He grabs my thighs and wraps my legs around his waist, pressing my back against the wall.

"Are you okay to keep going?"

I nod, and with a shaky voice, I reply, "Please don't stop."

He leans in and kisses my neck, whispering in my ear, "Good girl."

He moves his hips, and the sound of our bodies slapping together echoes off the tile.

"God, you feel so fucking amazing, Lou."

He leans his forehead into my shoulder, and he comes so hard that I feel him pulsing inside of me, and it pulls another small orgasm from me. My body can't handle anything more than that; I'm too exhausted.

He sets me down on the edge of the tub, sensing that my legs would fail me. He wraps one towel around his waist and the other around my shoulders. He scoops me up into his arms and carries me back to the bed.

Chapter Twenty-Seven

SAM

I look down at Lou as she snuggles into me. We're laying in my bed watching a movie. She picked Inside Out because it's one of her favorites, and I told her I'd never seen it, which she said was unacceptable.

After our shower yesterday morning, I drove Lou to her apartment to grab some things and change. She's been camped out here since, and I couldn't be happier.

Our limbs are tangled together, and her head is on my chest.

This movie has taken a really depressing turn, and I'm trying to hold in my emotions. My brothers always made fun of me growing up for crying during movies, but I can't help that I have a soft spot for fictional characters.

Bing Bong just jumped off the rainbow rocket so Joy could make it back to Riley, sacrificing himself. It takes me by surprise, and I have to choke back my tears. She must be able to tell because she looks up at me with tears in her own eyes.

I look up and blink away the tears like nothing happened. "What?"

"Nothing." She wipes away a tear that started rolling down my cheek. "I love that you aren't afraid of showing your emotions."

"Only around people who I know aren't going to judge me. So don't go telling Quinn I was crying at a cartoon; he will never let it go."

She giggles and wipes away another rogue tear. "I promise." She kisses me on the cheek and snuggles back into me.

I take a deep breath, trying to muster up some courage. Her head rises and falls with my chest.

"I've been meaning to ask...What are we?"

She lifts her head again to look at me.

I feel the need to clarify. "I mean, what do you want out of this?"

I've been afraid to ask out of fear of rejection. I'm afraid she won't trust me after what I did to her before. I just want her to be honest with me, and I'd rather know now before I continue falling for her.

"I really like you, Sam. I was really sad to lose you before, and I'd rather not go through that again. So if this is something you want to keep casual, it would be easier to know that now."

I let out a breath I didn't realize I was holding in. I smile at her and run a hand through her hair. "I don't want this to just be a casual thing. I'd like to have you all to myself."

I reach under her arms and guide her up so she's lying on my chest, our faces close.

"I don't know how this works at our age; I haven't been committed to anyone in a while." She looks at me skeptically, but I continue. "Do I have to officially ask you to be my girlfriend?"

She laughs and shakes her head. "I think you kind of just did." She gently brushes my lips with her fingers, and I peek out my tongue to wet them. "I'd love to officially be your girlfriend." She removes her fingers from my lips and replaces them with her own lips.

I wrap my arms around her and put a hand on the back of her neck to deepen the kiss.

She brings her legs forward, separating them so she's straddling me. I'm only wearing sweats, and she's only wearing underwear. I can feel the heat from between her legs, and I instantly start getting hard. Our lips never part as she grinds on me. I lift my hips up into her, needing to feel more of her.

My stomach growls, and I remember that we haven't gotten up to eat in a while. She senses my hesitation and pulls away from me. I rub my hand down my face, not wanting this to stop but knowing it will.

"I really want to fuck you right now, but I'm starving."

As if it heard me, her stomach rumbles. "I am too."

"How about I cook us some dinner, and then we can resume this?"

"Sounds good to me."

She moves her hips one more time just to tease me; I close my eyes, scrunching my face. It takes everything in me not to rip off her underwear and fuck her into this bed.

But she finally concedes and climbs off me.

———

LOUISA

We get up and start walking to the kitchen, but Sam hesitates. "I'll be there in a second." I can tell he's desperately trying to tame his raging hard-on. I giggle and make

267

my way to the kitchen, grabbing myself a glass of water. He joins me shortly after.

I sit on a stool at the island, watching Sam play master chef in the kitchen. Music is playing on a speaker, a hot guy is making me dinner, and I'm completely satiated yet somehow wanting more; who could dream up a more perfect scenario?

I'm so happy, but something about this makes me sad. I think about how I could have had this all along if he hadn't ended things. We missed out on so many happy months together. Would those unhappy things that have occurred in my life recently have happened if we never parted? Probably not.

I haven't brought it up yet because I've been on cloud nine, and I didn't want to risk losing it. But I have to know. I have to ask him why he did it.

"Sam, can I ask you a serious question?"

He stops chopping peppers for a second and looks up at me. "Of course."

"Why did you end things between us?"

He puts his knife down and wipes his hands off. "I've been wondering when you were going to ask that. You asked me this the other night when I picked you up from the club."

I did? Did he tell me?

"I told you I'd tell you when you were sober."

"Well, I'm sober now."

He lowers his head and doesn't say anything for several moments.

"You won't hurt my feelings, Sam; please just be honest with me. Was there someone else?" He's still silent, staring down at the cutting board. "Was it something I said or did?"

"No."

I wait a few more moments, and then I go to ask again. "Sam—"

"Jacob died."

I'm taken aback; my mouth falls open, and I have no idea what to say. I can see the tension in his body; he's clearly uncomfortable.

When he lifts his face to look at me, there are tears in his eyes. He is telling the truth. I'm such an asshole.

"I'm so sorry, Sam."

I pause a moment, then get up and walk around the island to where he stands. I go from behind, wrap my arms around his body, and rest my head on his back. His hand touches mine and gives it a little squeeze.

Letting go, I step back and give him space to spin around toward me.

"He died the night of Thanksgiving, and I found out the next morning. I was so out of it, I didn't even realize that I hadn't responded to you."

"Of course, that's completely understandable." I step forward and rest my hands on his chest, looking up at him. "You don't have to talk about it if you don't want to."

I would never want him to feel pressured to talk about that. Though it feels like I've known him for longer, we only reconnected less than 48 hours ago.

There's another long silence. Sam wraps his arms around me, kisses the top of my head, and rests his cheek there.

"I plan on keeping you around for a while, so you should know."

Though this is an incredibly sad moment, I can't help but get butterflies when he says that. I had hoped he felt the same way, and getting verbal confirmation makes my heart sigh in relief.

"I plan on keeping me around, too."

He squeezes me briefly before releasing me. I back up and lean against the counter across from where he leans against the island.

"Jacob died by...it was...he...did it himself."

I look at him, confused. I think I know what he's trying to say, but that's an awful thing to assume, so I wait for him to go on before saying anything. To confirm it's what I think it is.

"Suicide. Jacob died by suicide." He's clenching the edge of the counter, his knuckles going white, face pointed at the ground. This is clearly a painful thing for him to talk about. "That's how my therapist told me to phrase it. Instead of saying 'committed suicide', you say 'died by suicide'. Since it's brought on by mental illness."

I feel bile working its way up my throat. I feel sick. Sam lost someone he cares about so deeply to suicide. The exact thing I tried to do a week ago.

Me. I did that.

The thing that is tearing Sam apart, causing him so much pain and suffering.

"I've heard that before." What did I just say? "Rephrasing it, I mean."

"He and my dad got into it when we were at his house for Thanksgiving. It was a huge blowout fight, and Jacob left. That was the last time any of us saw him."

I know it's selfish to be thinking about me right now, but all I can think about is B. How she would be right now if my plan had worked, if Pepin hadn't intervened. My heart aches so badly for Sam and for what could have also been B.

How could I do that to her? Every time thoughts like

this have popped into my head, I shut them out completely. I can't bear it.

I reach out and grab his hand. "I'm here for you, Sam."

Until you're not, the voice in my head says.

What if Sam and I stay together, and I go through another hard time? What if I do this to Sam? Once is awful enough; I can't imagine losing two people you care about to the same thing. That's not fair to Sam. I have to tell him. He has to make the choice for himself if he's willing to live with someone else who may leave him too soon. I have to tell him.

But not now, I can't. I'll wait for the right time.

"Thanks, Lou. I'll tell you more in time, but I think that's all I'm ready to share for now."

"You take all the time you need." I reach up and kiss him on the cheek; it's damp with tears.

"I really did like you—a lot. It broke my heart to end things with you. I just didn't feel it was fair to put that type of burden on you that soon."

To be honest, I'm not sure how that would have played out had he told me. I would like to think I'd have been supportive. But what was I supposed to do, go over to his house to comfort him? Go to the funeral with him?

That's all a lot for someone you've only met in person once. Though I'm sad he didn't tell me the whole situation, I can't really blame him. I might have done the same thing. I sort of am doing the same thing right now, withholding information from him out of fear that it's too early to share a burden like that.

I go back and forth with myself, wrestling over whether or not to tell him. Eventually, I decide to wait. I don't want it to seem like I'm taking over his grieving with my own sob story.

"You don't have to explain it; I understand now. I appreciate you sharing that with me." I run my thumb over his cheek and cup the side of his face. He leans into my touch, and it breaks my heart.

This man deserves the world and to have his heart protected. I'm not sure if I'm capable of giving him that.

Chapter Twenty-Eight

LOUISA

Despite my doubts about whether or not I'm good for Sam, I can't stay away from him. He started coming over after work on the weekdays, but when B is home, it's hard to get privacy. So we started spending time at his house. I felt bad leaving Pepin home alone, so Sam insisted he come along.

Pepin loves Sam's house. He has a fenced-in yard where he can trot around in the grass. He'll be out there for hours, and when we check on him through the window, he's usually napping in the flower bed.

As one can imagine, the landscaping in Sam's yard is beautiful. The first time I caught Pepin in the flowers, I felt horrible. I ran out there and called him over. Sam just laughed at me and said a yard is meant to be enjoyed, and if Pepin enjoys napping in the flowers, then he's glad they're getting some good use. Sam is always sweet like that.

Pepin and Sam are besties. We take him on walks around Sam's neighborhood, which are much better than the walks I used to do with him near the apartment. There are trails, trees, kids, and lots of other dogs for him to meet.

When I decide to spend the night at my apartment, Pepin is always so bummed to be going back. It makes me feel kind of bad that I had him cooped up in there for a whole year. But I don't think he minded it until he knew what else was available to him.

Sam bought him a dog bed, food, and toys to keep at his house so we didn't have to drag it all back and forth. Pepin feels right at home here, and so do I. It's crazy to think that just a few weeks ago, I thought there was no way we would ever be together. And by a chance encounter, here we are.

I don't believe in soul mates, and I don't believe in fate. But those are the only ways I can describe how this happened. And if it truly was fate or we are soulmates, then this could be it. This is the happy ending.

But I can't shake the feeling it's not. I got lucky to find a guy like Sam in the first place. I was unlucky to lose him, but I got lucky running into him again. Now, I'm anxiously waiting for the other shoe to drop again. This time, I think it's going to be me who messes things up. I'm afraid that telling Sam about my depression and what happened before my birthday will scare him away; I wouldn't blame him.

A door slamming shut pulls me from my thoughts. I turn around and see Sam walking through the back door with Pepin. They were outside playing fetch while I was studying. I told Sam I failed the first exam, and since then, he has been really good about blocking out time for me to study, making sure I stick to it.

Of course, I'd much rather be outside with them, but I need to retake that exam so I can move on to the next one. I'm scheduled to take it next month.

"How's the studying going?"

"It's fine. Boring, but fine."

He walks into the kitchen and gets himself a drink. His shirt is off, and his chest is glistening with sweat. Muscles flex as he tips the cup back to chug the water. I can't get over how hot he is. I know I'm staring, but I don't care. He's mine, so I'll stare all I want.

He sets the glass down and walks over to kiss me on the forehead. "You ready for our date tonight?"

A few days ago, Sam and I realized that we hadn't actually been out on a real date since reconnecting. Sam took it upon himself to plan the entire evening, not letting me in on any part of it.

"Very! Can you finally tell me what we're doing?"

He smirks. "Nope." He looks over at the stove to check the time. "Only that it starts in an hour."

I playfully punch him in the shoulder. "Jerk."

He winks at me and heads to his room to shower. I follow him so I can start getting ready. I grab the dress I brought over and bring it to the guest bathroom. I need to do my makeup, and I can't do it in his bathroom with foggy mirrors.

I hang my dress up and plop my makeup bag down. I crawl up onto the counter and sit cross-legged in front of the big mirror. I throw on some music and get to work.

I keep my makeup simple and clean. Sam always tells me that I look great without makeup, so I'm doing a no-makeup makeup look for him. After I finish, I straighten my hair and pin the shorter pieces that hang in the front behind my ears. It's still warm out, so I picked a short floral dress and some short, chunky heels.

I zip up my dress and walk out to the living room to see if Sam is ready. According to the time he told me, we need to leave in five minutes, so he better be.

When I round the corner into the kitchen, I find him packing a cooler. He hears my heels and looks over at me.

"Damn. You look beautiful, Lou."

I walk over to him and start playfully touching his back.

"Beautiful enough that you want to just stay here all night and fuck me?"

His back shakes from laughter. He turns around and puts his arms around me, pulling me close. "No. I worked hard planning this, and I'm not going to let you spoil it with your sex appeal."

"You're funny." I go up on my tiptoes and press my lips to his for a soft, brief kiss.

"Alright, the cooler is packed. I'm ready to go, are you?"

I nod and examine his outfit to try and figure out what we're doing. Sam is dressed in nice navy pants and a white button-down short-sleeved shirt. Nice, but casual. My best guess is a picnic.

We let Pepin out one more time, and then we get into his truck and leave. I look in the back seat to see if I can spot any other hints.

None. Not even a blanket for a picnic.

"You can't handle not being in control, can you?"

"I'm just a curious woman, that's all."

He gives me a side-eye look. "Sure, whatever you say, Lou."

I playfully punch his arm. Ouch. It hurts me more than it hurts him when I do that.

We drive for a while until we pull up to a restaurant. Sam parks the car, and we walk to the entrance. It's an Italian restaurant I've never been to before. The inside is cozy, with only 15 tables max. It looks like a little Ma and Pa restaurant, which usually means the food is delicious.

Sam gives the hostess our name, and she seats us at a table for two in the back.

"Have you been here before?"

"No, my mom actually recommended it."

"You were telling your mom about our date?"

"Of course. Her and Quinn were sending all sorts of suggestions in the family group chat."

I know Sam talks to his mom on the phone several times a week, but I didn't know they talked about me. I grab the drink menu and hold it up to hide my giddy smile.

The waiter comes over, and we order our drinks.

Sam reaches his hand across the table, and I place my hand in his. His thumb rubs back and forth over my knuckles as he reads his menu. Is it pathetic that such a simple gesture means so much to me? That I'm swooning over a man because he's holding my hand in public?

Jay never took me to nice places. At first, I thought it was because we were poor and in college. But once we graduated and got jobs, things didn't change.

I'm still learning what life with Sam could be like, and I'm curious if this is a regular occurrence for him. "Do you go out to eat at nice restaurants a lot?"

"Not really. I used to go to some nice dinners when my brothers and I were with Joel."

"I sometimes forget that you have an incredibly wealthy father."

"Isn't that why you're with me, for the inheritance?"

"Oh, shut up." I shake my head at him and roll my eyes.

The rest of the dinner was lovely. We chatted about places we have traveled and the places we want to go. Sam went on a lot of vacations with his family when he was younger, always to extremely expensive places. But from what he told me, it sounds like it wasn't all that glamorous. It was a classic example of 'money can't buy you happiness.'

I traveled a few times in college with friends, and those were some of the greatest adventures of my life. Backpacking across Spain and hiking in Patagonia were life-changing experiences for me.

After we finish our tiramisu, we walk back to his truck, and he starts to drive without saying anything about where we're going. A few minutes later, we pull up to an old-fashioned ice cream shop.

"More dessert?"

"Well, this was the original plan, but you were so excited when you saw tiramisu on the menu that I wanted you to have that too. So now we get a second dessert."

"I'm stuffed. But I'm sure I can find some room in here." I pat my stomach, pushing it out to look bigger.

"Good, because this is the best ice cream you'll ever have."

"That's a bold statement, Sam Carlyle. Are you prepared for me to disagree with you?"

"You won't, trust me." He takes my hand, and we cross the street.

"Doubling down, so confident! I guess we'll just have to see."

———

It was the best ice cream I have ever eaten. I want to punch Sam in his adorably smug face when I admit it to him.

I watch the muscles on his arm flex as he turns the steering wheel. Why is that so hot? I tilt my head and lean into him, resting my head on his upper arm. He reaches his hand across his chest and strokes my hair. I take in a deep breath and let it out.

This is joy. This is bliss. Simple, attainable happiness.

On the drive home, Sam gets cut off and has to slam on his breaks. I hear something clunk off the back seat onto the floor. Looking back, I see the cooler that I forgot was back there.

"What was the cooler for?"

By the look on his face, I can tell he's been waiting for me to ask. "It was just to throw you off since I knew you were going to try to figure it out.

"That is cruel!" I let my jaw drop, mouth hanging open in disbelief.

"I did what I had to do. Sorry if I got your hopes up for a picnic."

"That's okay, we can do that next time." I squeeze his hand, and he squeezes mine right back.

We pull into the driveway and park the car. Sam goes into the back seat and grabs the cooler. We walk through the door, and Pepin immediately greets us. That's strange because usually he's passed out on the couch, and when we get home, it takes him a second to wake up.

"Hey Lou, I think I left the porch light on." He points to the back door, which has a faint glow behind it. "Would you mind running over and shutting it off?"

I walk over to the back door and look out to see which light was left on. I'm shocked by what I see. Sam comes up behind me and puts his hands on my arms.

"Do you like it?"

I turn around and give him a big hug. "I love it."

He grabs the cooler off of the counter and walks back with Pepin by his side, eager to get to the backyard. I open the back door and step outside to where Sam's surprise is waiting for us.

Strings of twinkle lights are strung from the fence to the gutters on the house. There's a sheet stretched out over a metal frame, and a projector shines on it with an image of Sam and me, a picture I took the other day. In front of the screen is a large, cushy loveseat with pillows and blankets strewn all over it. Flameless candles line the path to the setup.

Chapter Twenty-Nine

SAM

She steps onto the back patio and looks around. Pepin runs out right past her legs.

Without looking at me, she asks, "When did you do all this? I let Pepin out before we left, and I'm pretty sure none of this was here."

"I may have had a little help."

She starts walking down the path to the loveseat. "Who?"

"B and Quinn."

She whips around. "Both of them, together?"

"They've actually already met through Daniel. I texted them both in a group chat and asked if they'd be willing to help me surprise you. They went immediately into planning mode." I follow her, carrying the cooler I filled with her favorite drinks. "It was my idea to do an outdoor movie, but they're responsible for the decorating. I'm sure they were having a grand ole time together; I can't wait to watch that security camera footage back."

"It's beautiful. Remind me to text them and thank

them." She turns back around, walking away from me. "I didn't know you had security cameras."

She plops down onto the loveseat, saving only a sliver of room for me.

"Yeah, I had them installed after a house a couple blocks over got broken into. It gives me peace of mind."

I grab her hand, lifting her onto her feet so I can sit down without crushing her. I pull her down on my lap, and she snuggles in. Reaching over, I grab a blanket and put it over us.

I look around. "The remote should be here some-where...ah, here it is." I wake up the screen and hand the remote to Lou. "You pick the movie."

"Is this you trying to make up to me for when you forced me to watch all the Lord of the Rings movies?"

"No, I just want you to pick because I probably won't watch much of the movie anyway."

"Why's that?"

I put my hand on the back of her neck and pull her closer to me. I get my lips close to hers, barely touching. "I'll be too focused on you, sitting on my lap in this dress." I move her head to the side and kiss her neck.

She turns her head back to look at the screen noncha-lantly and clicks into a streaming app. "Okay, have fun with that. I'm going to be watching Pretty Woman."

Oh, she's testing me, teasing me. We'll see how long she can play that game.

I let her get a little ways into the movie before I start. This movie actually isn't that bad, but I want her more than I want to watch a millionaire fall in love with a prostitute.

Lou is sitting sideways on me with her ass hanging off my lap and her legs draped over me, leaning back on the armrest of the loveseat. My hand rests on her leg. I slide it a little further up her thigh, then a little more, until I'm just below her center. She stirs a little, moving my hand so it's touching her. I slowly run my fingers over her panties, and she stirs again. I pull my hand away slightly and leave it resting there for a while.

Just feeling the heat coming off of her on my hand is enough to drive me crazy. Mix that with her scent and how sexy she is, and I'm a goner. It makes me wonder if she knows how easily entranced I am by her.

I reach up and brush her hair off her shoulder, exposing it to me. The little sleeve on her dress is stretchy, so I pull it down with ease. I kiss her bare skin, and she shrugs like it tickles. I put my arm around her to pull her in close to me, continuing to kiss across her shoulder and up her neck.

She makes a little noise but pretends not to notice me. So I step it up.

I bite her ear lobe and lick the sensitive skin right beneath it. She shudders and extends her neck to give me better access.

My hand on her thigh creeps up again, this time slipping under her panties and lightly grazing her folds. She tenses up but is still committed to her game of pretending she's unfazed by me. But I know that's a lie because my fingers between her legs can feel how turned on she is right now.

I whisper in her ear, "You can't pretend when I can feel how wet you are." I slip one finger in, and she sucks in a breath, leaning her head back into my shoulder.

I take my hand that's wrapped around her right now and sink my fingers into the hair on the back of her head. I tug her head back, tilting her face around to look at mine. With my finger still working inside her, I add another.

Her eyes are heavy, and she's biting her juicy lower lip.

I look down at her and smile, knowing I've won. She releases her lower lip, and the corners of her mouth tilt up.

I lean into her and whisper, "Are you ready to be a good girl now and stop ignoring me?"

She nods and lifts her head slightly to kiss me, but I pull back, teasing her. She gives me a death glare that melts away when I add a third finger. I rock them back and forth a few times, then slowly remove them, knowing three is a lot for her.

I lean down and connect our lips. She opens for me, and I sweep my tongue across her bottom lip and gently bite it, pulling it out before releasing it. It bounces back, and she lets her mouth hang open for me. I go back in, and our tongues tangle in soft, sensual kisses.

I grab her hips and lift her up. Swinging one leg over, she now straddles me, her dress riding up around her hips. She rolls her hips and rubs against my hard cock that's straining under my pants. She grabs the blanket that fell to the side and wraps it around us.

"Now that I know you have cameras," she teases me. "Though this might be fun to watch back later." She leans forward and touches her lips to my neck, biting, sucking, and licking.

I put both hands on her hips and pull her down as I lift my hips up into her, needing to feel her. In response, she reaches down and starts to undo my belt, then the button and zipper of my pants. She opens my pants and pulls my cock out of my underwear. She strokes it with her hand a few times, and it starts pulsing in anticipation, dying to feel her wet and warm around me.

I move my hands to the front of her panties and curl my fingers in the delicate cotton fabric. With one swift motion, I pull my hands apart and tear them. I tear the fabric until she is free of them and toss them to the ground.

She shifts herself so she's over me and slides her wet pussy back and forth over my cock. The feeling of her makes my body tense up and want to slide right into her, and I almost do.

With all my willpower, I lean forward around her and reach for the cooler. I can barely reach the strap, but I get a hold of it and pull it toward me. I reach into the side pocket and pull out a condom.

She looks slightly disappointed, but we haven't had that conversation, and I'd rather not have it in the heat of the moment. Still, it absolutely kills me to put one on. I'd love to feel her around me with no barrier, nothing to dull the blissful sensation of her sliding up and down me.

I roll the condom on and lift her hips, setting her down on top of me. I slide into her slowly, and she pauses for a moment, letting herself adjust to me.

"Fuck, you're so tight, baby."

She continues settling the rest of the way. I'm fully seated now, and I can feel my cock completely fill her.

She rides me for a while, angling herself just the way she likes so I hit that sweet spot. I rub my thumb over her clit; it's wet and slippery, allowing me to move around it with ease. She moans and starts moving faster.

I reach behind her, gather a large chunk of hair, and pull her head back. She clings onto my shoulders to hold herself up. She's breathing hard, and her moans are louder than ever.

"Shhhhhhh, you don't want to wake up the neighbors, do you, baby?"

She tries her best to shake her head, but it's still bent back from me pulling her hair.

She presses her lips tight together to stifle her moans.

"Good girl."

I'm getting so turned on by this that I'm about to come with her. I grab one of her hands off my shoulder and place it between her legs so she's touching herself. I use both hands to grab her hips to lift them, then slam them against me. I lift my own hips off of the seat and move under her at a rapid pace.

She screams as she folds over onto me and comes all over my cock. I can't stop myself from busting inside her. I hold her down and lift my hips so I'm as deep in her as I can be. Our muscles pulse against each other, and it's a feeling I can't describe.

She slides off of me, and I run inside to grab a damp towel for her. She cleans herself off, and we crack open another drink, getting snuggled up on the loveseat again. Lou grabs the remote and starts rewinding to the part where we left off.

"You really don't have to do that."

She looks at me with one eyebrow raised. "Oh yes, I do; you're not missing a second of this classic."

We finished the movie, and I have to admit that I actually liked it. I'm glad she rewound it because I would have missed the iconic scene where Vivian is shopping and tells those women to fuck off.

I check the weather app to make sure it isn't going to rain tonight and confirm that I'm okay to leave everything out for the night and put it all away tomorrow. I grab the cooler and follow Lou inside. Pepin, who was sleeping on his dog bed next to us, trails behind.

While we're getting ready for bed, Lou walks up to me, lifts up onto her tiptoes, and hugs her arms around my neck.

"Thank you for tonight. It was the best second first date

I've ever had." She giggles at her own joke, which I find adorable.

I grab the back of her neck and tilt her head to kiss her. Her lips are soft and warm, her scent is intoxicating, and I just can't get enough of this woman. I want to be around her all the time and never leave her side.

Finishing up the summer season was difficult after Lou's birthday. I hated having to leave her, but she also had to work. I pull away from her and stare into those beautiful brown eyes, wondering how I got so lucky.

Chapter Thirty

LOUISA

Pepin runs across the park to fetch the ball Sam just threw. He stops when he sees a little girl playing off to the side. I run over to him because I don't want her mother to get nervous. Pepin just stands there staring at her, waiting for me to give him permission to approach her.

On my way over, I see the mom lean over and say something to the girl. The little girl looks nervous, but it's clear she wants to pet him.

"You can pet him if your mom says it's okay. He's very friendly."

Her mom nods to her, and the little girl approaches, and Pepin wags his tail with excitement. She sticks out her hand and pets the top of his head. He licks it, making her giggle. Pepin lifts up onto his hind legs and sticks his paws up on the arm of her wheelchair to get closer to her face.

She doesn't shy away from him, even though, in this position, he towers over her small frame. Instead, she wraps her arms around his neck and gives him a big squeeze. My gentle giant always has the power to make people feel special. I thought about getting him certified to go into hospitals and nursing homes; I just haven't gotten around to it yet.

While she pets Pepin, I chat with her, asking her name and what grade she's in. Eventually, her mom calls her back over, saying they have to leave. The girl reluctantly says goodbye and wheels away. Pepin wants to follow his new friend so badly, but I hook the leash on him and walk back toward Sam.

The three of us walk around the lake on a new path near Sam's house. The fall colors are gorgeous this time of year. When I moved out of state for college, I missed the fall season in Minnesota. Between the view of the trees and the views of this beautiful man walking by my side, I'm not sure how I got so lucky.

Sam and I have been dating for a couple of months now, and I couldn't be happier. Sure, I still get down sometimes, but nothing compared to how I felt before Sam. I still haven't told him about my depression or the bathtub incident. I just haven't found the right time, or the right time comes, and I chicken out because I don't want to ruin this beautiful thing we have.

It weighs heavy on my mind, though. I often remind myself that even as Sam gets to know me better, he doesn't know every side of me. He doesn't know about the side he won't like. The side that could lead to heartbreak.

Sam squeezes my hand. "Everything okay? You look deep in thought."

"It's nothing. Just thinking about my exam."

That's not what I was thinking about, but it very well could have been. I passed the first exam the second time I took it. I've just taken the second one and am waiting for the results. Sam's been doing his best to keep my mind off it, but it's hard.

Instead of mansplaining and telling me how pointless it is to worry, he's supportive.

"Is there anything I can do to take your mind off it?"

We stop, and he puts his arms around me, turning me so we face each other. Pepin sits beside us, patiently waiting to continue his walk.

"Well, I could think of a couple things…" I give him the look that usually leads to us being sweaty and tangled up in the sheets.

He looks down at me and tucks my hair behind my ear. We're hidden behind some bushes, so nobody is being subjected to our PDA. His face changes from suggestive to something I can't quite read. Is it concern, worry?

"I've wanted to say this for a while…"

I'm getting slightly nervous.

"I love you, Lou. So much." He's staring into my eyes, and I realize that the look he's giving me isn't concern or worry; it's the look of someone painfully in love, not knowing how the other one feels.

I can feel his heart pounding in his chest, and I stand there just staring back at him, silent.

"You don't have to say it back. I just needed to tell you before I exploded."

When he senses that I'm not going to say it back just yet, he breaks the silence by leaning down to kiss me.

I don't know why I didn't say it back.

Well, maybe I do. I want to say it to him; I want him to know how crazy I am about him and how happy he makes me. But I can't. I can't take the next step, knowing he doesn't know all of me. I'm sad he got to it first because now I worry it's only going to make that talk more difficult.

He releases me and takes my hand, continuing down the path. He starts up a conversation like nothing happened. I appreciate him not making me feel bad about not saying it back. My heart flutters when I replay the image of him saying it. I want to say it; I want to rewind and say it back to him, but I can't.

We're a block away from the house when Pepin startles me with a sneeze. Or was it a cough?

"Bless you, buddy." I reach down and pat his side. It feels firm.

Next thing I know, he starts gagging, and I realize it wasn't a sneeze. I've seen him throw up before, so I'm not that fazed. I bend down and rub his back.

"Let it out, buddy."

Nothing comes up. He stops heaving, and we keep walking. Until it happens again. This time, the coughing produces white foam.

I'm starting to get concerned. Sam whips out his phone and starts typing.

I continue to pet Pepin on the back as he keeps coughing and gagging. It almost seems like he's choking, but I know he didn't eat anything. I feel his stomach again and notice his abdomen is distended.

My heart is racing, and I can feel my throat close up from trying to hold back tears.

"Lou, I think we should take him in. From what I'm reading, this could be bad."

I start to cry because I feel so helpless.

"I'll run and grab the truck; you stay here." Sam sprints down the block toward his house.

A couple minutes later, Sam rolls up to the curb and jumps out. The coughing hasn't stopped, and he's starting to look like he's in pain. My face is soaked with tears, and my vision is blurry.

Sam lifts Pepin into the back seat, and I climb back there with him. He places his head on my lap, and Sam peels out, taking off down the road. I don't even know where we're going because Pepin's vet is closed on week-ends, but Sam has GPS navigating somewhere, and I trust him.

"It's okay, Pep." I continue petting him and trying to make him comfortable. I keep hoping that it'll stop, but it never does.

"Hey Lou," he gets my attention, "would you be able to call them ahead of time to start the check-in process."

I nod and take out my phone. He gives me the name of the place we're going, and I call them. The lady on the phone is extremely calm, and I feel like she's not under-standing the urgency of this. I'm sure she deals with crazy people who over exaggerate all the time, but Pepin is *not* okay.

She makes me give an email, make a deposit, and go through the financial responsibility of these visits. I tell her I don't care how much it costs, I'll pay it. She then tells me that the estimated wait time right now is three to four hours. I tell her he can't wait that long, and she attempts to reas-sure me that the triage team will assess him when we get there and make that call.

It takes us 15 minutes to get to the emergency vet, and I'm still on the phone with someone when we pull up. Sam grabs Pepin out of the back and carries all 65 pounds of him like he's a newborn baby.

When we walk in, the front desk staff can clearly see that Pepin is in distress, and they rush around the counter and help Sam get him onto a padded cart.

Finally, someone understands the urgency!

I hear people running down the hall calling for an open room, but it's muffled. My ears are ringing, and I can feel my heartbeat in my toes. I see Sam talking to the vet tech and signing papers. I'm still right by Pep's side, petting him and kissing the top of his head as he lays on his side, still wheezing.

Someone in scrubs comes over and says something to me. The ringing continues, and I don't hear her.

"What?"

I feel Sam grab my arm. "Lou, they're going to take him back now."

They start to wheel him away, and he tries to sit up to look back at me. I give him one last kiss on the head and gently lay him back down on the cart. "I'll see you soon, Pep. I love you."

They take him to the back, then Sam and I are instructed to wait in the lobby. We sit down on two chairs next to each other, and I lean into Sam. He puts his arm around me and rubs my head with the other.

I'm feeling a little better now that we're here, but I'm still so worried about him.

After sitting in silence for a while, a woman in scrubs comes out and calls our name. I shoot up and walk over to her as quickly as I can without running, and Sam follows behind me.

"How is he?"

"I'll walk you back to one of our consult rooms, and the doctor will be in shortly to discuss Pepin's condition with you."

Why couldn't she just say he's fine? Is he not fine? I look back at Sam, worried, and I can tell he's trying hard to be calm for me. We sit down in the room and wait.

A woman walks in and introduces herself as the vet. This time, I don't bother asking how he is because now that she's here, I'm not sure I want to know.

"Pepin is sedated right now and stable. We were able to get some scans done and determined that he has gastric bloat. His breed, his gender, and his age put him at high risk for it. Essentially, what happened is that Pepin's stomach flipped. When the intestines get cut off like that, it causes gas to build up in their abdomen."

"How did that happen?"

"It's usually a freak accident; it likely wasn't anything you did."

I nod, even though I will continue to run through the entire day in my mind, trying to figure out what could have gone wrong.

"So how do we fix it?"

"He needs surgery immediately. We will need to remove the parts of the intestine that have already died and then put the healthy bits back together."

"Okay, let's do it."

"I think that's a smart choice. While I'm prepping him, my assistant will come in and go over some stuff with you. If you have any questions, just let the front desk know, and they will come ask us."

The assistant comes in and goes through the financials with us. The surgery is $4,000, and that's not including aftercare, medicines, and spending a few nights here to recover. I sign the papers, only thinking about Pepin and how much I need him to make it.

"The surgery will take several hours. You guys can go home and rest. We will call you with updates. There's really no point in waiting here since you won't be able to take him home tonight anyway."

I don't want to leave him here alone, but I'm exhausted.

Sam puts his hand on mine. "We can wait here if you'd like."

"No, we should go home. There's nothing we can do here."

We gather up our few things and walk to the car, hand in hand. As we drive home in silence, I stare out the window at the leaves starting to change colors. Fall is my favorite time of year; something about it just feels so warm and cozy to me. But looking out at the beautiful fall colors right now, I don't feel any joy. Just sadness.

———

SAM

When we get home, I make dinner, but Lou barely eats anything. I can tell she's riddled with anxiety, and I feel helpless. She's been in a daze ever since I pulled up to the curb with my truck and loaded Pepin in the car. I tried to handle a lot of the logistical things for her so she wouldn't get too stressed.

It's been three hours since we left the clinic, and still no word. We're sitting on the couch with a movie playing on the TV, but I know neither of us is watching it. Her head is lying on my lap, and I'm playing with her hair and rubbing her back. Every now and then, I feel a tear drop onto my thigh.

Her phone rings on the coffee table, and she shoots up, almost hitting her head on my chin. It's an unknown number, so I assume it's the clinic. My mind flashes back to last fall when I got the call about Jacob. My heart squeezes in my chest, and I feel sick. It makes me wonder if that trigger will ever go away.

She answers, and I can barely make out the voice on the other end; all I hear is Pepin's name, so I know it's the vet.

Lou puts her hand over her mouth, trying to choke back a sob. Her eyes fill with tears, and I can't yet tell if she's relieved or devastated. She doesn't say anything, just mumbles "mhmm" occasionally. I put my hand on her back and try to lean in closer to hear what they're saying. All I hear is, "...give us a call back when you make a decision." Then Lou drops the phone down to her lap, and she breaks.

I know now that it can't be good news.

I wrap her in my arms and hold her close. She can barely breathe through her sobs, tears soaking my shirt. My heart aches for her, and my own eyes start to fill with tears. Though a brother and a pet may be different, I know what loss feels like. I know the pain and the disbelief that this is happening to you. I know the feeling you get, like you can't breathe, like your head, your heart, and your lungs are all going to implode.

I try to control my breathing, taking deep, slow breaths in hopes it will help slow hers. After a few, she sucks in a deep breath, holds it, and slowly lets it out. I say softly into her hair, "Thatta girl. Just try to breathe." Her rhythm matches mine, but her body still shakes. I pull her onto my lap and tuck her head into my neck. We sit there for a while before she finally speaks.

She pulls back and looks at me. Her words are choppy and muddled with sobs, but I can still understand her. "Too much of his tissue has died." She sniffles. "She said they could finish the surgery, but there's a chance he wouldn't make it long or wouldn't have a great quality of life." Her breath catches, and she takes a moment to clear her throat. "She asked me to decide if we want to try or if we want to let him go."

I tread carefully, knowing there is no right thing to say in this moment. "Are you leaning one way or the other?"

Her palms press into her eyes as if she's trying to stop the tears from falling out. "I know what I *should* do, but I just can't do it."

She has an incredibly hard decision to make, and I almost just wish he would have passed. Giving her that decision may seem like a good thing, but no one wants to be the one making a decision to end a life. No one.

"He's old, and I just don't want him to be in pain for a few weeks or months and then pass anyway."

"I am not trying to sway your decision one way or another, but I do think that Pepin had a pretty awesome day today. Some people don't get the chance to give their pets a great last day, and if we were to wake him up, you can't guarantee he'll go peacefully. But I completely understand if you don't want to...let him go." I almost said "give up on him," but that's not what she'd be doing, knowing the odds look so bleak.

"I know, that's exactly what I was thinking." She curls up in my lap again and cries.

"And Lou..."

"Yeah?"

"You didn't just give him a great last day; you gave him a whole year of being loved and cared for."

She sniffles and nods, too choked up to reply.

She grabs her phone and calls the number back. My heart starts racing. I know what I just said, but dialing the number and officially giving a decision carries such a heavy weight, even more than it did minutes ago. A tear falls down my face and lands on Lou's cheek.

She lifts her head and catches me crying. I was really trying to hold it in for her, but it's just coming out of me. She touches my cheek and wipes away another tear with her thumb.

"I'm supposed to be the one doing that for you, not the other way around." My voice is weak and shaky.

She huffs, "I'm glad you're letting me see you. All of you."

The phone rings in her hand, and someone answers on the other end. Lou talks to the receptionist, who forwards her to the vet.

―――――

LOUISA

I walk through a sterile feeling hallway lined with doors. The tech leads us into a room on the left, opposite the one where we talked to the vet a few hours ago, with hopes that Pepin would be okay. We walk through another hallway and enter a room that is somehow less welcoming than the hallway. Of course the operating room needs to be this way, but I never imagined walking into one under these circumstances.

There he is. My baby. My Pepin.

I reach back and grasp Sam's forearm, unable to move closer.

"It's okay; you can come up and touch him." The tech's voice is sweet and encouraging, clearly having done this several times.

My hand is over my quivering lips, and I can already feel my face soaked with tears. I'm surprised there's anything left in there.

Seeing him lying there like this isn't what I expected, though I hadn't actually put much thought into this. He's covered in a polka-dot fleece blanket from the neck down.

All you can see are his head on one end and his fluffy tail poking out the other.

I walk up to the table, still squeezing Sam's arm. At some point, his other arm came up to rest on my shoulder, which is also shaking. Or is it Sam's hand that's shaking? I can't tell.

I reach out and pet his soft head that I've kissed too many times to count. I lean down and kiss the face I've held in my hands many times as I look into those big dark eyes that I know were staring back at me, into my soul. Pepin always had a way of making me feel seen, especially the times I felt most lonely.

Getting this dog was the best decision I ever made, and I honestly don't know if I'd be here today without him.

"Hey, Pep." My voice cracks, my throat tight and hoarse from crying. I take a peak over my shoulder; Sam's now standing a few steps back, giving us a private moment.

I look back down at my baby, who I hardly recognize with the tube down his throat. But if I close my eyes and lay my head on his, I can almost pretend we're snuggled on the couch back at the apartment.

I gently stroke his soft ear as I whisper to him. "I just wanted to tell you how much I love you." An uncontrollable sob breaks loose. "And I wanted to thank you. You know what for."

I know he doesn't—because he's unconscious—but I can feel him nuzzling his head into my neck the way he always does. I can hear his soft, deep bark. I can see him running through the park, well, more like frolicking.

I can't tell if it's a laugh or a sob, but some kind of noise comes out of me. I bury my face into his neck, letting his fur soak up my tears. "Goodnight, Pepin. I love you."

———

IT's BEEN a few hours since we got home from saying goodbye to Pepin. I can't even say his name without crying.

Eventually, I crawled out of Sam's loving arms, though I could have stayed there for the rest of my life. He makes me feel so safe, so protected. I can't thank him enough for his support. I could not imagine going through this alone.

I know I wouldn't survive it.

Sam and I are sitting on a blanket on the floor of his living room, having a picnic. After I finally released him from my tearful clutches, he went to the kitchen and brought back fruit, cheese, and crackers. He also made us each a mixed drink, and I asked him to make mine extra strong.

We've talked for a while, and my tears have slowed. But my mind continues to race. So many thoughts flooding my brain. So many things I want to say while, at the same time, I don't want to talk at all.

I take a sip of my drink, then take in a big breath. Looking at Sam, I swallow my pride and decide to do something I should have done a long time ago.

"I feel dumb making this comparison, but all that's happened with Pepin has had me thinking a lot about Jacob. I know losing a pet is nothing compared to losing a brother, but there's something I want to talk to you about."

"Lou, do not minimize your grief for my sake. I know how much Pepin meant to you."

"That's the thing, I don't think you do."

He looks at me with curious eyes.

"I mean, you know that I adored him and spent a lot of time with him. You know that I got him after my break up and that he helped me feel less lonely when B wasn't around. But there's more that you don't know..."

Chapter Thirty-One

LOUISA

Sam still gives me that same questioning look.

"Pepin didn't just bring me comfort and happiness...he saved my life."

I take another big sip of my drink, trying to calm my nerves.

"I need to tell you about the time I tried to kill myself," I say in a hushed and embarrassed tone, knowing full well he knows nothing of what I'm about to tell him. This conversation has been weighing heavy on my mind for months now, but I need to tell him. No more waiting.

I'm holding my breath for what seems like minutes, waiting for him to respond. In reality, it's probably only been a couple of seconds.

He sits up a little straighter. "Okay."

He pauses, waiting for me to continue. But I can't seem to get the words out.

"You don't have to if you don't want to," he reassures me.

My body heats like a furnace, and I can feel the sweat

running down my sides. The baggy sweatshirt I'm wearing does nothing to soak it up.

"Well, I don't particularly want to, but I think it's important for you to fully know what you're getting into with me.

"I'm all ears, Lou."

I take in a deep breath that strains my lungs and let it back out. Lifting my glass to my lips, I take a sip, letting it burn on my tongue for a moment before swallowing. I start at the beginning...

———

I TELL him about that night. How the thoughts swirled in my head and how my world went dark. How nothing was in focus, nothing seemed real or right. I explain to him what happened at the cabin with Tony. I tell him about meeting Erin at the charity ball and how even though that was an amazing opportunity, it scared the shit out of me about the exam. I tell him about feeling alone and unaccomplished. But most importantly, I tell him how Pepin saved my life.

Sam, bless his good heart, sits and patiently listens to it all. I don't think he's said a single word the whole time, and I feel so seen, so heard. His face doesn't hold any judgment, nor does he look like he wants to run. He holds my hand, rubs my back when I struggle to get the words out, and holds me as I break down.

So tell me why I just finished, and I'm sitting here panicking, waiting for his response.

We now sit face to face again, and he's holding both my clammy hands.

"I'm so sorry you went through that alone."

"I wanted to tell you sooner, but I kept getting scared

you would leave me. And I would still understand if you didn't want to deal with all of that."

"All of that? You mean all of *you*? Lou, I said it this morning because I meant it; I love you. And that means *all of you*."

"But you didn't know about this part of me."

"That's true. But Lou, I'm 27. I've lived enough life and known enough people to know that everyone has parts of them that they don't show everyone. I knew there would eventually be things we'd have to work through. This is something that you've been painfully struggling with alone. But now you have me, and I want to be there for you."

I sniffle, and he lifts his hand to wipe the tears from my cheeks, kissing one then the other.

"But you've lost someone you love like this already. Doesn't it terrify you to be with someone who has similar struggles?"

"Of course it does."

I knew it.

He continues, "But I'm also terrified that you'll die in a car accident on your way home. I'm terrified that you'll get some grand job offer and move away, leaving me behind. I'm terrified that you'll never share the same feelings I feel for you. There are a lot of things about you that terrify me, and all of them have to do with losing you. This is no different. Could it be something we deal with for the rest of our lives? Yes. Does that make me want you less? Absolutely not."

"But..."

"I'll say it a million times until you believe me or until you know what these words mean to me. I love you, Lou."

I get choked up again because only in my dreams did I think this conversation would go like this. My chin quivers, and I close my eyes because the sight of him makes my heart want to burst. I feel his arm engulf me, and he tucks my head into his neck.

His touch, his scent, his warmth. It's like a drug. One that makes everything else fade away and transports me to a place where nothing can hurt me.

"I don't want to force you to do anything you don't want to do, but I want you to know that I'll be there every step of the way if you decide to seek help outside of me."

"Like what?"

"Like antidepressants, therapy, or anything else that you think will help you avoid those dark places."

I sit up straight, and his arms fall down my sides, his hands resting on my thighs. His thumbs stroke lazy circles on my skin.

"I guess I haven't really thought about any of that. You came around right after my low point, and I've been feeling really good."

He gives me a soft smile. "I'm really glad that being with me has helped you feel better. Of course, I hope that you never go to a dark place again, but from what I've read, some people deal with this off and on throughout their whole life. I just want to know that we're doing everything we can to keep you happy and to keep you feeling safe in your own skin."

"How do you know so much about all this?"

"After Jacob, I started going to therapy. I've learned a lot, but I'm definitely no expert. Like I said, I don't want you to feel forced into anything. Just let me know if you want my support with stuff like that."

I nod and put my hands on his. I don't have words to tell him how grateful I am for him. How much his support means to me. How relieved I am that he didn't run. I express these feelings in the only way I know how—with a new sense of confidence now that he knows every part of me.

"I love you, Sam."

Chapter Thirty-Two

SAM

Lou and I are back in her hometown to spend Christmas with her family. We did Christmas Eve with my mom and Quinn last night at my house again. It was just the four of us, and I couldn't be happier.

My mom has met Lou several times now, and they are two peas in a pod. We played games all night, and I swear they were ganging up on me.

We cleaned up the house this morning and then got on the road. I've met her parents before, but I haven't been back home with her yet. Since Thanksgiving was a difficult one this year, being the anniversary of Jacob's death, Lou insisted we stay and spend the entire weekend with my family. She was right by my side the whole time.

We pull into the driveway of her parents' house, and B comes running out the front door to greet us. I watch her running, and one second she was there; the next, she wasn't. Lou and I both look at each other and jump out of the car. As soon as my door opens, I hear B laughing hysterically.

We walk to the front of the car and find B flat on her back, having slipped on a big patch of ice.

Lou shakes her head, laughing. "You idiot."

I can't help but laugh too because only B would sprint on a driveway in winter and not look for ice.

B is still laughing and crying. "Quit laughing at me and help me up, you jerks."

We each grab a hand and hoist her up carefully. Despite our efforts, in a matter of seconds, we are all on the ground, roaring with laughter.

We manage to crawl our way to the car and stand. We unload our bags and make it to the salt path that their dad made leading to the garage door.

We walk in and are greeted by the sweet smell of cookies baking in the oven. The Christmas tree is lit up in a multitude of colors, filled with mismatched and handmade ornaments. I walk closer to get a better look.

There's one that's from Lou's first Christmas, several that were clearly made by a child, and a few that look so old and delicate, likely family heirlooms.

Lou walks up behind me. "Welcome to my childhood." I turn around to see her arms spread wide

I spin around, taking in all the decorations, all the pictures on the walls, and the cozy feel that the real fireplace gives it. "It's adorable."

"It's a lot." Lou lifts her eyebrows, opening her eyes wide.

I get what she means. You can definitely tell B grew up here, but Lou's style is completely different. She hates chaos and thrives on simplicity. But I like it; it feels lived in. It feels like a home.

Growing up with Joel's endless rotation of sleek and

modern homes was stale and depressing. The contrast is comforting. And even though I lost a parent when I chose never to speak to my dad again, I at least have a wonderful replacement with Lou's family.

They have been so warm and welcoming every time they've come to visit. I keep asking Lou if they are always like that, and she reassures me that neither of her parents has a mean bone in their body.

Lou walks me to the kitchen, where her parents are busy cooking. The rest of the extended family is arriving later today, and I'm anxious to meet them after hearing all of Lou's stories about them last year.

When Mrs. Blake turns around, she squeals and runs over to hug Lou and pepper her cheeks with kisses. "I thought I heard you come in. We are so glad you made it safe." She lets go of Lou, and now it's my turn. "Oh, Sam. I'm so glad you could come. Are you sure your mother isn't going to be missing you today?"

"I'm sure she will, but we had dinner with her and my brother last night. Thanks for inviting me."

"Of course—"

She gets cut off by her husband. "Sam! How are you?" He walks over and gives me a hug.

The first time her dad hugged me, I was really taken off guard. My family, besides my mother, have never been big huggers. Joel, especially, was not big on affection of any kind. But over time, the hugs have become more natural.

He turns to Lou and wraps her in a hug, picking her up off the floor.

"Dad, you're crushing me."

"I missed you too." He plants a kiss on her forehead.

We spend the rest of the afternoon catching up and

watching her parents cook. I offered to help several times but was denied. Only once did her mom give in and let me chop onions, but only because she didn't want to ruin her makeup with onion tears.

Slowly, family members start arriving. First, it was her grandpa, escorted by a young nurse who he referred to as his new BINGO girlfriend. Then her cousins, who are slightly older than us, came with their children. And lastly was her aunt and uncle. I've been warned about her aunt several times and have been dying to witness her extravagant personality in person.

The first thing her aunt says to me is, "So you're the boyfriend." Not quite the welcome I was expecting, but I brush it off.

Now, as we're all sitting around the dinner table, she says to me, "So Sam, should we be expecting a proposal any time soon?"

Lou almost chokes on her mashed potatoes. "Sam, you do not have to answer that."

I just look at her aunt with a smile and confidently say, "You can expect one whenever Lou tells me she's ready."

The whole table looks over at us. Her aunt, who is staring at me with a straight face, says, "Good answer." She then turns to look at Lou with a smile. "I like this one; keep him."

Lou takes a drink of her wine, clearly in shock by how this interaction just played out. Everyone goes back to chatting with one another, and her aunt goes back to telling B how she used to get guys when she was her age.

Lou leans over and whispers to me, "Sorry about that. I warned you she has no filter."

I whisper back, "What I said to her is the truth, you know."

She looks up at me with those sweet, caramel brown eyes, and I can tell she's trying to hold in her reaction, fighting a smile. "I'll keep that in mind."

I subtly kiss her on the cheek before sitting back up and continuing my meal.

———

LOUISA

When we're getting ready for bed, I walk from the bathroom to our bedroom, locking the door behind me. When I turn toward Sam, I see him holding a little red box in his hand. He extends it out toward me.

"Here's your final present."

I freeze, my eyes widening. "Sam..."

He opens the box, and I sigh with relief. A little silver key sits inside, and I instantly know what it is. The lease is going to expire soon at the apartment where B and I still live. I've been talking about renewing it but haven't made a decision yet.

Part of me was hoping he would ask, but I wasn't sure if he would think it was too soon since we've only been together for five months. But to me, those five months have seemed like five years. I am so in love with this man, and I trust him with my whole heart.

When he responded to my aunt like that at dinner, I instantly got butterflies. We've talked about marriage, but never in a super serious way. More in the sense of daydreaming about what our future could look like together. And I can absolutely picture a future with Sam in a way that I never could with Jay or anyone else.

Sure, I planned to marry Jay, but I never really thought about what married life would be like with him. I thought we would have kids, but I never imagined what raising children would be like with him.

With Sam, I've pictured it all; with him, I want it all.

"Do you want to officially move in with me?"

"Of course!" I get giddy, and his smile in response to my answer makes my heart so happy. I walk over and crawl onto his lap. "I was nervous for a second that you were proposing."

"I know," he giggles, "I wanted to tease you a little to gauge your reaction. Then, after your aunt's comment earlier today, I knew the look on your face was going to be priceless."

"You're cruel." He leans in to kiss me.

He grabs my face in his hands and pulls me closer to deepen the kiss. What started out as a kiss is now escalating at a rapid pace. I rip off my nightshirt, and he palms my breasts with both hands and plays with my nipples while running his lips down my chest.

I tug at his shirt, and he releases me briefly to pull it over his head and throw it on the floor next to mine. I press my body into his, melting over the warmth of his bare skin on mine.

I run my hands all over the soft skin of his abs, down to his shorts. I pull on the elastic band of his shorts, and he lifts his hips up, me with him, and pulls them down.

All I'm wearing under my nightshirt is a pair of panties, which he now pulls to the side. He touches me between my thighs and massages in gentle circles at first.

He brings two fingers up to my lips, and I open my mouth to suck on them. He takes those fingers and enters me, moving in and out, getting me really wet. I stroke his hard cock while he plays with me, running my fingers over the tip to spread his precum.

I try my best to quiet my moans since B's bedroom is right next door, and my parents' bedroom is down the hall. I know from personal experience that these walls are very thin, or B was just really loud.

Once he gets me to come like this, he wraps an arm around me and quickly spins us so I'm lying on the bed, and he's standing at the end of it, between my legs.

He leans over me and grabs my panties with his teeth, pulling them down my legs. He straightens up and grabs the base of his cock, pushing it into me.

A few months ago, we had a talk about not using condoms during sex. Sam told me he hadn't been with anyone since me and that he got tested before we met up. I told him about Ruth, B's nurse friend at the clinic, and how I got tested regularly between partners. I've also been on birth control since I was a teenager. We agreed that we trusted each other and wanted to occasionally do it without a condom.

Even after months of having sex with him, it's still a tight fit, so he goes in slowly. Once he's all the way in, he grabs my legs and holds them up for me while thrusting from a standing position. I reach above my head and grab onto the bed to stabilize myself.

The sound of his hips smacking my ass with every thrust echoes throughout the room, but I don't care right now.

Sam clearly notices it too because after a minute, he switches things up to a position that doesn't make as much noise. He flips me over on my stomach and pulls me down so my legs hang off the bed. He enters me from behind and places his arms on either side of my head to support his weight.

He aggressively rolls his hips, and I put my face into the comforter so I can let out the sounds I've been holding back.

He picks up his pace even more, and I grab onto his wrists. With the way he positioned me, my clit is rubbing against the bed with every thrust, and I can feel myself reaching another climax.

I release one of his wrists and put my hand between my legs to help myself along. He takes his now free hand and gently presses down on my neck, pinning me to the bed.

Being gently dominated by him always gets me hot. My hips start shaking, and he can tell I'm close, so he starts thrusting harder. A light smacking sound comes from his hips hitting my ass, but not nearly as loud as before.

I turn my head and bite his meaty forearm as I come. At that, he releases my neck and pulls his cock out. Stroking it a few times, he finishes all over my back.

He leans forward and brushes the hair out of my face to kiss my cheek, and I turn more for him to kiss my lips. I remain face down so I don't spill his come all over the sheets. He goes across the room to grab the towel I used to shower earlier. It's still a little damp, which helps him clean me up. He wipes my wetness off of him and then crawls into bed with me.

I snuggle into his bare chest and kiss his soft skin.

"I love you, Sam. And I can't wait to live with you."

"I love you too, Lou." He kisses my forehead and runs his fingers through my hair.

The only way that this Christmas could get better is if Pepin were here to celebrate with us today and if Jacob were there yesterday when we celebrated with Sam's family.

But life didn't deal us great cards this past year. I hope that this next year is filled with a lot more happiness and less loss. But now, I have Sam here by my side to fully support me through whatever obstacles threaten to keep us from experiencing true joy.

To anyone who feels like they need to quiet all the noise with a painfully irreversible decision...

Please don't.

Epilogue

SIX MONTHS LATER

SAM

"Mr. Carlyle, you better hurry, or you'll be late for your own party."

"Denise..."

"Sorry...Sam."

"When you call me Mr. Carlyle, it makes me think of Joel. And you know how we both feel about that man."

Denise's eyes widen, and she nods her head. She, more than anyone, had to put up with my dad's shit, and for far too long.

A few months ago, I got a call from Denise asking if I was still willing to offer her a job at my landscaping company. I, of course, said yes and hired her immediately. It took her a few weeks to get up the courage to tell my dad she quit, but we eventually got her out of there.

She's been working as my secretary, and I don't know how I managed without her. Not taking so many calls or answering so many emails has allowed me to spend more time with Lou doing the things that I enjoy. Don't get me wrong, I enjoy my job, but I enjoy days at the beach with the love of my life better than getting sweaty and playing in dirt.

I start to walk out the door when Denise calls me back.

"Sam, you forgot something!"

I turn around and walk back into the office to where Denise is sitting, holding a little red box.

"Fuck, thank you! That is not a good thing to forget."

I asked Denise to hold onto it for the past few weeks because I didn't trust Lou not to find it. I could just picture her deciding to deep clean the house one day and stumbling across it, completely ruining the surprise.

She hands me the box and holds my hand a second longer, looking up at me. "Good luck. I know she'll say yes."

I'm not nervous about her saying no; I'm nervous about everything going to plan. I recruited B and Quinn to help me plan out the perfect engagement, followed up by a party with our close friends and family. Per usual, they crushed it. And B only almost spilled the beans twice.

I get in my truck and start driving to the restaurant.

———

LOUISA

It's my birthday, and Sam told me to meet him at Orion's for dinner since he would be running late. I told him a while ago that I didn't want to do anything big for my birthday, so we made these reservations at the last minute. Luckily, Matt was able to get us a table.

After running into Sam on my birthday a year ago, I texted Matt, telling him I'd found someone and that our little arrangement had come to an end. At that point, I didn't even know if Sam wanted to be with me, but I didn't care. I knew, for better or worse, nothing could be the same after we reunited.

Months later, Sam and Matt met at one of David Perez's parties. They actually get along really well, and I'm not sure how I feel about that just yet. Sam knows about my previous relationship with Matt, and he doesn't seem to be jealous. It could have something to do with the fact that Matt has doubled Sam's business by hooking him up with several wealthy clients. Daniel Perez also hired Sam for a job, which led to several doors opening for him. I'm so happy he hired more help; otherwise, I would never see him.

I walk into the restaurant and wait for Sam in the entry-way. I have his location, so I know he's only a couple of blocks away, likely parking.

When I see him walk through the doors, I smile and give him a hug. He's wearing a perfectly tailored navy suit that makes me want to drag him back to the car and lay the seats all the way back.

"I was wondering if you would be clean." I kiss him and feel him laugh on my lips.

"You think I would show up to a place like this in my work clothes?"

"I wasn't up when you left this morning, so I didn't know if you had brought a change of clothes with you. You said you had to work late, so I brought you some in case you didn't have anything."

"That was nice of you, but I had it covered. I wouldn't show up to your birthday dinner all sweaty."

He kisses me on the cheek and tells me how beautiful I look. We hold hands as we're escorted back to our table. Even after a year of being together, he still gives me all the affection I need.

After dinner, he says he has a surprise for me. As we walk toward the kitchen, I genuinely have no clue what to expect. I know he asked me for Matt's number to make the reservation, so maybe they conspired to surprise me.

We get to an elevator, and I give him a skeptical look as we step in. He pushes a button, and my mind starts racing with ideas. Why do I have to be so nosey?

"The roof?"

"Mmmhmmmm." He manages to keep a very neutral face the whole ride up.

The doors open, and we walk down a hallway to the door leading out to the roof. I walk through it, and a warm summer breeze rushes in, lifting the skirt of my dress. I laugh as I flatten it back down and step out onto the roof.

When I look up from my dress, I see a blanket laid out with a bottle of champagne in a bucket of ice. Two glasses sit next to it, along with a speaker. It's dark outside, and despite the city lights, the stars are out.

"It's the picnic I promised you."

"Sam, this is so sweet."

I turn to him and wrap my arms around his neck. He leans down and kisses me.

We walk over to the blanket, and Sam turns on the speaker, connecting his phone to it. He starts playing a song that he knows I love. I've made him dance with me around the kitchen to this song many times, and I always joke with him that we're practicing for our first dance at our wedding.

Sam stands up and reaches out a hand to me. I place my hand in his, and he twirls me around and pulls me close. We dance slowly, and my cheeks are starting to hurt from smiling so much.

Looking into his mesmerizing eyes, all I can think about is how happy I am. A year ago, I was at an all-time low, but

Sam came into my life again and changed everything. My eyes start to fill with tears.

"Everything okay?" he asks.

"Everything is perfect. I just love you so much, and I'm so happy I get to share this life with you."

He twirls me again, but this time, he doesn't pull me in close after. He holds my hand and stretches out his arm to keep me at a distance. He's beaming from ear to ear, and I can't help but blink away my tears and smile back at him.

"It makes me incredibly happy to hear you say that."

As I start to take a step toward him to continue our dance, he stops me and starts to kneel.

Holy shit. Is this really happening right now? My heart starts to race, and I get a little dizzy. He reaches over behind the bucket of ice, pulls out a little red box, and opens it.

"I want to do forever with you, Lou. Will you marry me?"

The tears return to my eyes, and I choke out my answer with not a single doubt in my mind.

"Yes, of course."

———

SAM

After she said yes, I felt like I could breathe again. We celebrated by popping some champagne and spent a little more time on the roof together, dancing under the stars. I don't recall ever being this happy in my life.

The elevator reaches the main floor again, and we step out and walk through the kitchen. She thinks the surprises are over and that we're just headed back to the car. But when we step out into the dining room, it's been completely transformed in the 30 minutes we spent on the roof.

Lou jumps back, startled by all the people standing around waiting for us. Everyone yells surprise, and she looks like she just had a heart attack. I didn't want to scare her like that, but she loves surprises, and I wanted to make tonight as special as possible.

She turns to me and rests her forehead on my chest while the shock settles.

"You...." Her eyes glare at me, but her mouth spreads into a huge smile.

"Happy Birthday, Lou."

She looks around at all the people who came to celebrate with us, and people start to come over to wish her happy birthday and to congratulate us. All three of our parents are here, as well as several of our friends. I was so happy when people told me they could come. I only told the family that I was planning to propose; everyone else just thought it was for Lou's birthday. But based on the mixed decorations, I'm sure everyone has figured it out by now.

We're chatting with B when I hear a familiar voice behind us.

"Congratulations, you two! And Happy Birthday, Lou!"

We turn and find Sarah, the woman who used to live above Lou in her old apartment. She wraps Lou in a big hug.

"I'm glad you could make it."

"Me too! I was so glad when Sam said I could bring the kids. I didn't have anyone to watch them."

I look over and see her kids chasing each other around one of the tables. It looks like the oldest boy is trying to smash a cupcake into his sister's hair. I chuckle to myself before turning back to the conversation.

"You know, I heard you scream that first night."

Lou almost spits out her drink and gawks at Sarah for making such a bold comment. "Excuse me?"

Sarah nods and looks at me. "Oh yeah. I was genuinely concerned you were going to kidnap her, so I listened. I heard screams." She looks at Lou. "But you told me you'd yell my name, and I never heard it, so I just let it be. So, you're welcome."

Sarah has never shared those details with either of us, and I'm shocked she has kept it to herself for this long. In the year I've known her, she's never been able to keep many of her thoughts to herself.

Lou is laughing so hard, but I can tell she's dying on the inside at the thought of someone overhearing us.

I think back to that first night we spent together, and I have to shake the thoughts from my mind because I start getting hard at the memory of Lou riding me. Now is not the time to be getting turned on. We have plenty of time for that once we get home, and I fully intend to properly celebrate Lou's birthday. Thoroughly. Fast. Slow. All the ways she likes it.

Fuck. As happy as I am to be surrounded by loved ones celebrating us, I can't wait to get my fiancé back home.

Acknowledgments

If you made it this far: thank you, thank you, thank you.

My readers - Thank you for taking a chance on an indie author publishing her debut novel. I have no idea where this journey will lead, but I am so grateful to each of you for being a part of it. I have had so much fun sharing my stories with you all, and I hope that at least one of my characters resonates with you. If not, maybe you just haven't met them yet.

My husband - If it weren't for you, I would have never published this book. I would have never pursued this dream I didn't even know I had. Your endless love and support through all my self-doubt and imposter syndrome means more than you know. Thank you for being my biggest fan and always encouraging me to tell my stories.

My friends - You have been my ultimate hype-girls and guys. All the times I thought I was crazy for thinking I could be an author, you guys were there to tell I'd be crazy not to try. Thank you for reading my spicy scenes and not cringing. Thank you for being my beta-readers and providing me with valuable feedback. And thank you for living such interesting lives that help inspire my stories.

My parents - I know having a daughter that writes smutty romance books wasn't on your BINGO card, but thank you for accepting my new-found passion. Thank you for supporting me and being proud of something I'll never allow you to read.

About the Author

Emma Pathy

Emma is a contemporary romance author based in Minneapolis, MN, where she lives with her husband and their two dogs. A newcomer to the world of writing, Emma has always had a deep connection to love stories. After devouring dozens of romance novels in just a few months, she discovered her passion for creating her own heartfelt and emotionally rich tales.

For Emma, writing isn't just about crafting fiction, it's about giving life to the characters who already feel real in her head. With each book, she brings her readers on a roller-coaster ride of emotions—blending spice, laughter, and deeply relatable situations that tackle heavy topics with care and sensitivity.

Her stories offer not only escapism, but a raw reflection of the highs and lows of love, creating an experience that readers won't soon forget. Emma's warmth, empathy, and infectious optimism shine through both in her books and in her life.

When she's not writing, you can find Emma sharing her journey on social media (@emma.pathy.author). She'd love to hear from you, so don't hesitate to say hello and share in the joy of her characters' love stories.

Also by Emma Pathy

Coming Soon...

2. Please Stay With Me

3. Please Wait For Me

4. Please Think Of Me